Immortal Grave

Nichole Chase

Printed in the United States of America

Immortal Grave
Book Three of
The Dark Betrayal Series

ISBN-13: 978-1480083974
ISBN-10: 1480083976

Find out more about the author and upcoming books online at **http://www.nicholechase.com** or friend her on Facebook at **http://facebook.com/nicholechase.author**

Dedication:

For my husband, my very own guardian.
I will always go where you go.

CONTENTS

Prologue

Tristan looked around the large living room in disgust. It was the week before Christmas and the students were enjoying their short-term freedom. Teenagers lounged about on the furniture, while others danced in the corners or made out in the shadows. Running a hand across the back of his neck, Tristan tried to not think about the thirst that consumed much of his thoughts. His gaze stopped on the back of Shannon's dark hair. She was sitting on Michael's lap, her hand wrapped around the idiots' thick neck. Red crept into Tristan's vision and he had to quickly avert his gaze. If she wanted to act out the charade tonight, that was fine by Tristan. Taking a swallow of the beer he was holding, he choked it down and wondered what else they might have to drink at the party.

"Hey, Trist." A girl from his chemistry class sidled up next to him and ran her hand up his arm. "You don't seem to be having much fun."

"Hey, Emma. You're looking good tonight." He smiled down at the voluptuous girl and tried to not focus on the lush skin of her neck. He turned his attention to other interesting body parts and slid an arm around her shoulders. She giggled and pressed against his chest. Shaking her curly hair, she leaned back in a calculated move that gave him a good look at her cleavage.

"Maybe we could go hang out somewhere else. You know, if the party is boring you." Licking her lips, she smiled at him and placed a hand on his chest.

"Well, we could always go work on some chemistry homework. I always thought we might make good lab partners." If he couldn't quench his thirst, he could get lost in other things. Emma would be a fun distraction.

"I was thinking along the same lines." Grabbing a fistful of his shirt, Emma turned and sauntered toward the stairs leading to the second floor. They passed Paden, who rolled his eyes at Emma and shook his head at Tristan. Winking, Tristan tried to not be bothered by his best friend's disgust. There had been a time, not that long ago, when Tristan would have never disappeared with a girl like Emma. Paden would never understand what it meant to be the scholarship kid. It didn't matter that Tristan was the star soccer player. The only things he was good for were taking the school to state or serving as a distraction for the rich girls before they settled down with someone their family would approve of.

Unintentionally, Tristan's gaze moved back to Shannon. She was still sitting on Michael's lap, but now her scrutiny was focused on Tristan and Emma. She narrowed her dark eyes. Tristan could almost smell her anger and jealousy from the other side of the room. He stumbled on the bottom step making Emma giggle. Yanking his gaze from Shannon's, he set his cup down on the banister and swooped Emma up in his arms. She threw her hands around his neck and laughed as he took the stairs two at a time.

The bedrooms were already taken, so Tristan pushed into the bathroom and kicked the door shut behind him. Emma immediately started untucking his shirt and running her hands across his stomach. When she pressed her mouth to his, he tried to focus on the kiss instead of the thud of her heartbeat. It seemed unbelievably loud in the small bathroom. Pushing away from the wall, he shoved Emma against the counter and smiled when her eyes grew large. His gaze focused on the thumping of the artery in her neck. Moving back to her, he ran his hands up into her hair before yanking her head to the side.

"God, you smell delicious." Using his tongue he traced a path down to her shirt collar.

Her hands reached between them and began to unbutton his pants. Even though he could taste the spike of fear in the air, she wasn't going to miss her chance to score with the school's soccer captain. While he was excited by her desire, he was even more excited by the thought of her blood. His turning couldn't be far now; he could smell the girl's blood through her skin.

With his hands still fisted in her hair, he scraped his teeth along her neck. She groaned and pushed her body closer to his. Testing, he bit her as gently as he could and tensed when she gasped in pain.

The door to the bathroom slammed open and Shannon stood glaring at them both. The light from the hallway framed her in a glowing halo, and Tristan could taste her fury. He lifted his head slowly away from Emma, his tongue darting out once more to trace her neck as he pulled away. Shannon's nostrils flared, and her hands fisted on her hips.

"Geez, Shannon. This bathroom is occupied." Emma yanked her hands out of his pants and tried to readjust her shirt.

"Get out." Without waiting for them to move, Shannon walked into the bathroom and yanked Emma off of the counter.

"What the hell is wrong with you?" Emma glared at Shannon. "Couldn't you just use one of the other bathrooms?"

"I don't need to use the bathroom. I just need you to get the hell out of my house." Though she barely stood five feet tall, Shannon dominated the tiny space. Emma backed out of the bathroom and flipped her hair over her shoulder.

Tristan could see his bite mark even in the dark of the bathroom. He tensed and wondered if Shannon had seen it too.

"God, you act like you haven't fooled around with Michael while you were at my house. We were just having a little fun." Emma's eyes went past the tiny girl blocking the doorway and she smiled at Tristan. "What do you say, Trist? Wanna talk about our homework somewhere else? Seems we're not welcome anymore."

"I didn't say anything about Tristan, idiot. I just said for you to leave." Shannon crossed her arms and tilted her head. "Or are you so stupid you couldn't understand the simple words I used?"

"What?" Emma looked at Shannon and then at Tristan. "Are you going to let her tell you what to do?"

Shrugging his shoulders, Tristan leaned back against the bathroom counter and folded his arms across his chest. "It's her house."

Emma set her jaw and glared at Shannon and then Tristan. "Whatever." Turning on one heel, she flounced away, her hair swinging angrily.

"Emma?" Closing the door, Shannon turned to glare at Tristan. "And you bit her! Jesus, Tristan. What has gotten into you?" Stepping up to him, she poked his chest with one small finger. "Get a grip, will you?"

"I'm not far, Shannon." Scrubbing his eyes with the palm of his hands, Tristan leaned his head back against the wall. "It's got to happen soon. I could smell her blood. I wanted to bite her, wanted to do much worse."

"You think they're going to turn you now?" Shannon's voice grew quiet and something in her eyes looked sad. "Are you sure this is what you want, Trist?"

"I want this." Standing up straight, he placed his hands on her shoulders and leaned down to look in her eyes. "I want you. And this is the only way I can have you. The only way your father will ever let you be with me. I'm tired of watching you pretend with that giant idiot. You're too good for Michael and it makes me sick to watch him touch you."

"Tristan…"

"Don't you want it too? I thought that's why you introduced me to your dad. Told him who I was." His eyebrows drew together.

"I do. I want you, Tristan. You know I do. But, will you still be you when you turn? I think we're in over our heads."

"You think your dad would let something bad happen to you?" Tristan snorted. "Never mind. Of course he would. He would sell you to someone if it would get him a good deal. But he's right about one thing. I'll never be more than a soccer player or a mid-level employee stuck in a dead-end job. You deserve more than that, and this is the way that I can give it to you."

She stepped forward and leaned her forehead against

his chest. "I don't deserve you, Tristan."

"No, I don't deserve you. But that's all going to change soon."

"I still think we don't know enough. I don't think my father is telling us everything."

Leaning down, Tristan kissed the top of her head. "It's going to be okay. We already know the worst of it. Blood drinking creatures of the night, right? I can handle that."

"He hasn't had any of their blood. Not one drop. But he encourages us to drink it all the time. You especially. He never lets me drink as much as you and Michael."

"Don't talk about Michael to me." Stiffening, Tristan pulled back from Shannon a little. Rage coiled in his belly and he knew that his eyes were taking on the black smoke that marked him as a darkling.

"Don't be stupid, Tristan. It was your idea for me to stay with him. To keep people off our trail." Shannon turned away from Tristan and pretended to check her makeup in the mirror. Raising her eyes to meet his reflection, her mouth twisted sardonically. "I think it's time you leave. Otherwise people are going to start talking."

Brushing past Shannon, Tristan yanked the door knob and heard something crack as the door swung open. Without turning around he said, "You've always been a bitch, Shannon."

"That's why you love me." Shannon's voice was soft, meant for Tristan's sensitive ears.

Chapter 1

Scrubbing the sleep out of her eyes with the heels of her hands, Ree blinked in the sun filtering through the window. Moving slowly so that she wouldn't wake Melanie, Ree sat up in the bed and looked around the room. If she was quiet enough, she might be able to sneak to the bathroom and change out of the borrowed pajamas that she was wearing and back into her clothes. Shifting her weight carefully, she stood up and tiptoed across the wood floors to the chair with her clothes.

Melanie rolled over, but her breathing stayed slow and even. Biting her lip, Ree left the room and continued her careful journey down the hall to the bathroom. She threw her clothes on the edge of the bathtub and turned on the water in the sink. Dark circles under her eyes spoke of the long night she had before finally getting to sleep. Even though she didn't feel bad physically, her mind was beaten down by everything that had happened in the last couple of weeks.

Cupping her hands under the water, Ree let the cool liquid pool in her palms before splashing it on her face. Barely two weeks ago, she and her friends had been attacked by a monster; threatened by a myth. Something from a Hollywood movie set. The attack, car chase, and fear in her friend's expressions ran through her mind and she splashed some more water on her face.

The world had been dumped on her shoulders. Literally, the world depended on her and she had to come terms with that responsibility. She had been lied to, mislead, and worst of all, betrayed. It was the darkest form of betrayal; the kind that can only come from someone you love, someone who is supposed to love you. Her brother had sold his humanity so he could be something inhuman. Even though it meant that it would be the death of Ree and her friends if he won.

Ree looked up in the mirror and smoothed the hair away from her face and turned the water off. She shed Melanie's pajamas and pulled on her dirty jeans. They smelled like smoke and there was a blood stain on the left knee from where she had knelt in Sophie's blood. Pulling her shirt over her head, Ree was glad to see that the blood stains were mostly hidden by the dark color. She snagged a rubber band from the back of the sink and swished some of the mouth rinse before finally cracking the door open and sneaking downstairs.

Roland was asleep on the couch. His back to the room and his face half buried under a pillow. His foot twitched when she hit the bottom stair and Ree froze. She wasn't in the mood for company, and she knew if anyone woke up she wouldn't have the opportunity for some alone time. There was too much going on in her head, and she needed to do some sorting.

When he didn't move again, Ree stepped carefully to the landing and quickly tiptoed out the back door. She knew if she tried to cross Ellie's boundary line, it would wake everyone in the house, but she could find somewhere in the little garden to sit and think. Taking the stairs two at a time, Ree slipped at the bottom on some smooth gravel that littered the ground.

"What the…" Ree managed to catch her footing quickly. Looking around the yard, she shook her head and was glad no one was awake to see the smile and blush that covered her face. The only good thing to have come from the mess of the last two weeks was the change between her and Paden. Last night he had kissed her senseless, making her lose control of her powers and floating the pebbles from the pathway.

She looked over her shoulder at the windows and back door to see if anyone had noticed her escape. Not seeing anyone, she turned back to the scattered gravel and took a deep breath. The power flowed into her smoothly and quickly. There was no need to pull energy from anyone or anything around her now. The Death Gift Sophie had passed to her last night multiplied her own reserve. She had to concentrate a little harder to keep from using too much power and to keep her feet from lifting off the ground. It was quick and easy work to pick up the tiny pebbles and arrange them back into the shape of the pathways. When she was happy with her work, she headed for a wooden swing that hung from a giant oak limb.

It was a little chilly, but Ree wasn't willing to go back inside for a jacket. She swung her legs up next to her and rested her head on the armrest of the swing. The leaves rustled as the wind blew through the tree and Ree concentrated on the quiet sound. It was a simple thing, but one she had always enjoyed. She had always liked the weather like it was today. Slightly overcast, with a breeze and not so cold that you didn't want to be outside. Now, with so much at risk, the stakes so high, Ree had a new appreciation for things. She wasn't sure when it had happened. Maybe after last night, when everything had seemed so hopeless. But now she knew it was important to take a moment to enjoy the little things.

Taking a deep breath, she thought about what had happened after everything had calmed down. The goddesses Brigid, Hecate and, to all of their surprise, Athena had made an appearance at the bed and breakfast. They came to check on them all, but Ree was certain they were there to see how the Death Gift had affected her. Athena, particularly, had seemed interested in her reactions, and her serious eyes had followed Ree's every move. Brigid had also watched Ree, but was much more covert. Her words had been kind and warm, as if she was worried about how they were all going to hold up after the deaths of Sophie and Teagan. Honestly, Teagan's death had been a shock and it was painful to think of her dead body, but it was Sophie and her sacrifice that brought tears to Ree's eyes.

Using the edge of her sleeve, she wiped her eyes and tried to reel in her emotions. It would do no good to get emotional about Sophie at this point. The older Guardian wouldn't want Ree to focus on her death. Sitting up, Ree took a deep breath. Even though the goddesses had checked on them and insisted they leave for the island, Ree was certain they had come for some other reason. And after thinking it all out, she was pretty sure she might know what they had been looking for after all. She hadn't mentioned it to anyone else and knew Paden would be completely against letting her test her theory. She also felt she needed be a step ahead of the gods and their plans.

The sound of crunching gravel had Ree sitting up and reaching for the power. She didn't see anyone around the yard, but her power told her there was someone or something just outside the large brick wall at the back of the property. Slowly, Ree stood and walked toward the wall. This might be her chance to test her theory. And, if nothing else, it might give her the confidence she needed to face the ugly battle coming her way.

She could hear the person on the other side of the wall breathing, but it was the power that told her it was a darkling. Reaching further with the power, she realized there were several other darklings spread around the surrounding streets. Tristan and the Dark Ones had set their day-time eyes on the bed and breakfast. She heard a sound come from inside of the bed and breakfast and she made up her mind up quickly. Moving quicker than she ever had before, she jumped to the back of an old bench and vaulted over the wall. A smile of pleasure curved her mouth as she realized how easily she had made the jump. The triumph was short-lived as she looked up. The darkling was disappearing around the corner, and the sound of raised voices from the house drifted to where Ree was crouched. Firming her resolve, Ree darted down the tiny alley after the darkling.

Chapter 2

The night before, Paden had been in danger. A terrible nightmare came to life before Ree's eyes, but she had somehow been able to move faster than any human possibly could. She had shoved the Dark One, a full-fledged Dark One, away from Paden. It shouldn't have been possible, but she could remember the feeling of her arms and legs moving in fast forward. Paden hadn't mentioned anything about it and Ree suspected he may not have really understood what had happened. However, it had bounced around in Ree's mind for hours last night. What if Sophie had passed on more to her than her ability to touch magic?

Ree skidded around the corner and watched as the darkling shoved past pedestrians. He was headed toward one of the nearby squares, and she was intent on catching him. She wanted to know what he had been up to behind the house. Instead of following him through the crowds of people and drawing attention to herself, she headed for a side street that would keep her out of the public. It took less time than she had planned, and she belatedly realized that she may have been moving at speeds faster than a normal human. She looked over her shoulder and hoped no one had noticed. Slowing to a walk, Ree reached for the power and felt the darkling nearing the square in front of her.

Stepping out into the light, she tried to keep her pace casual and hoped none of the people recognized her face from the wanted pictures on last night's news broadcast. She felt it the moment the darkling saw her in the square. She had her back to him, but his shock was palpable. Surprise warred with worry as he tried to decide if this was a trap or good timing. She caught his movement out of the corner of her eye as he checked behind him to see if someone was coming for him. Ree almost smiled as she understood he hadn't realized it was her following him. Apparently smarter than he looked, he pulled a cell phone from his pocket and made a quick call.

The off-kilter, cold spots of darklings Ree had felt around the city began to move in her direction. Ree's step faltered and she openly looked over her shoulder at the darkling. A young man in his early twenties, he was thin and angry looking. Ree picked up her pace and thought about trying to get back to the house. There were five darklings nearby, and even though she had wanted to test her new abilities, this may have not been her smartest move. Paden's going to go crazy when I get back, Ree thought.

Her heartbeat picked up, and she thought about running for it, but decided her new abilities were her only surprise weapon. If she could get away without showing her hand, that was what she needed to do.

The darkling smiled at her and started to walk after her with slow, predatory steps. Something in his expression scared Ree, and she realized it was the mixture of lust and confidence. She could feel his nasty thoughts as she picked up her pace. He wanted her to run, wanted to see her panic. Stuttering to a halt, anger bloomed in her chest. Why the hell should she be afraid of a darkling? She was the Alastriana. She had a power on her side he would never be able to understand. Turning to look at him, she spread her feet and prepared to make her stand. She had a thing or two to show this darkling, and she would be damned if she was going to run now.

As if the humans in the square understood something ugly was about to happen, they quickly left the area. Ree snorted and tried to not think about it. Whether they sensed there was more than meets the eye, or generally didn't want to be near a domestic dispute, every single one of them had hightailed it out of there. She opened her hands at her side and watched as the darkling came toward her.

"Not going to run?" He spit on the ground. "I like it when they run."

"Where the hell do they find you guys? Assholes-R-Us?" Ree pulled on the power in her chest and felt her feet try to leave the ground. Letting go of a little power, she tried to keep herself calm as she waited for the darkling to get closer.

He didn't answer, just snarled as black crept into his eyes. When he was a few yards away, he made his move. Darting toward Ree with his hands outstretched, he never expected her counter-attack. Spinning, quickly, she ducked to the side and planted her foot on his butt. He barely caught himself before nose-planting on the cobblestone path. Snarling, he turned toward her and moved again. She tried to not snicker as he telegraphed his upcoming attack. His fist swung up toward her jaw, and she grabbed it midair. Using his momentum, she flung him over her hip and onto his back in a move Roland had taught her on the island.

Keeping hold of his hand, she twisted it until he

hollered and placed her foot on his chest. "Now, what should I do with you before your friends get here?"

He struggled and sputtered, but couldn't break her hold. Ree wasn't sure if that was because of her technique or her new suspected powers. Either way, she was happy with the results.

"What were you doing behind the bed and breakfast?"

"Spying."

"And what did you learn?"

"Get off me, bitch."

She twisted his arm until she heard something pop and he howled in pain. She didn't let up, or move so he could catch his breath. Instead, she kept on with her interrogation. She could feel her Guardians zeroing in on her location and she would be damned if they would take this moment from her. For the first time, she didn't feel like the weak human that would break if someone looked at her wrong.

"What did you find and who did you tell?"

"Barrier. Can't hear through it. Can't see much." Heavy pants filled the pauses between his words.

"What else?"

"Guardian and you are together." That made Ree pause and her stomach clenched. This jerk had watched her with Paden.

"Not a big secret, so you have to do better than that." She tried to keep the disgust out of her words. She didn't want him to know what he had said bothered her.

"Roland is your lap dog." For just a moment his eyes

cleared of pain and smiled viciously. "You must be a good fuck. Don't know why all those guys want you otherwise."

"Who did you tell?" It took all of her self-control to not beat the daylights out of him.

"Ree!" Paden was pissed and she knew he was only seconds from reaching her.

Leaning down she looked the darkling in the eyes. "Who did you tell?"

"Your big brother." Laughing, the Dark One closed his eyes. Unable to stomach the sound, Ree let go of his arm and placed a swift kick to the side of his head. The vile sound cut off just as Paden reached her.

"What. The. Hell. Are you doing out here?" His hands closed on her shoulders and forced her to look up at him.

"My job." She could feel his fear and love, so she tried to quell her irritation. "I'm the Alastriana, Paden. I can take care of myself too."

As if to prove her point, she shrugged out of his grasp and looked around the clearing as the other darklings emerged. When they realized she wasn't alone, they stopped and watched them warily. It was apparent they knew better than to mess with her Guardians. Darklings just didn't stand against the immortal warriors.

Not wanting them to leave with nothing to show for their encounter, Ree grabbed the power and felt her head snap backward. As green rippled out from her body, she carefully maneuvered it around Paden and toward the cold spots of dying energy. Lifting her head, she watched as they flew backward and were pinned to the ground by her power. Surprise made her mouth open slightly. Under the cold of the alien disease, many of these darklings had a large amount of their human soul intact.

Turning to Paden, she shook her head. "They're mostly human. I can feel their souls still glowing under everything."

"What are you saying?" His eyes looked from Ree to the darkling at their feet.

"I'm saying I think they can be saved." Ree felt relief well up inside of her. She didn't want to kill anyone if she could help it. And darklings weren't completely dead yet.

"What? No, Ree. That's insane." He reached out to grab her arm, but stopped. For a brief moment, Ree could feel his awe for her and the fear that clenched his heart. "You can't do that, Ree."

"I think I can, Pay." Looking down at the darkling at her feet, she grimaced. He didn't deserve it, but she would rather him rot in a prison than spend eternity as a nightmare preying on innocent girls. She looked at Paden and nodded her head as if making her decision. "We don't have a lot of time. Let me do this."

Not waiting for his reply, she turned her attention to the darkling and closed her eyes. She knew Paden would watch out for her while she worked. Letting the power fill her, she pushed it toward the darkling. It was like a light in the middle of the night. Darkness fled as she worked from his center and pulsed outward. The disease was more stubborn near a newer bite and in his mind. She added more power as she cleaned, letting it scrub away at the shadows and stains. Within moments, she opened her eyes and looked up at Paden.

He was staring at her with bright eyes, his expression full of wonder and fear. "You did it."

"I did it." She realized she was floating a few inches from the ground and forced her feet back to the ground.

"We don't have time for you to do the rest, Ree. We have to get back to the house. There are police everywhere. I have no idea why they aren't all over this square. That's what I was trying to tell you earlier."

"What about the others?" She looked at the darklings still pinned to the ground.

"They'll just have to wait. Can you leave them pinned to the ground? Maybe the cops will arrest them for public intoxication or something."

"Yeah, I think I can do that." Closing her eyes, she used some of the techniques Sophie had shown her when imbuing things with a purpose. The one she knew best was that of protection, but with a little tweaking she was able to convince the ground energy it needed to keep the people in those places. Working as quickly as possible, she made the energy bend to hold the darklings still. Her intent was clear, but she didn't know how long it would hold.

"Okay. Let's go. I think that's the best I can do for now."

Without hesitation, Paden grabbed her hand and headed for the same alley she had used earlier. Looking back over her shoulder, Ree almost tripped. Sitting on a bench as if she had been there the entire time was Athena. She nodded her head at Ree and, with a crack of energy, disappeared.

Getting her feet back under her, she picked up the pace and hurried alongside Paden. They moved quickly, but not fast enough to draw unwanted attention. He was still worried about getting her safely to the house, and she could feel his fury rising to the surface. Her pleasant morning had certainly taken a turn for the ugly.

Chapter 3

Ree and Paden made it back to the bed and breakfast in record time. The sound of sirens filled the air, and a cop car roared past the alley entrance. Paden held his arm to keep Ree from stepping into the road and she couldn't help but roll her eyes. Sensing her annoyance he turned and looked at her.

"We're fugitives now." Raising his eyebrow, Paden smiled wickedly. He moved toward Ree until she was backed against the brick wall. Placing a hand on either side of Ree's shoulders, Paden barricaded her between his arms. "For being a good girl, you get into an awful lot of trouble."

Ree snorted. "Who said I'm a good girl?"

Paden smiled down at her, obviously disagreeing. She could feel his humor bubbling under the surface.

"Okay. Maybe I was a good girl. But I'm turning a new leaf. Rebellion here I come!"

"Bar fights, murder, and arson. You don't do anything small, huh?" Paden moved closer to her and she could feel the heat radiating from his body.

"Go big or go home." As if to prove her point, Ree reached up and pulled Paden's head down. Feeling brave after her morning adventure, she ran her lips over his and slid her hands through his hair. He was all too eager to let her work out her left-over adrenaline and slid his hands down her arms before moving to her waist. When his fingers bunched her shirt so it slid up her lower back, she gasped at the cold air on her skin. He took his opportunity and plundered her mouth.

Not wanting to let him be the one to take control of the kiss, she ran her hands under his shirt and up his back before sliding them around to his stomach. Hooking her fingers into the top of his pants she pulled him to her and enjoyed his grunt of pleasure. She leaned back to nip his bottom lip and moaned when his hands slid up her back and under her shirt. His fingers drifted beneath the clasp of her bra but stilled and didn't move. He pulled back a little and placed a slower, gentle kiss on her swollen lips before leaning his forehead against hers.

"I'm still mad at you, you know."

Not trusting herself to talk quite yet, she pursed her lips in annoyance... Slowly he pulled his hand back out of her shirt and raised it to touch her cheek. "What were you thinking, Ree? You could have been hurt."

"I know, but I needed to test myself and I knew you wouldn't have let me."

"Test yourself how?" He leaned back so he could see her face clearly and moved his hand away from her cheek.

"When Sophie moved her Death Gift to me it gave me… a lot more power. I wanted to know just how much." Ree winced. She had almost told him she suspected Sophie had given her more than just power.

"What? Slow down. You wanted to see how much

power you could hold?" Paden's eyes widened and his breath left in a rush. "Ree, you didn't have to sneak away to do that. Did you run out looking for a darkling?"

"No. He was hiding behind the wall at the back of the yard. I heard him moving around and he started to run. I wanted to know what he had done and decided it was a good opportunity." Adjusting her shirt, Ree looked down the alley before letting her gaze turn back to Paden. "Look, I know it wasn't the smartest move. I should have just told you what I was thinking."

"Yeah, you should have. We're a team, Ree. You can trust us. You can trust me." Reaching out, Paden grabbed her hand and ran his thumb over her knuckles.

"You're right. I'm sorry."

"That figures." Paden smiled at her when she looked at him questioningly. "No one here to hear you say that."

She punched him in the arm and watched as he rubbed his bicep in surprise. His eyebrows drew together and his eyes looked her up and down. She could see the wheels spinning behind his eyes, but he didn't say anything.

"I think it's time to head back to the house. I don't see any cop cars." Ree peeked out of the alley and looked up and down the street. "I feel like we need to get to the island. The cops have got to decide Melanie's house would be a likely hideout."

"You're right. Of course, I think Ellie's warding is helping keep them distracted. And don't forget there are members of the community working to keep us hidden." Paden rubbed his jaw and looked at the bed and breakfast across the street.

"I don't like depending on other people to keep us hidden. We're the ones that are supposed to be taking care of them." Ree narrowed her eyes. It was her job, and she was ready to accept the responsibility. "No more hiding, no more running. It's time to make a plan."

Paden didn't say anything, just grabbed her hand and nodded. After another quick check, they left their alley and crossed the street. As they neared the surrounding gate, Ree turned toward Paden to ask if the wards had been replaced, but didn't have the chance to form the words.

Lightning seemed to erupt from the house, the power of the explosion knocking Ree and Paden off of their feet. Gravel and brick rained down on the street like fiery bombs. Paden rolled over Ree and covered their heads with his arms. His body was tense and Ree could feel the rubble that landed on him as he sheltered her. After the initial shock, Ree threw a shield over where they lay on the ground. Paden scrambled off of her and they both stared at the bed and breakfast in shock. As the air cleared and they were able to see a little better, Ree dropped the shield and they ran for the house. Smoke filled the street, turning the bright sunny day into a malevolent dusk. Dust still littered down on the area and the sound of screams and panicked voices began to drift to Ree's ears.

Jumping the tattered remains of the fence, Ree threw herself into the smoldering remnants and called for her friends. Pulling at plaster and chunks of wood, Ree shifted through the debris, trying to get into the damaged house. The main portion seemed to still be standing, thankfully.

"Paden!" Roland's hoarse voice cut through the odd silence and Ree darted toward the staircase. The Dark One was pulling chunks of plaster and wood off Ellie, making soothing noises when she grunted. "Get your ass over here, godling."

Paden jumped over some of the furniture blocking his way as Ree scrambled behind him. She watched as Paden let his gaze run over the older woman, his hand going to Roland's arm when the Dark One went to lift Ellie. He murmured something that made Ree's heart stop.

"Don't." Paden frowned. "Her back is broken." Kneeling down, he let his hands move gently over the woman's body. "Ellie, this is going to hurt some. The vertebrae in your back are moved and cracked. You're going to feel it when they shift back into place."

The sound of things being thrown around toward the back of the house drew Ree's attention away from the small group on the stairs. Knowing Ellie was in good hands, she left to help the others. Melanie was making her way through the rubble, blood dripping down her face. Taking a running jump, Ree leaped onto the debris and threw her hand out to help Mel.

"Are you okay?" Ree pulled her friend over the upturned furniture and trash.

"I'm okay. Where's my mom?" Melanie looked around the front of the house. "Oh my God. Gran." Melanie jumped over the fallen chandelier and grabbed her grandmothers' hand.

"She's okay, Mel." Paden didn't look up at his friend. Instead he kept his eyes on Ellie's face as he worked over her body with his hands.

"I'm fine, girlie. Where's your mama?" Ellie's voice was faint and it made Ree's jaw clench. She hated hearing such a vibrant woman's voice reduced to a hoarse whisper.

"I'll find her, Melanie. Stay here with your Gran." Roland stood and closed his eyes for a moment. Taking a deep breath, he turned and looked up the stairs. As if gravity had no hold on him, he leapt onto the landing above Ellie. Wanting to find the others, Ree headed for the back of the house.

Juliette and Bryce were on the tattered back porch. Bright red blood covered his shirt and ran down along his arms. Juliette lifted his shirt and checked him for injuries, while he looked at her cheek that was covered with a large purple bruise, already in the stages of healing.

"Are you guys okay?" Ree waved a hand in front of her face. There was a lot more smoke in the back yard. Turning to look at the destruction of the yard, she could understand why. What was left of the carriage house was engulfed in flames.

"We're fine." Bryce grabbed Juliette's hands and looked her in the eyes. "I'm fine, Jules." Nodding her head, she slid his shirt down and back into place. Wiping a hand across her forehead, Jules turned in Ree's direction and frowned.

"Are you okay?" Jules didn't meet Ree's eyes, instead squinted at the blazing fire.

"I'm fine." Ree looked at Bryce and then back to Juliette, who still wouldn't make eye contact. Her friend was upset with Ree and she knew there wasn't much she could do about it at the moment. "Do you guys know where Weylin is?"

"No. We were out in the backyard, watching for you." Bryce gave her a sad smile. "I thought he was out front."

As they turned around, another explosion slashed through the air, knocking them all back to their knees and sending another plume of angry smoke through the yard. Coughing, Ree squeezed her eyes shut against the dust that assaulted them. The roar of flames made her scramble to her feet in fear. Bryce's hand closed on her shoulder, his fingers digging into her skin, and dragged her into the house and toward the front yard.

"Everyone okay?" Bryce's voice demanded a response.

"Ree? Is Ree with you?" Paden's form materialized out of the smoke. His hands reached out to cup her cheek while his eyes traveled over her face.

"I'm fine." Coughing, Ree squinted as moisture gathered in her eyes. "We've got to get out of here."

"Let's go." Paden tugged Ree away from Bryce and headed for the front door.

Outside, the sound of sirens was unmistakable, which didn't really surprise Ree. There was no way the humans could have missed the destruction and fire.

"What do we do?" Ree sought Paden's eyes.

"We run. Now." Paden turned to look at their bedraggled gang of immortals. Melanie was supporting Ellie, who looked much better than she had on the staircase. Roland was holding Melanie's mother in his arms like a child. She seemed to be unconscious. Ree hoped it wasn't anything serious. They couldn't take the time to let Paden heal her right now.

"Weylin?" Ree's eyes searched the yard for her friend.

"Last I saw him, he was heading out to look for you." Paden shook his head. "Don't worry, Ree. We will find him, but right now we have to go."

Their ragged friends followed them into the alley that Paden and Ree had recently used and headed away from the square. Ree realized Paden was taking their group toward one of the safe houses nearby. They needed to regroup and decide how to move from there. It was apparent to Ree they needed to get to the Island. She wasn't sure what had caused the explosion, but it was obvious they couldn't stay in the city.

Chapter 4

The golem, that they met just the day before, sat at the front counter, his expression neutral. Despite the dirt they shed as they shuffled through the door, despite the two human women that were half carried up the stairs, the creature barely acknowledged their entrance. He merely grunted as they hobbled up the steps to the door at the top.

Paden took the lead, as usual, carefully opening the door and giving the area a quick scan before motioning for everyone to enter. Roland immediately set Melanie's mother down on the small bed. She gave a painful cough and grimaced. Paden went to her quickly and ran his hands over the older woman's head. His hands glowed gently as he worked to heal whatever was causing the woman discomfort.

Roland moved away from the bed, taking a place near Ree as Paden worked. Melanie sat on the edge of the bed frowning, her eyes on her mother's face. Ree looked away from the scene in front of her and met Roland's weary gaze. It bothered her to see his eyes clouded, his expression so somber. Gone was his normal smirk and teasing eyes. The weight of his years seemed to be sitting on his shoulders, the loss of his longtime friend eating at his frame of mind. But there seemed to be something deeper, something confused and forlorn in his expression as he stared back at Ree.

Clearing her throat, Ree looked back at Paden, and Melanie's mother. "Where did you find her?"

"She was trapped under a large armoire. She was unconscious and I suspect she suffers from a concussion. There was also a great deal of smoke upstairs. She probably breathed in too much of it." Roland tilted his head down to speak quietly in Ree's ear. She could tell from his voice he didn't want to upset Ellie or Melanie with the details. "I could hear her heartbeat, but could also tell her breathing was labored. Something happened in the initial blast that caused a fire in the upstairs area. The flames were devouring the old walls and flooring." He took a deep breath, and in an uncharacteristic show of frustration, shoved a hand through his hair causing it to spike in odd directions.

"What's bothering you Roland?" Ree leaned closer to him, worried at his show of vulnerability.

"Those flames were not normal flames, little Ree. Those were the green and blue flames of the gods. Something is very wrong that they would attack a place of safety." A deep note of anger crept into his voice. "Even worse is the fact that those who should be keeping us safe should have noticed something was wrong. Where were they, Ree?"

"The bed and breakfast wasn't really a safe house, though, was it?" Ree lowered her voice so it wouldn't carry to those around her.

"Perhaps not in the sense of it being sanctioned by the gods, but Ellie's magic protected us from the Dark

Ones just as well. It's the lack of protection from our supposed allies that have me worried." Roland shook his head and looked back to where Melanie and her mother sat on the bed. Paden was still checking for injuries, his attention on the woman in front of him.

"If we go to the island, will we be safe?" Ree searched Roland's eyes. "If we are on sanctioned land, it would be harder for the gods to miss something that happens to us."

"Honestly, I don't know why they didn't act this time. I would have thought Brigid or Hecate would have responded on our behalf. And the way Athena was eyeing you last night, I'm surprised she didn't show up either." Squinting at Ree, he titled his head to the side. "What was she looking for, little Ree? She didn't show up until Sophie had died. Not until after..." His eyes widened fractionally. "Not until after you received Sophie's Death Gift."

Ree kept her gaze locked on his and hoped her heart didn't speed up. Had he guessed what was bouncing around in her head? Was it even possible for what Ree suspected to happen? It seemed crazy, and yet, he'd obviously had the same thought. She could see it written on his face. Maybe Sophie had passed on her Immortality too.

"I'm not really sure what she wanted." Keeping her voice bland, Ree looked at Roland and shrugged.

"Not sure, or don't want to say?" Roland's eyes bored into hers, making her want to squirm.

"What are you two talking about?" Juliette had slipped next to Ree without notice.

"Honestly? I don't really know." Turning away from Roland's penetrating stare, she tried to not think about how well he seemed to be able to read her. She'd rather face Juliette and her anger than Roland's thoughtful assessment. Or maybe not.

Juliette had her arms crossed and a frown on her face. She was pissed and Ree could tell it was going to take a lot to calm her down. There was only one thing that would make Juliette this upset.

"I'm sorry Bryce got hurt. Is he okay?"

"Uh-huh." Juliette narrowed her eyes at Ree and uncrossed her arms. "You're real sorry. You know, he was out in the back yard looking for you, Ree. If you hadn't been out there gallivanting around, he wouldn't have been nearly killed by flying debris." Juliette poked Ree in the chest.

Frowning, Ree rubbed the spot Juliette had touched. "I'm sorry, Jules. I'm really sorry Bryce got hurt."

"You know, this stuff doesn't affect just you. We're all caught up in this mess, too. Bryce could've been killed, Paden could have been caught by the police while he was out looking for you. And who knows what's happened to Weylin. All because you freaked out and tried to run away?" Juliette moved closer to Ree and poked her again.

"What?" Ree felt a surge of anger. "I didn't run away, Juliette. I was chasing a darkling. And if I hadn't chased him, then I would be dead. I was sitting right under the tree next to the carriage house."

"You should have called one of us. It isn't like you could keep up with the darkling anyway." Juliette poked her one more time and Ree snapped.

"My puny human legs somehow managed to keep up, thank you very much. Not only that, but I managed to remove the Dark One taint from him too." Without thinking, Ree reached out and pushed Juliette's shoulder, only to watch her stumble back a step.

Roland sucked in air somewhere behind Ree and Juliette looked at her with large eyes. "How—"

Ree leaned toward Juliette, her shoulders tense and her spine stiff. "I'm sorry Bryce got hurt. I'm sorry all of you have been dragged into this mess, but don't you dare accuse me of running away. I might've had a freak out or two. I might have been scared out of my mind, but not once have I tried to duck my responsibility." Ree took a deep breath and looked away from Juliette. "Not once, Jules."

Rubbing her shoulder with a look of confusion, Juliette nodded as if understanding. "I'm sorry. I should've known you wouldn't run away. I freaked out, okay? He was covered in blood and there was this huge splinter stuck in his side. Can you imagine what it was like to see that?"

"Yeah, I can." Ree remembered all too well, the bullet holes in Paden's shirt and jacket. She remembered feeling his body jerk against hers with each shot. "I get it."

"If you two are done we need to focus on what we're going to do next. Like finding out where Weylin has disappeared to." Paden placed a hand on Ree's shoulder. She hadn't even realized he had left Melanie and her mother, but knew he must've responded to Juliette's posturing. Which was silly, because no matter how mad Jules had been, she would never hurt Ree.

"We also need to talk about what just happened." Roland's smooth voice cut through Ree's thoughts.

"I think they've already settled it, Rols." Bryce was standing behind Juliette.

"Oh, not that. I mean the fact that Ree gained a little

more than extra power from Sophie's Death Gift." Roland's smirk was back in full force, the light in his eyes causing Ree's stomach to flip.

Paden leveled thoughtful eyes on Ree. "I thought you kept up with me earlier today pretty easily."

"It could just be all the exercise I'm doing now." Ree looked away from everyone. She didn't like the way they were looking at her, as if she had done something new and weird. Which, if she was being honest with herself, was exactly what they were thinking.

"And you were able to catch that darkling yourself." Paden looked at her shrewdly.

"Ree, you caught the darkling?" Melanie grinned at Ree enthusiastically. "Way to go." Paden glared at Melanie until she schooled her features into a serious expression. "I mean, you could've been hurt!" When Paden turned his attention back to Ree, Melanie winked and flashed a thumbs-up.

"It occurred to me last night something had changed. Do you remember the Dark One that came out of nowhere? I was able to push him away from you. I did it without thinking, but he should've brushed me off like a fly, right?" Ree shook her head, still awed by what had happened. "That's why I went outside this morning. I was thinking about everything, trying to get a grasp on why Athena had been watching me so closely." Should she mention seeing Athena in the square earlier? She still wasn't sure what the goddess had been looking for.

"Ree." Paden looked down into her eyes, obviously aware she was keeping something from them. "Tell us."

"I saw Athena today. In the square as we were leaving. She was sitting on a bench, watching us." Someone mumbled an explicative, and Ree was surprised to realize it was Bryce. He was usually the last one to freak out. Raising an eyebrow, Ree cocked her head at him in question.

"The goddess of strategy was watching you kick darkling butt? She was waiting to see if her plan had worked." Bryce shook his head. "I would bet money she had planned for Sophie to make a Death Gift to you all along."

Ree couldn't help the gasp that escaped her mouth, nor the tears that gathered in her eyes. "She told me. Sophie told me it had always been the plan, and she did it anyway."

Roland growled deep in his chest and walked away. He stood staring blankly at the wall before letting loose a roar and slamming his fist through the drywall. Leaning forward, he let his forehead rest just above the hole, his shoulders shaking with each breath. Silence was thick through the air as everyone watched Roland work through his anger.

Pain and fear washed over Ree in waves, making her wrap her arms around her chest. For over a thousand years, Roland and Sophie had been used and manipulated. She hated seeing him hurt so much. She hated knowing Sophie had been another pawn in this war, just another tool in the gods' closet.

Taking a deep breath, Ree looked away from Roland and her gaze fell on Melanie. Two tears made tracks down her friend's cheeks, but it wasn't the sadness that surprised Ree. It was who Melanie felt sad for that caused her to pause. Even without her extra sense to make it clear, Ree could see the longing on her friend's face.

Ree turned to look at Juliette, their argument forgotten. She wanted to know if she was the only one aware of how Melanie felt. When Ree raised an eyebrow,

Jules gave a soft jerk of her chin in acknowledgment. Ree frowned, knowing her eyes communicated her confusion. When had this happened and how had she missed it? Guilt and frustration rolled in her stomach. Here was one of her best friends, in love with someone that had feelings for Ree. To make matters worse, Ree had mixed-up feelings for Roland, too. And Melanie had never said a thing.

Cutting her eyes to Paden, she saw the compassion in his features as he watched Roland. In that moment, she understood the true extent of the gods' plan and the cruelty it depended on. Ellie had even told Ree, just because you loved someone in one life, it didn't mean you were soul mates. You could love many people, but only your soul mate truly completed you.

There, in Roland's most desperate moment, the gods had capitalized on his love for Tria, promising he would be with her again. They never promised they were soul mates, never promised the love they felt for each other would be the same in her new reincarnation. For centuries, Roland had been waiting for Tria, thinking they were soul mates.

"Ree?" Paden must have felt her anger and sorrow. Turning to her, he reached out to touch her cheek. In his eyes she saw his worry over the possibility that she wanted to go to Roland, but that wasn't what she was feeling. She did want to go to Roland, to comfort him, but not in the way Paden worried.

The gods had provided two protectors for their surprise weapon. Two men that both loved her for different reasons. Two men that would give their lives for her, perform amazing feats of strength to safeguard Ree. The inhumanity of their decision, the cruel manipulations and calculations left Ree breathless. Was this what Roland was realizing in this moment?

Looking past Paden, she watched as Roland's shoulders jerked with each ragged breath. Had the gods overplayed their hand? Would he handle this well or would he defect? Could he turn his back on everything?

Turning his head slightly, Roland's blue eyes met Ree's. For just a moment, she could see the ragged edges of his pain, frustration, and rage; then, just as quickly, everything disappeared. A blank expression slid over his features, and the Roland she knew disappeared behind a mask of icy consideration.

Cold crept into Ree's stomach and left her with an empty feeling. Love walked a fine line with hate, and from the way Roland was looking at her in that moment, she couldn't read anything other than resentment in his expression. Part of her wanted to cry, part of her was so bruised and beat up inside she could only feel resigned. Somewhere deep in her heart she felt the memories of Tria, knew they were teasing them both, and she wanted to scream.

The sound of footsteps on the stairs broke the connection that held them, and the door flung open to show a filthy Weylin. Taking a deep breath that was purely for show, he gasped and held a hand to his chest.

"There are entirely too many safe houses in this city."

"Where have you been?" The relief in Ree's voice was obvious as she went to hug her friend. "We've been so worried."

"Me? Well, I was arrested, broke out of a cop car, and then stole a truck." Lacing his hands together, Weylin popped his knuckles and smiled. "So, are we ready to go? Or are we going to wait for someone to realize their vehicle has gone missing?"

Chapter 5

The truck had a cover over the bed, thankfully, but it was still a very uncomfortable ride to the boat dock. Weylin, Melanie and her grandmother rode up front. The rest of their group piled into the truck bed and tried to keep their heads down.

The roads in the historic district were swarming with cops and it didn't feel safe to breathe until they had gotten into the more modern areas of the city. No one spoke for the entire ride. Roland looked like he was ready to explode at any moment, his hands opening and closing on his knees. His expression was calm and nonchalant, belying the short fuse that lay just beneath the surface. Weylin still hadn't explained the details of his close call, and Melanie's mother seemed to be lost in thought.

Paden squeezed Ree's arm, but his eyes were scanning the windows as they drove past one of the malls. When they finally pulled into the neighborhood with the dilapidated Victorian house, the tension was almost unbearable. Part of Ree was so tired she wanted to find a place to crawl into and hide. It wasn't a physical sense of exhaustion, but rather a mental and spiritual fatigue. So much had happened, with so little time to process anything, she felt as if she was constantly running. By the time the gravel of the driveway crunched under the tires, Ree was up and throwing open the tailgate.

Before the truck had even come to a stop, Ree had jumped out and was walking toward the dock. The sleek boat that had originally taken them to the island bobbed gently in the waves. Roland walked past Ree and hopped gracefully over the boat's edge and started checking different switches. Her steps halted and she watched the Dark One. He was obviously ignoring Ree, and she didn't really blame him. It was obvious he must've come to the same conclusion she had in the safe house. She was just glad he hadn't started screaming at her. Knowing she had caused him pain made part of her soul wither. She might not love him the way Tria had, but she remembered it. And she could understand why Tria had loved him, which made it so much harder to ignore.

A warm hand squeezed her shoulder and she looked up into Paden's green eyes. There was a question in them she didn't know how to answer. Instead she covered his hand with hers and squeezed.

"I don't like this, Paden. We're running again; letting them dictate our actions. We have to stop allowing that happen." Changing the subject let Ree push the guilt aside for a minute.

"Let's regroup and go from there. You're right, though, we need to start making the calls." Paden frowned and looked out over the water.

Ellie walked past them with Bryce and Melanie. "Now, that is a nice boat. Much bigger than the last dingy I went fishing on. Do you remember, Mel?"

Melanie groaned. "No wants to hear that story, Gran."

"Of course we do," Weylin said from where he knelt next to the truck. With a firm yank, he pulled the license plate off of the truck and balled it up in his hands. Ree watched, amused, as the metal folded like paper. Standing up, he threw the metal into the water.

"Weylin! That's littering!" Ree pointed a finger in his direction and glared at him.

"What was I supposed to do? Put it in the trash can?" Weylin shrugged. "At least I didn't push the truck into the river. We really need to get rid of it, or they will track us here."

"We could leave it at one of the other houses. Or maybe the abandoned lot we passed." Juliette offered.

"That's still pretty close to the house. There's a share-ride lot near the highway. We could leave it there and run back." Paden suggested. "That would also keep us from being tracked by the cameras on the stop lights."

"I can go and be back pretty quickly." Weylin stood up and headed for the truck cab.

"No one should go alone. I'll ride with you." Paden squeezed Ree's shoulders. "I'll be back soon." Leaning down, he brushed his lips over her forehead. "Stay close to Roland."

With that, he joined Weylin in the truck and they were gone. The breeze from the coast slid through Ree's hair and she shivered. Turning to look at the boat, she caught Roland's cold gaze on her. After a moment, he jumped back on to the dock and headed for the old house. He brushed past Ree and she felt his grief and anger like a cold knife between her ribs.

Her breath shuddered through her clenched teeth and she wrapped her arms around her middle. How had it ever come about that she could be the cause of so much pain? Her eyes followed his lithe form as he ducked through one of the rotten doorways. As if she couldn't help herself, she began walking toward the door.

Stepping through the entrance to the house, Ree stopped and looked around. The interior was mostly gutted, but instead of everything being old and destroyed, it was clean and neat. Dark hardwood covered the floor and the walls were painted a light gray. There was a small kitchenette on the other side of the cavernous space and a small room that looked like a bathroom in one corner. Weapons of all kinds lined the walls and there were mats stacked up against one wall. But it was Roland, leaned against the wall with his arms crossed, that made her heart stop. Dangerous and sexy, he would make any girl's heart flutter, but it was the pain in his expression that made her wince.

"I figured you'd follow me." His voice rumbled deep in his chest, but he didn't look up at her.

"You're mad at me." Ree wasn't sure why she said that, because it wasn't exactly what she felt radiating off him. It was what she feared.

His eyes cut up at her sharply and he grimaced. "I'm not mad at you, Ree." Pushing off the wall, he ran a hand through his hair and looked away from her. "Not mad at you, but definitely mad."

"I'm sorry, Roland."

"Don't you dare." Turning to look at her, his eyes held a fire that made her want to take a step back. Instead, she straightened her spine and walked further into the house. "I don't want your pity, Ree. Not yours, or anyone else's."

"Fine, then stop acting like you deserve it." Ree winced as soon the words left her mouth, because he did deserve it. He deserved so much more than he had been dealt in life. And in death.

"I don't want to talk to you." Letting his hands hang at his sides, Roland's features shifted into the blank expression that she hated.

"You know what? I don't really care what you want. I think you need to talk to me." Ree walked toward him and tilted her head back so that she could look up into his eyes.

His hands grabbed her waist and pulled her against him. "I don't want to talk, Ree."

"Why did you get so upset at the safe house?" Swallowing, she ignored his statement and tried to steer the conversation to a safer place.

"You know why I was so upset. They played me this whole time. Tell me Paden isn't your soul mate. Tell me I haven't spent hundreds of years waiting for someone that was never meant to be mine." His voice cracked on the last word and his hands clenched at her sides.

"Roland—"

"Better yet, show me." Without waiting for a response, his head dipped down and deftly captured Ree's mouth. She gasped in shock and he took advantage of the moment to plunder her mouth. When one of his hands slid under her hair to cup her neck, she closed her eyes and melted into the kiss.

A surge of memories pounded through her head, transporting her to another time: Tria as a tiny girl with a dark-haired boy in a field of tall wheat, laughing and giggling. It was replaced with a girl of twelve or thirteen standing in the corner at a party, watching a devilishly good-looking boy dancing with her friend. There was the image of Roland bringing her a flower, his face wreathed in a happy smile, while Tria's heart beat rapidly in her chest.

Then, as if her memories were running parallel to the present, she saw their first kiss. His hands shook when they cupped her face and Tria laughed at his nerves. So many moments ran through her mind, filling her with a sadness that made tears run down her cheeks.

Something in her soul felt as if it was shriveling. One of the threads that held her tied to this body seemed to snap, dying from the pain of the moment. She was sharing her first kiss with Roland as Ree, but Tria was kissing him goodbye. Part of her would always love Roland, there was no denying it. But he needed to start over, to find the one that really held the other half of his soul.

As if sensing where her thoughts were going, his kiss intensified, demanding her attention. Running her hands over his chest, she laid one against his neck before slowly pulling away. He pressed his forehead against hers, his breathing heavy, his eyes closed as if he was in pain.

A growl ripped through the room and Roland spun so Ree was behind him. Paden slammed into Roland with the force of a freight train, knocking Roland back into Ree. She stumbled, but it only took Roland a split second to regain his footing. Grabbing Paden by the shoulders, he flung him away from them both. Stepping away from Ree, Roland intercepted Paden's next strike and blocked the punch aimed for his face.

"Paden!" Ree's heart slammed into her chest and she moved to try to intervene. She was too slow though, and Paden managed to connect his fist with Roland's jaw. The Dark One was knocked backward to slide along the floor. Paden stayed on him as if they were tied together. Jumping onto Roland's chest, Paden raised his fist to hit him again. Instead of fighting back, Roland deflected the blow. Paden's knuckles crashed through the hardwood floor with a loud crack and sent splinters flying. His first punch was followed by the second and third, leaving the floor around Roland's head obliterated.

Bryce and Weylin flew into the room and tried to pull Paden off of Roland, but he shrugged them both off like flies. Ree stepped forward and grabbed his shoulders. Paden tensed, but didn't stop his assault on Roland.

"Paden, stop!" Ree pulled at his shoulder, but he didn't budge.

"No." Paden's voice growled the word and his attack grew in ferocity. His pain filled every crevice in Ree's mind and she would do anything to make it better, but she couldn't let him beat Roland. She had let Roland kiss her and she deserved Paden's wrath more than anyone else. Grabbing the power, Ree threw it around Paden and Roland, using it to pull them apart. She lifted them both into the air a foot from the ground.

"Put me down, Ree. I'm not done." Paden snarled in her direction and Roland brushed some of the blood away from his eyes.

"We had a deal, Paden." Roland's voice was tired, his movements weary. Ree couldn't help but notice he didn't refer to Paden as godling, and that made her nervous and sad.

"I don't care. I'm going to rip you apart."

"Don't be a sore loser, godling." Roland sneered at Paden with more of his normal attitude. "You took the bet, and I won."

Paden growled again, but didn't say anything else. Ree was surprised there was a trace of guilt sliding through his anger and hurt. What did he have to feel guilty about?

"I don't know what you two are talking about, but if I put you down can you behave?" Ree looked at Paden, letting him know she was mainly concerned about his behavior.

"I don't know. Can you keep your hands off of him?" Paden's angry voice sliced at Ree's heart, but it was no less than she deserved.

"Yes, I can." Ree looked at Paden, knowing he could feel her guilt and shame. Yes, she let Roland kiss her, but she would never love someone the way she loved Paden. After a moment Paden jerked his head in agreement and Ree lowered the shield separating them. Ree looked around the room and realized the others had left them alone, obviously not wanting to be there for whatever was about to happen.

"We had a deal, Paden." Roland wiped at his nose and grimaced. Paden merely growled and looked anywhere but at Ree.

"What are you talking about?" Ree looked between Roland and Paden.

"We made a bet at your parent's house. I killed the most Dark Ones and he agreed to my terms." Looking far more uncomfortable than Ree had ever seen Roland, he looked down at the floor.

Suspicion gnawed at Ree as she remembered their last bet; Paden had won and had taken her home with the intention of staying the night. Not that anything untoward would have happened, but he'd wanted to be the one to protect her.

"What were your terms, Roland?" Ree looked at him and put her hands on her hips.

"To kiss you." Roland frowned and looked at Paden. "And I thought it was without recourse on his part, but apparently I should have been clearer."

Ree sucked in a breath and tried to not lose her tenuous hold on calm. Turning her wide eyes to Paden, she caught his grimace. Paden had bet a kiss with Ree, like she was some type of object to trade, as if her kisses were a commodity. No wonder he was feeling guilty.

"You bet a kiss with me?" Ree felt her face fill with her hurt.

"I didn't think you would really kiss him." Paden looked away from her face. "I didn't think he would win."

"He did win! If my kisses meant something to you then you wouldn't have taken the chance." Shaking her head, Ree took a deep breath.

"No, Ree. That's not it. It was stupid." Paden took a step in her direction but stopped when she glared at him.

"Who else did you make that bet with? Weylin and Bryce? Melanie and Juliette?" Ree crossed her arms and cocked her hip. "Is there anyone else I owe a kiss?"

"It was wrong, Ree. But you did kiss him. How could you do that?" Paden looked at her with sad eyes. "I thought…" His voice trailed off, leaving her to decipher what he was thinking.

"Paden, I'm sorry." Ree felt tears welling up in her eyes. No matter how angry she was about the bet, she had done something unforgivable.

"She was letting me say goodbye to Tria." Roland cleared his throat, drawing both of their attention. "I needed to let go." A staggering breath escaped him and Ree knew he had felt the same thing she had. There would always be something between them, the memory of what had been in one life, but it wasn't what either of them deserved. And Ree had found that person in this life. The gods had sent him to protect her. She could only hope she hadn't messed it up royally at this point.

Paden's eyes snapped to Ree's face and she could feel his emotions wavering between anger, hurt, guilt, and oddly enough, understanding. Not sure what to say or how to act, Ree turned on her heel and walked out of the house. She wanted to throw herself at Paden, to plead for him to forgive her. She wanted to hit him for treating her like a prize in a bet, and she wanted to comfort Roland.

Since she didn't think any of those things would go over well, she left. For the first time in the last few weeks, she felt like a true coward. She needed to regroup and she couldn't do that while she was around either of those guys.

Without slowing, Ree made her way down the dock and hopped onto the boat. She avoided eye contact with everyone and sat down next to Ellie. The older woman smiled and put her arm around Ree's shoulders.

Roland and Paden were the last to embark. A tense silence blanketed the boat as Roland pulled away from the dock and headed for the island. In an odd way, Ree was grateful no one was talking. At this point, she didn't feel like she could hold a conversation without completely losing it.

Chapter 6

Everyone disembarked quietly. The trip had been uncomfortable at best, no one speaking unless they had to. Ree was the first to scramble out of the boat, her mind in a million places and an intense desire to be alone pushing her toward the large house.

She didn't stop until she was closing the door to her room, where she leaned her forehead against the heavy wood. Her breathing became difficult, tears slipped out from under her closed eyelids and down her cheeks. In the span of hours, her life had gone from really bad to even worse.

Her parents were running for their lives, her protector and friend had died saving her, and she had cheated on Paden. To top it all off, her friends were on the lam . Snorting, she dragged her hand across her nose and turned around so the back of her head could lean against the door. It was too much for any person to handle, too much for anyone to really process. It would be easier to just keep plowing forward, but today had shaken her to her core.

Wanting nothing more than to take a hot shower

and to go to sleep, Ree headed for her bathroom. Stopping midstride, she looked around. Something was off and she couldn't put her finger on what it was that bothered her. Slowly, she ran her eyes across the room, hesitating on the chair next to the bed.

A velvety chuckle glided through the air and where the empty chair had caught Ree's attention, a dark haired woman sat with her legs crossed.

"So, your senses really have heightened." Smiling, the goddess leaned further back into the chair. "I was wondering if you'd be able to tell I was here."

"Who are you?" Ree narrowed her eyes at the woman. She was not in the mood for company, and a god was the last person she would want to talk to even if she wasn't in the mood for quiet.

"Aphrodite." The woman pursed her lips. "Goddess of love. Yadda, yadda, yadda." She waved her hand flippantly, looking bored with her introduction.

"Aphrodite." Ree stated the name calmly, but the last thing in the world she wanted to talk about was love.

"Of course, dear. There are important things happening right now and I figured you might need a motherly figure to talk to." Smiling wickedly, Aphrodite motioned at her body. Ree couldn't help but snort. There was nothing motherly about Aphrodite. She looked like a runway model, complete with designer outfit and awkward-looking shoes.

"Actually, I'm not really in the mood to talk to anyone. But, thanks for the offer." Ree thought about walking out of the room, but didn't want to turn her back on the goddess. "Maybe another time."

Aphrodite uncrossed her legs and tsked under her breath. Standing up, she walked toward Ree and gently wrapped her fingers around her wrist. Tugging carefully, the goddess pulled Ree over to the bed and sat on the edge.

Fighting the urge to pull herself free of the goddess's hold, Ree sat next to the lovely woman on the bed and frowned. She wasn't sure what the goddess wanted and it made her nervous to sit so close to a deity that could kill her with one thought.

"Now, tell me what happened." Aphrodite cocked her head to the side, her expression open and interested. Pulling up one leg up on the bed she turned to face Ree, looking like a girl at a sleep over party dishing for details.

"I'm not sure what you want to hear about." Ree brushed a hand over her face.

"I'm the goddess of love, Alastriana." Narrowing her eyes, Aphrodite poked Ree in the shoulder. "Tell me about the kiss."

"I guess you mean my kiss with Roland? Why do you really care?"

"I have a soft spot for Roland. Let's say I'm one of the few gods that actually care about how he has been treated." For the first time, Aphrodite looked fierce. "He's been treated poorly from the beginning and I have a habit of rooting for the underdog."

"Then why did you send Paden to watch over me? Why did you put us in this horrible place? Both of them are going to hate me before this is all over!" Ree stood up and glared at the goddess. "Why did you let Roland think he was my soul mate? Why didn't you keep me from kissing him and hurting Paden?"

Aphrodite stood up suddenly. She seemed much taller than Ree, and there was an angry fire flashing in her eyes. "Sit down little girl. I might be underestimated by my brethren, but I am a goddess and will be given the respect I deserve."

"You have to earn respect and so far all I've seen is manipulation and pain! I'm tired of hurting. I'm tired of watching the people I love hurt!" Ree screamed at the goddess, her rage taking over her common sense.

"Sit down, Ree. And let's talk." Aphrodite suddenly looked tired and waved a hand at the bed. "Let's see if we can't clear up this mess."

Startled by the goddess's change in temperament, Ree's rage left her and she was even more tired. Sitting back down on the bed, Ree turned to face the goddess and watched her with cautious eyes.

"Casualties in war are an expected consequence." Sitting down next to Ree, Aphrodite's eyes stared off into space. "Mothers left with children to rear by themselves, innocent people caught in the cross fire, and heroes that are willing to give their lives so others will be safe. Sometimes when you are coming up with a strategy, there are things sacrificed for the greater good."

Ree watched the goddess's face closely. This was the most a god had spoken to Ree, and she didn't want to miss anything.

"When the dark gods decided to take Roland from Tria, they were hoping Tria would be too soft to kill someone that she had loved. They had hoped his face would make her weak. In some ways, they were right. She hadn't been able to kill him, but she had proven stronger than anyone could have hoped. She gave her life to return his humanity. She was the exact reason we were fighting for our planet. Humans have an amazing capacity for love. It's one of your greatest strengths." Pausing, Aphrodite opened her eyes and looked at Ree shrewdly.

"It's also a weakness." Ree looked at the goddess with open eyes.

"A double-edged sword." Aphrodite nodded. "But I think you are strong enough to use it in the right way."

Running her hand over her face again, Ree grunted. "I don't feel strong enough. I have no idea how to navigate this mess, and I feel like I need to figure it out before it explodes in our faces."

"You already know who your soul belongs with." Aphrodite stated it calmly and Ree nodded. She did know Paden was the person that completed her. It shouldn't be possible to know that, it should be harder to tell, but it wasn't. Something in her knew he fit her in every way, but she also didn't want to hurt Roland.

"But Roland…" Ree trailed off, not sure what she really felt for her friend.

"Ah, yes." Aphrodite frowned. "Roland has been led to believe he waited all this time for you." Something in the goddess's voice made Ree look up. Aphrodite was clearly angry about how Roland had been misled. "I was overruled on that one. Some felt he was a weapon we could not afford to lose."

"So, what? He's an acceptable casualty?" Ree shook her head in anger. "I love him, Aphrodite. It isn't what it should be, but I love him. Me, not just my memories of Tria. He is a good man and he deserves better than this. He deserves better than hundreds of years of torture and disappointment."

Nodding her head, Aphrodite looked pleased with Ree's announcement. "I told you I have a soft spot for Roland. I think he has suffered more than enough. That's why I'm here to talk to you. I worked out a deal with one of the other gods."

"Hecate." Ree breathed the word as understanding pulsed in her heart. There was a small tug of jealousy, but it wasn't enough to outshine the relief that ran through her body. "You sent Melanie for Roland."

Aphrodite nodded. "Yes, just like I made sure Bryce and Juliette wouldn't be alone. I knew they would both be watching you, and I wasn't willing to split them up for eternity." Narrowing her eyes. "I've been pushed around enough. Love can be your strongest ally, your sharpest weapon, and your biggest weakness. It's time the other gods learn a little respect."

"What if we lose? Or if one of them dies?" Ree asked, her voice trembling.

"If you lose, it won't really matter, will it?" Aphrodite shrugged. "And I have a feeling it's going to take all of you to win. That's why I'm here. They don't understand the true power of soul mates. They thought to hedge their bets with having two men in love with you, but that kind of drama would only serve to distract, rather than empower you. "

Ree took a few breaths to try and calm her racing heart. Was it possible one of the gods was actually worried about their happiness, not just what they could accomplish?

"How do I fix this with Paden? I betrayed him." Ree swallowed and looked at Aphrodite, for the first time really trusting a goddess.

"You'll figure it out. And trust me, Paden feels like he has messed up just as badly." Aphrodite smiled. "I think he always figured you would end up kissing Roland at some point. Roland needed to say goodbye to Tria, needed to be able to let go."

"I let him kiss me, though. I made the decision to

kiss him back." Ree shook her head, feeling forlorn. The worst part was, while she regretted hurting Paden, she didn't really regret kissing Roland. It had been coming, it had to happen, and she was glad they had moved past it.

"He's attractive and intelligent." Aphrodite made an amused noise. "You remember how Tria felt for him. Of course, you kissed him. Love comes in many shapes and sizes, Alastriana."

"How can Paden forgive me?" Ree's voice was small and tired. "How could I kiss someone that wasn't my soul mate?"

"That's a question you will have to ask him." Aphrodite smiled. There was no condescension, or pity. "As for kissing someone that isn't your soul mate? People do it all the time. Not everyone incarnates together for every life. People often date and enjoy other people until they find their soul mate."

Nodding, Ree looked down at the floor. She would have to talk to Paden soon, but she still didn't know what to say to him. The bed shifted next to Ree and Aphrodite stood up.

"Thank you for explaining so much." Ree looked up and met her eyes.

"You're welcome." Aphrodite smiled. "I know things feel like a complete mess right now, but I think you will be able to figure it out."

"I hope so." Ree gave the goddess a small smile. Aphrodite winked and disappeared just as another thought crossed Ree's mind. "What about Weylin?"

No one answered.

Chapter 7

After a long, hot shower, Ree climbed into her bed and fell asleep almost immediately. Unfortunately, her dreams were anything but restful. She flitted between scenes of Roland and Tria, to images of Paden and Ree in different lives. Some of the moments were happy, others were bittersweet, but in each one the amount of love was palpable.

After a while, the images started to fade and were replaced with a fog Ree could barely see through. Voices drifted to her, and she moved in their direction. Taking careful steps, the fog started to clear and she found herself in an ornate hallway. A large golden doorframe bracketed the end of the hallway, and she crept cautiously forward.

"She needs to be punished!" Ares's angry voice rang through the hallway and Ree froze, her heart beating rapidly in her chest.

"We need her." A man's calm voice carried to Ree's ears, and she felt her feet moving again. Inching toward the door, she carefully peeked into the room. It was filled with thrones, most of which were occupied by different people. Recognition came quickly, and Ree bit her lip to keep from making a sound. This was the gods' throne room. The same place Hecate had warned her not to return. Unfortunately, she had no idea how she had gotten there the first time and no idea how she had gotten there this time either.

"She cannot show so little respect. I am the god of war. She should fear me." Ares's angry voice made Ree wince. He was talking about her and she knew it.

"I think you've already managed to scare her, Ares. Perhaps that's why she called the power in the first place." Hecate's calm voice was smooth and peaceful.

"She is human." He spat the last word out as if it was an insult. "I can do as I please to her."

"She is the Alastriana and should not fear us. We need her to fight for us." Hecate's tone turned placating, as if she was talking to an unruly child.

"Fear is a good motivator." Another god spoke from the other side of the throne room. Ree couldn't see his face, but his voice made her shiver.

"Anubis, your tactics would defeat our purpose." Athena's voice was calm and collected. "The Alastriana is not someone who will take well to fear. She is likely to rebel and fight against us."

Hushed whispers spread through the room, and Ree wished she could get closer to hear what they were saying about her.

"You should not have chosen such a headstrong soul for this job." Anubis said again. His voice was dark and heavy with an accent Ree had trouble making out. "She may buck your carefully laid plans."

"Nonsense. Only a strong soul would be able to take on the demands we have laid at her feet. She had to be someone that would rise to the challenge." Hecate's voice cut into the conversation.

"We are not here to discuss your strategy." Ares's angry voice echoed through the room. "We are here to discuss her punishment."

"Why did the Alastriana feel the need to call the power in your presence?" Another woman's voice asked, this one filled with bitterness.

"Hera, I think the better question is why Ares was bothering the Alastriana in the first place." Aphrodite's bored voice made Ree's eyes widen. Was the goddess really as bored as she sounded, or was she actually taking up for Ree?

"Stay out of this, Wench." Ares's voice was disgusted. "Why don't you go find someone to play with?"

"Don't be angry that I don't like your idea of fun. Chains and whips aren't my style." Aphrodite's voice stayed bored, but there was an undercurrent of disdain. Ares growled when a few chuckles followed her comment.

"Settle down, Ares. Aphrodite has a good point. Why were you bothering the Alastriana?" The man that had originally said they needed Ree spoke up, and it was obvious the people in the room respected him in some way, because the room quieted down immediately.

"I wanted to see if she was ready for the upcoming battle." Ares's voice was quieter, more controlled.

"Perhaps." The man's voice sounded dangerous and Ree wished she knew who was doing the talking. "Or perhaps you were trying to further some other agenda."

"Mighty Zeus, what would Ares have to gain by hurting the Alastriana?" Loki's voice made Ree's skin crawl.

"Not as much as he might think." Athena's voice replied calmly. "It should be understood that anyone seen as a traitor will be treated as such. I give my solemn vow I will hunt down anyone that would see this world taken out of our control."

"Peace, sister." Loki laughed as if enjoying some private joke. "No one would want you on their trail."

"I am not your sister, Loki. Do not address me as such." Athena's voice stabbed through the room, and Ree was glad she couldn't see the goddess's face.

"I will be on the hunt as well. I will not stand for a traitor." A much younger-sounding voice echoed through the room. "Athena would not have to hunt alone."

"No one would want to be on the opposite end of your hunt, Artemis." Loki's voice sounded respectful, but Ree would never trust that god. Maybe he did fear the young-sounding goddess, but Ree didn't doubt he would think it a game to try and outfox her.

"Zeus, I would ask that you forbid Ares to visit the Alastriana." Hecate's voice changed the subject.

"You would dare to tell me what to do, Hecate?" Ares stood up from his black and bloody throne, his back to Ree. "Who are you to dictate my actions?"

"We cannot afford for you to endanger our plans. We've made many sacrifices to get to this point." Hecate sounded like a mother scolding a child. "Now, sit down and let your father answer."

The attention in the room seemed to shift toward a corner Ree couldn't see, but it obviously housed Zeus's throne. No one said anything as Zeus pondered the request.

"Ares, it is best for you to avoid the Alastriana and

her Guardians. They need no distraction from the task at hand." Zeus's voice made it clear he would brook no argument, but Ares sputtered.

"Father, I am a god of war! Shouldn't I be a part of the preparations for an upcoming battle?" Ares leaned forward in his chair, as if to look at Zeus better.

Unable to help herself, Ree took a step closer to the door to try and see better. Hecate's eyes snapped to hers and widened slightly. Ree froze, her heart stuttering. Would the goddess announce that Ree was present? Carefully, Hecate turned her head as if she had not seen anything, but Ree knew better.

"It is not your place to question me, Ares. I have declared you are to avoid the girl. This is a time for strategy, not battle." Zeus stood up and walked into the middle of the room. He was taller than any human Ree had ever seen. His skin glowed and he carried a golden staff shaped like a lightning bolt. He came to stand in front of Ares, and Ree moved away from the doorway, afraid that the god's silver eyes might see her. "If you go near the girl again, and I have proof, then you've signed your own death warrant."

There was a loud gasp, and murmurs circulated through the room, but Zeus was not finished talking. Turning away from Ares, he looked at the other gods and goddesses. "That goes for anyone else who would harm the girl in any way."

Was it her imagination, or did Zeus's eyes rest in the direction of Loki's throne? Deciding it was time to get as far from that room as possible, Ree slowly tiptoed back in the direction she had come. The fog was still at the end of the hall, and Ree hoped it would take her away from the home of the gods. Last time she had been here, Hecate had sent her back. She still wasn't sure how she had gotten here in the first place, but she was glad to have gleaned some more information. Everything she knew brought her closer to getting her friends out of this mess alive.

The fog closed around her feet, which she was amused to note were wearing the thin, gold sandals from her last visit to the god's home. The further she walked into the thick, fluffy cloud, the sleepier Ree became, until eventually she wasn't aware of anything around her.

Ree sat up in her bed and took a deep breath. Her eyes searched for the clock and frowned at the numbers. It was almost midnight. She had been asleep a lot longer than she thought. Throwing the covers off of her, she hopped out of bed and padded over to the wardrobe against the wall. She opened the drawer and was relieved to find clean clothes. Pulling out a pair of jeans and long sleeved t-shirt, she quickly threw them on and looked around for her tennis shoes.

As she finished tying the laces, someone knocked on her door making her jump. If she was immortal, shouldn't she have heard them coming? She was going to have to work on that soon. Letting the power wash out of her, she walked over to the door and took a deep breath.

Paden was standing on the other side, his face blank and she could feel him trying to hide his emotions from her. "I heard you get up. Can we talk?"

Chapter 8

"Sure." Ice settled into Ree's gut as she looked up into Paden's face. She had messed up her chance with her soul mate. How could he possibly ever forgive her for kissing Roland back? "Um, do you want to talk in here?"

"Why don't we go for a walk?" Paden took a step back and jerked his head toward the garden.

Nodding, Ree stepped out into the hallway and pulled her door shut behind her. Stuffing her hands into the pockets on the back of her jeans, Ree followed Paden out of the house. He held the door open for her and her heart ached. Even with everything that had happened he was being polite to her. He was much calmer than he had been earlier and it scared her down to the bottoms of her feet.

They walked for a while, the moon shining through the branches of the trees to dance across the sandy path near the beach. Eventually, the trees thinned and Ree could see the water. Paden seemed to have a destination in mind, so she just let him lead the way. After a while, Paden sat down facing the water, his legs pulled up in front of him and his arms braced on his knees. Ree sat down quietly next to him and looked out at the water. Her stomach was clenched and her heart was thudding in her ears. Had he brought her all the way out here, so the others wouldn't hear if she made a scene? She felt as if she was standing on the edge of a cliff, waiting for him to push her off, all the while knowing she deserved it.

After a while, she cut her eyes toward Paden and watched the sea breeze ruffle his hair. His face was stoic, but she could feel his carefully concealed turmoil. She hated to watch him suffer, even if it was to find the words to break her heart.

"Paden, I'm sorry. I understand if you—"

"Do you love him?" Cutting her off, he glanced at her and then quickly away.

Ree became conscious that her mouth was hanging open, so she snapped it shut and shook her head no. When she realized he might not have seen her response, she cleared her throat and his eyes cut back to her face.

"No. Not like that. Not like…" Her voice caught, but she pushed on. "Not like I love you." Paden closed his eyes for a moment and Ree tried to keep from crying. "I'm not trying to make this harder on you. I know you deserve much better than me. I don't even really know why or how it happened. It was stupid and I wish… I wish you could forgive me, but I know that's not possible. I won't make things difficult."

He opened his eyes so they were barely slits and looked at her. "You don't love him." His words were odd, and didn't make sense to her at first.

"No, no. I mean, I care about him. I want good things for him, but I'm not in love with him. I remember how much Tria loved him and it made things kind of confusing, but that's gone. Roland was meant for someone else." Ree took a deep breath and wrapped her arms around her waist. She almost told him she was meant for him, but that wasn't fair. She didn't need to make things harder on him.

Paden's breath came out raggedly and he hung his head so she couldn't see his face. Biting her bottom lip, she looked away and tried to keep the tears from running down her face. Part of her wanted to find a place to cry, while another part of her wanted to yell and kick things.

"Ree, I'm sorry." Paden didn't look up at her, and Ree felt her heart sink. This was it, the end. Her tears ran down her cheeks, but she didn't say anything. She'd let him finish and do her best to not make a scene. "I never should have made that bet with Roland. I shouldn't have treated you like you were an object to be won."

"Why did you?" Confused, Ree wiped at her cheeks with her sleeve.

Looking up at her, his face looked terrified. "No, Ree, don't cry. Please." He moved as if he was going to touch her face, but stopped. He shook his head and licked his lips. "I thought I would win. I wanted to win, to be better than him. It was stupid, but I thought it would prove that you were supposed to be with me." Running a hand through his hair, his eyes got a wild look to them. "God, Ree. Do you know what it felt like to see him holding you? Kissing you?" His breath came out raggedly. She shook her head, but didn't say anything.

"And it was my own damn fault." He looked at her seriously, his eyes wide and earnest. "But, you're not in love with him?"

Again, she shook her head no and waited to see what he would say. "Do you…" He stopped and seemed to struggle for words.

"I love you, Paden." Reaching a shaky hand out, Ree touched his fingers and gasped when he yanked her into his lap. His arms crushed her to him, his fingers tangled in her hair and he tucked her head under his chin.

"I love you, Alastriana McKenna. And I never want to see you in someone else's arms again. You belong right here. Right here with me." He turned so he was talking against her hair. "I love you."

"I'm so sorry, Paden." Ree mumbled into his shirt. "I love you so much. I never meant to hurt you."

Paden pulled back and used a finger to lift her chin so he could look into her eyes. "No. Don't be sorry. I think… I think it had to happen for you both to move on. And I made just as big a mistake, okay? I should never have made that bet. You are worth so much more than my pride. Do you understand that? You're my life, Ree."

"So, you're not breaking up with me?" Ree bit her lip and felt the stirring of joy and relief in her heart.

"Break up with you?" Paden gave her a small smile before tucking her head back against his chest. "How does someone break up with their own heart? To not have you would be like living half a life. Only death will keep me from you, and then only for a little while."

Ree laughed weakly, her tears choking her as she buried her face in his shirt. His arms tightened around her, and he shifted her gently so he was lying down, and she was tucked against his chest. They didn't say anything for a while. Instead Ree stared at the stars and enjoyed being in Paden's arms. His free hand toyed with her hair and she cuddled up to him as closely as she could get.

"I meant it, Ree. I would fight all of the Dark Ones by myself to keep you." Paden's voice rumbled through his chest, making her body ache to be closer to him.

"And I would fight the gods for you." Ree moved so her leg was thrown over his and she wrapped her arm over his chest.

"Those are dangerous words." Paden said quietly, but he turned his head so he could kiss her hair.

"Those are true words." She looked up at him, so he could see the fierceness in her eyes. He nodded and smiled at her before tucking her head back down onto his chest.

The sound of the lapping waves seemed to soothe their hurts as they lay under the stars in each other's arms. After a while, Ree started to drift to sleep, only to jerk awake when Paden shifted.

"I guess we need to head back to the house." Ree sat up and brushed some of the hair out of her face.

"Why?" Shrugging out of his jacket, Paden held his arms open in invitation to her. She melted back into him and smiled when he covered the two of them with his coat. "I want to spend the next few hours holding you."

"Sounds perfect." Cuddling back into him, she put her hand on his chest and smiled when he covered it with his own.

After a while, Ree's eyes fluttered open and she saw Aphrodite tending a small campfire. The goddess smiled at Ree and put a finger to her lips. Snuggling closer to Paden, Ree closed her eyes and went back to sleep.

Chapter 9

The sound of hissing may have woken Ree, but it was the stinging cold water droplets that kept her awake. Rubbing a hand across her face, she looked around the area in confusion. Soft rain fell from the early morning sky, causing the fire to sputter out. A rumble of thunder woke Paden, who cussed under his breath and pulled Ree up and out of the sand. He held his jacket over their heads as they ran for the cover of the trees.

"And this would be why I never wanted to go camping." Ree laughed.

"Congratulations. You just spent your first night roughing it." Paden winked at Ree.

The clouds opened up just as they reached the large tree Ree had fallen out of not so long ago. Laughing, Ree fended off the wet assault when Paden shook his head, sending water flying in all directions. Paden narrowed his eyes at her before pushing her against the tree and rubbing his wet hair along her face. She couldn't help the squeal that escaped her lips as she tried to shove him away. Somehow during their struggle, Paden's leg ended up pressed between hers and her heart started to flutter in her chest for very different reasons. Paden seemed to be experiencing the same thoughts, because his mouth touched hers in a scorching kiss. His hands tangled in her wet hair, tipping her head backward so he could reach her easier. Tiny pricks on her lips meant his fangs were down, but that only urged Ree onward. Running her hands over his wet t-shirt, she traced the outlines of his muscles with her fingertips.

Her heart stuttered when his hands followed the same path hers had, only over her shirt. When his hands hesitated along the lines of her bra, she leaned into him, wanting more. She could literally feel his resolve weaken as his hands ran over her body freely. When he lifted the hem of her shirt so his fingers could touch her skin, she moaned into his mouth.

His breath stuttered against her skin while he trailed kisses down her neck. When his fangs scratched gently over her skin, she felt a small sting of pain that quickly disappeared as he healed her. His mouth continued its downward journey, his hot breath teasing her skin through the wet material of her shirt. She gasped in pleasure, her hands tangling in his hair.

Water from the rainstorm dripped through the leaves and ran along their faces and down their bodies as they stayed pressed against the tree. The soft sound of wind filled their little area, and Ree knew her power was swirling through the fallen leaves at their feet. There was no way she could control the power at this point, but if all it did was churn around them happily, then she decided it would be fine. At least out here no one would notice.

Running his hands under the back of her shirt, he played with the clasp of her bra. After a moment, it snapped open and his breath shuddered out of him. Almost timidly, his hands slid around to the front of her body and her back arched in pleasure.

Ree could barely form a coherent thought as Paden's hands and mouth touched her hot skin. The only thing she was capable of deciding was that she wanted more. She wanted to touch him and never stop. Moving her hands out of his hair, she slid them down his chest and grabbed the top of his jeans. With nervous jerks, she undid the button and traced her fingers along the top of his boxers. Paden sucked in his breath and grabbed her wrists. Very slowly, he lifted her arms so they were pinned above her head.

"You can't do that, Ree." His breathing was heavy as he nuzzled her neck.

"Why not?" Ree pulled her hands down and lifted his face so she could see him better.

"Because I don't think I would be able to stop. I want… I want you so much." His eyes stared into hers intently, and she could feel the truth under his words.

"Then why stop? I want you, too." Ree ran her thumb over his bottom lip to catch a drop of water that had travelled down his face.

"Because now isn't the right time." Paden slid his hands down so they wrapped around her waist. "Not here, not in the mud."

"Our whole world is a mess. We could die tomorrow. Why not here, in the mud?" Ree widened her eyes.

"Did you really just pull the 'we could die tomorrow' card?" Paden's body shook against Ree's with laughter. Leaning down he kissed the top of her head. "God, I love you Ree."

"So, is that a no?" Ree couldn't help but laugh, even if she was disappointed.

"That's a 'not right now'. When I make love to you, I

want to be able to take my time. And I don't have any protection. The last thing we need to be worried about right now is you being pregnant." The laughter left Paden's eyes and he looked at her seriously. Ree shivered, the word pregnant bouncing around in her head like the sound of a gunshot.

"So, I guess we should head back to the house?" Ree sighed.

"Probably. It's after dawn and the others are most likely up." Paden kissed her gently, his own feelings of disappointment making her feel a little better. Stepping back, he fixed the button on his jeans. Ree blushed a little and looked away. She reached behind her to redo her bra clasp and tried to shake the image of Paden with his pants undone.

She had done that, unbuttoned his pants and been ready for more. Consequences had been the farthest thing from her mind. Trying to calm herself, she turned and ran her fingers over the rough bark of the tree.

"So, when did you start a fire?" Paden asked.

"Hm? Oh, on the beach? I didn't. That was Aphrodite." Ree didn't turn to look at Paden. Her mind caught by something familiar surrounding the tree.

"Aphrodite?" Paden moved closer to her, his voice confused. "Uh huh."

"The goddess of love. I guess we looked cold." Paden sounded odd, so Ree looked at him and smiled. "It is their island, you know."

"Kind of creepy when you think about it." Paden shook his head and looked to where Ree was touching the tree.

"You know, this tree is really spectacular." Ree let

her fingers travel over the rough bark with interest. "It feels alive, like it has a personality."

"I know what you mean." Paden touched the bark next to Ree's hand. "I swear it's happy when you're around."

Ree used her senses to reach out to the tree and was surprised to feel it did indeed seem happy she was there. And even more importantly when she looked with her extra sense, she could see the fog that surrounded her when she travelled to the god's realm. Could this tree be a bridge of some kind?

"Paden, last night before we talked I visited the god's realm again. And I think this tree is the reason I've been making trips over there." Ree looked over her shoulder at him and realized he was frowning again. "What?"

"You were over there with them again? Why didn't you tell me?"

"We had other stuff to talk about. We needed to get through our mess before we could talk about the rest." Turning around, Ree grabbed his hand. "I couldn't function, thinking that I had ruined my chance with you."

"You can't ruin your chances with me, Ree. I'm a sure thing." Paden touched her cheek gently. "But, please tell me if anything like that happens again. I can't take care of you if I don't know what's going on."

Ree nodded, but didn't say anything. She was pretty sure that there was nothing Paden could do about her traveling to the god's realm and she felt that, in a way, it had helped her to understand more of their situation. Obviously Paden could sense what she was thinking, but he didn't say anything, just tightened his hand around hers.

"So what happened last night before our talk?" Paden

started walking toward the house, his fingers urging her to come with him.

So, she told him about Aphrodite, about Melanie and Roland, about the gods being worried about her power. She explained what she understood about the gods' plans, how there were connections between them all, how they had acted like politicians playing with her and her friends' lives.

"Paden, they sat around discussing us like we were things. Nothing more than tools or pets that needed to be kept in line. All of it, everything they do, is probably to point us in some direction, or in hopes of getting us to react a certain way." Ree kicked at a rock as they walked and watched in shock as it flew much further than she thought possible. She looked at Paden with big eyes.

"I think you're going to need to do some of the training we did while you were learning to use the power. It takes some getting used to." Paden's fingers squeezed hers reassuringly.

"Even this." Ree gestured at her body with her free hand. "Even this change is because of something they planned. I don't like being used like a toy."

"We need to just get through this war, then we try to claim our lives." Looking at Ree as they walked, Paden frowned. "We don't really even know what all you got from Sophie. You didn't get the fangs, but what about the healing?"

Ree thought about that for a moment. She hadn't even thought about the fact that she hadn't gotten the fangs. She wasn't used to having them, so not having them hadn't been something to worry about. "Did you heal me, back at the tree? I felt your fangs scratch me, but it went away really quickly."

"I think it was automatic. I knew I had hurt you, so healed you at the same time. Maybe I didn't need to." Paden stopped walking and turned her to face him. "I'm sorry about that. I got a little carried away."

"It's okay." Ree touched his face. "But, maybe we should test the healing thing. We can do something small, and if it doesn't work then you can heal me."

"I can't hurt you, Ree." Paden's brows drew together. "I don't know if I can keep from healing you. It's part of who I am."

"We can start small." Ree looked around the little path.

"Start small? What do we need to do to prove you heal? Cut out a lung?" Tugging on Ree's hand, Paden demanded her full attention. "We can try something, but we aren't going to do something crazy. A paper cut would let us know."

"Maybe. Let's see if I heal at all first. But, I want to know what I've got to work with. I don't have fangs, and there might be other things my body didn't transition for. Let's face it. You had the genetic makeup to change into a Guardian. My lowly human genes weren't made to do this."

Paden looked around the clearing in frustration, before he finally reached into his pocket and pulled out a knife. He flicked it open and looked at Ree seriously. "Fine. But, something small. Don't cut off your finger."

Ree frowned at him and took the knife. She thought about it for a moment and then lifted the blade to the skin on her arm. Biting her bottom lip, she dragged the blade quickly across the soft skin and tried to not hiss. Paden made an odd sound that had her looking up at him and away from the cut. His hands were glowing, but he backed away from her slowly so he couldn't heal her. His eyes looked slightly panicked, but otherwise he seemed in control. She looked back at her arm and smiled. The cut was mostly healed, just an angry pink line was left.

Feeling relief, she lifted her arm to show Paden and gasped when she found him standing right in front of her. His fingers wiped away the blood and he looked carefully at the skin.

"I heal!" Ree looked at her arm, feeling smug.

"Yes, but I don't think it's as fast as we do." Paden's green eyes looked troubled.

"Well, any healing at all is better than what I had to begin with, right?" Ree pulled her arm back and pulled her sleeve back down.

"Of course it is. But I don't think you will heal quite the same way we do. You might not be able to take as much damage as we can." Paden took her hand in his and started back toward the house.

"So, I still have to be careful." Ree twisted her mouth in thought. "But, it's better than before, Pay. I mean, now I don't have to worry about someone kicking me and collapsing my lung. Or hitting my head and getting a concussion."

"True. But let's stay on the cautious side. We still don't know how your body would handle a large wound. Even we can only take so much." Paden didn't look at her, just kept his eyes on the trail. Ree could feel his confusion and worry floating around them, and it frustrated her. This could be one of the best things to come out of all this mess, and he wasn't excited. Obviously attuned to her the way she was to him, he raised an eyebrow and frowned. "What's wrong with you?"

"Me? What's wrong with you? Do you realize what

this means?" Ree lifted her arm. "I heal Paden. What if I don't age anymore either?"

Paden stopped in his tracks and turned to look at her with bright green eyes. For a moment, he just stood there looking at her. Then he had her in his arms with his mouth pressed to hers. After a moment he pulled back and looked down at her, his face almost boyishly happy.

"That means I wouldn't have to live without you. I couldn't even think about it before, because I didn't know how it would be possible." He framed her face in his hands and kissed her again gently. "This may be the best thing that's ever happened to me. To get to have you forever."

Ree laughed, relieved he finally understood her excitement. "As long as you can put up with me."

"Promise me." He kept her face in his hands, his eyes bright with something Ree couldn't define. "Promise that I can have you forever."

"Forever." Ree whispered the word. She knew in her heart, that this was a very important moment for them. Their declaration of forever was as serious as the war happening to them. If she couldn't be with Paden in this life, she would find another way.

Chapter 10

The others were up and about, working in the training room, or in the office going through Sophie's things. Ree went to the office while Paden headed for the gym, she needed some time to think, to figure out the next step and she hoped that maybe she would find something in Sophie's office to help point her in the right direction.

Melanie and Roland were glaring at each other when she walked into the room, and Ree stopped dead in her tracks. The tension was almost overwhelming, and she needed a minute to sort it from her own feelings. Melanie was the first to acknowledge Ree's presence. Nodding her head at Ree, Melanie closed the file cabinet and walked out of the room. Her friend's back was rigid, her head held at a haughty angle. Ree stepped out of Melanie's way, her eyes following her slow, angry steps. When her friend's back disappeared from view, Ree's eyes snapped back to Roland.

He stood there with his hands clenched at his sides, his face devoid of expression. His eyes slid to Ree's and his shoulders drooped, as if all of his years weighed on him in that very instant.

"You and Paden have made up, I take it?" His voice was blank, as if he was past caring about anything.

"Yes." Ree forced her arms to hang calmly by her sides. She wasn't sure what to make of Roland's emotions. He had them held tightly inside, and Ree's heart clenched. She hoped one day he would be able to forgive her for the situation they were in and be friends again, because at this moment she had no idea how to proceed.

He jerked his chin to signal he understood, but just stood there staring at her. After a long silence, she looked away and bit her lip. There was nothing she could do to make this better. She would always be the girl he had suffered for; the girl that loved someone else. How could she right all of those wrongs?

"I'm trying." Roland's accent became more pronounced, as if struggling with his emotions made it difficult to keep his words clear. "I don't blame you. I'm just trying to figure out what I do now. I waited for so, so long, only to have you love another." He stopped, stumbling over his words. He looked at her with large, blue eyes, every inch the nineteen year old boy he appeared to be.

"I'm sorry." It was Ree's turn to clutch her hands at her sides. She wanted to comfort him in some way; she wanted to take away the pain in his eyes, but she would only make it worse.

"Never be sorry for loving someone, Ree." Taking a deep breath, he looked away and stared into the empty fireplace. "We've all been put in this position by others. All we can do now is make the best of it."

"Melanie…" Ree trailed off at Roland's glance.

"Melanie is… angry with me. We're all under a lot of

stress right now." He shrugged his shoulders as if trying to work out the kinks. "I came in here to see if perhaps Sophie knew anything that might have been helpful."

"Did you guys not share information?" Ree walked over to the desk and flipped through some of the papers on the Guardian's desk. There were receipts for the antique shop, addresses scribbled on edges of paper, names underlined, and bills for the utilities.

"I thought we did." Roland let out a harsh breath as he opened the file cabinet. He ruffled through the folders for a moment. "I never suspected Sophie was waiting to make a Death Gift to you. It never occurred to me they would use us in such a way." His hands stilled and he took a deep breath. "I believed their lies."

"We all believed their lies." Ree kept her voice quiet, sensing the stress under his words.

"Sophie didn't. Sophie knew they were planning on using her death to help save the world." He swung his fist into the side of the filing cabinet, buckling the metal with a loud screech. "She knew she was walking around, waiting to die when she finally got her sister back. Some kind of sacrificial lamb waiting for slaughter."

"She must have believed it was the right thing to do, Roland. Sophie was an amazing woman. I can't believe she would have fallen in line with that plan if she didn't think it was a good idea." Ree felt tears well up in her eyes, but blinked them away. "Now, we just have to make her sacrifice worth something."

Roland lifted his head to look at Ree. There was so much pain in his eyes, Ree had to clench her hands to keep from running over to hug him. She didn't think they were at a point yet where they could hug and have it not be uncomfortable. She wasn't at that point yet. After a moment, he nodded his head and looked around the room.

"I don't think she would have had some secret plan for beating the Dark Ones that she was waiting to spring on us. Well, other than the whole Death Gift deal." Roland ran a hand through his hair and looked around the office as if lost.

"What we need is a plan, but you're right. We aren't going to find one outlined in her files. We need to come up with one ourselves." Ree looked back down at the paperwork in front of her and frowned. She pulled out a piece of paper that was barely visible. "What was the name of the guy with the two twin boys?"

"The one from New Year's?" Roland's eyebrows drew together as he thought. "John, I believe. John Hansen. Why?"

"She has his name scribbled down on the side of this paper." Ree held it up so she could look it over. Roland came around the desk and read over her shoulder.

"That's a list of people we know have an immortal bloodline." Carefully, he pointed at the top two names. They had lines drawn through them. "Those two families were killed while we were on the island the first time. I bet Sophie made this list to try and keep track of everyone."

"Do you think she was going to try to get them out of here?" Ree turned to look at him, hope filling her chest.

"I don't know, Ree. If she was, she didn't tell me. And I know she told you it was dangerous to go against the gods' will. She was right." His eyes leveled on hers, his expression serious.

"I want—"

"Don't Ree." He covered her mouth with his hand. He looked around the room and shook his head. "You never know who is listening."

Ree closed her eyes and let the power surge out of her body and fill the room. She didn't get that uneasy feeling she had when Aphrodite had been waiting in her room. "We're alone."

"I don't know how you know that, but it doesn't matter. They don't have to be here to listen in. Just keep whatever you are thinking to yourself." He ducked down so she could see his face clearly and mouthed, For now.

She nodded her head so he would know she understood, and she folded up the piece of paper and stuck it in her jean's pocket. She was going to look at that list later to see if she could figure out what Sophie had been thinking.

"Okay, then we should find the others and decide on a plan." Ree stepped out from behind the desk. The office felt so empty without Sophie.

"Let's not forget that you need to train. There are things you need to know. And I'm looking forward to getting you set with some weapons." Roland headed for the door, but not before throwing her a smile over his shoulder. "It's always interesting to see what people are called to."

Ree smiled in return and felt her heart lighten just a little. Roland's smile had been very close to his normal cocky grin, and it set Ree's heart at ease. There was hope they would all make it out of this after all.

The others were in the workout room training with the equipment. Paden was beating the practice dummy into an unrecognizable lump, while Melanie and Juliette worked on throwing knives at the other end of the room. Ree's eyes focused on Weylin and Bryce, though, and the weapons they were fighting with.

Each held a long, slightly curved blade at the ready

and circled the center of the mat slowly. Ree was pretty sure they were Samurai swords, but she wasn't willing to ask and interrupt. There was something special about the way they moved. It was slow and graceful, yet there was an unspoken strength and certainty in each step. If she had to guess, she would say Bryce was the more confident. When they finally moved, it was a blinding flash of steel and male bodies, but her newly developed eyesight kept track easily.

Bryce was definitely the aggressor in the battle, but Weylin managed to hold his own. As Bryce ducked forward, swinging his blade in a quick sweep, Weylin flipped backward and brought his sword down in an arc. Blood splashed the mats lining the floor and Ree gasped. Roland placed a hand on her shoulder, keeping her in place. She didn't look at him, worried she might miss something vital.

Bryce didn't stop his movement; instead he dropped to the mat and swept his leg through Weylin's. Weylin landed hard on his back and had barely managed to raise his sword to protect himself before Bryce had the tip of his blade pressed into his neck.

"You almost got me that time, Wey." Bryce moved his sword and held a hand out for Weylin.

"I did get you. Just not good enough." Weylin took Bryce's hand and let his friend help him stand.

"Bryce, are you okay?" Ree shook off Roland's hand and walked over to her friends.

He looked down at his shoulder and shrugged. "Yeah. He barely nicked me."

"But, all the blood…" Ree looked down at the floor and frowned. There was red splattering a good bit of the mats.

"That's not a big deal. We bleed a lot when we're training." Weylin walked over to a closet that had brooms and mops.

"Oh. I see." Ree's eyebrows drew together and she bit her lip.

"No one's going to make you bleed, Ree." Paden stood next to the practice dummy, his arm propped on the smashed head.

"Don't promise her that, godling. She needs to learn just like you all did." Roland looked at Paden with steady eyes. There was something passing between the two, but Ree couldn't be sure what. It really wasn't her place to try and understand it either.

"There's no reason for her to get hurt." Paden stood up straight and frowned at Roland.

"Paden, don't make this difficult. I'm sure Weylin wasn't trying to hurt Bryce just to hurt him. They were practicing. It's the same kind of thing Ree needs. She'll be stronger for it." Melanie threw a towel over her shoulder and broke the seal on a bottle of water.

"I was too trying to hurt Bryce!" Weylin groaned. "I just didn't do as well as I would have liked."

"She's right, Pay. I need to train, and I need to do it fast." Ree pulled off her jacket and threw it on a bench. "So, what first?"

"Katas and learning your new strength." Roland pulled off his shirt, revealing a white tank top. He threw it near her jacket and pointed at the mirrors. "Take a stance, and let's move through the katas you already know."

Chapter 11

"When do I get to use weapons?" Hours after they had started, Ree bounced on her toes and smiled at Roland in the mirrors. She had picked up all of the katas easily, remembering each step as if she already knew them.

"You guys are always so eager for the weapons. The real power comes from knowing your strengths and weaknesses." Roland threw Ree some water and shook his head. "No. We start with hand-to-hand sparring. Then we move to weapons."

"How did you guys get good so fast?" Ree looked over at Paden and Weylin. They were sitting on the floor and sharpening some of the weapons.

"I was born this way, baby." Weylin winked at Ree.

"Sadly, he's right." Paden rolled his eyes and smiled at Ree. She was thankful to see him so relaxed, even though she was spending so much time with Roland. Hopefully this new calm would last while she sparred as well. She smiled at Paden, but it didn't last. A brick wall slammed into her and sent her spinning across the ground.

She shook her head but jumped to her feet quickly. Her eyes jerked around the room, while she tried to shake the shock. Roland stood back on the other side of the training mat, his hands at his side and small smile twisting his lips. Ree dropped into an open stance, and lifted her hands into defensive positions.

Roland's muscles barely tensed before he was flying across the open space between them. He reached for her left arm and she scarcely had time to think. She dodged to the right and swung her arm at the back of his head. She almost stopped moving when she made contact, but managed to use her momentum to spin behind him instead. Deftly she slammed the side of her foot into the back of his knee and sent him sprawling. She jumped on his back and slammed her elbow into the back of his neck. He grunted, but didn't move.

She looked down at him suspiciously, not convinced she had actually beaten him at his own game. She looked up when someone snorted and saw Paden and Weylin both trying to not laugh. She looked back down at Roland and frowned. When he made a grunt of frustration, she hopped off him and took a few steps backward.

Paden squatted down next to Roland and smiled. "I think she won."

"She broke my bloody neck." Roland lifted himself up onto his forearms and moved his head slowly in a circle.

"Your eyes are huge! Like, wombat huge." Weylin looked at Ree and laughed. She stood there shocked, her eyes going back and forth from Roland and Paden to Weylin.

"Weylin, wombats don't have big eyes." Roland rolled over onto his back and moved his head to pop his neck.

"They don't?" Weylin looked at Roland and frowned. "Are you sure?"

"I'm not a zoologist, Wey. I'm a Dark One. But even I know a wombat has little eyes." Roland looked over at Ree and smiled. "But he's right. Your eyes are huge."

"Are you okay? I don't know what I was thinking." Ree rubbed her palms on her pants.

"Don't worry, Ree." Paden held his hand out to Roland to help him stand. Roland took it and nodded his head in thanks. "That wasn't going to kill him. He just needed a few minutes to heal." Paden laughed when Roland jerked his neck to the side. "You certainly surprised all of us though."

"I… I… I just reacted." Ree looked at her friends and felt a laugh bubble up and out of her throat. "I totally kicked your ass." She pointed at Roland and continued to laugh.

He rubbed a hand across the back of his neck and gave her a crooked grin. "Well, I wasn't expecting you to be so damned proficient."

"She looked a lot like Sophie. I wonder what else you got from our talented leader." Paden grabbed a sword off the wall and tossed it at Ree. She caught the handle deftly and looked at the blade in question.

"That was kind of hot, you know." Weylin winked at Ree. "I like a woman who knows how to use a sword." Ree laughed at him and winked back. It was the only way to handle the guy.

"Weylin." Paden and Roland both said his name in exasperation before looking at each other thoughtfully.

"C'mon, you guys were thinking the same thing." Weylin gestured at Ree. "Well, go ahead. Do one of the Katas with the sword."

Ree looked down at the sword in her hand and enjoyed the gleam along the blade. It was long, but not as long as the broadswords hanging along the wall. Giving a few practice flicks of her wrist, she gauged the weight and noticed it felt longer than it should.

"This was made for Sophie?" She shifted her feet into the first position and held the blade in a pointed angle toward the ground. She slid her right foot forward and shifted the blade angle as if deflecting a lower slash.

"Yes." Roland's voice was quiet and thoughtful.

Ree slid into another stance, sweeping the sword through a more complicated maneuver. She closed her eyes and let the movements come naturally.

"It's a little longer when I hold it." Ree tried to keep her mind clear and focus on the muscle memory she was experiencing. It made her sad to think Sophie had died to give her this, but it also strengthened her resolve to use it. Increasing her speed, she slid through the maneuvers quickly, relishing the sharper movements. When she finished the kata, it was with her sword held high and her breathing calm and centered. She opened her eyes to find all three of the guys watching her.

Paden cleared his throat and looked sheepishly at Ree. "Well, Sophie was taller."

Ree lowered her arms and brought the sword down to her side. She looked away from the guys and back at the wall. Walking over, she grabbed one of the other swords and walked back to the mat.

"Who wants to try me?" Ree held the sword out to her side and smiled at the guys.

Weylin raised his hands and took a step back. "No thanks. I've had my ass kicked enough for the day." Ree swung her gaze to Roland and Paden. Paden's face was frustrated as he tried to war with his need to protect her and his fear of hurting her.

Roland stepped forward and held his hand out for the sword. "I'll do it." Paden's face relaxed with relief, and he nodded his thanks to Roland.

Ree stepped back and fell into a stance she shouldn't have known. Lifting her sword into a ready position, she waited for Roland to make his move. He shifted into position and lifted the blade above his head. He didn't move, his blue eyes trained on hers.

Something in Ree's mind pulled at her instincts, making her want to be the one on attack. Instead, she took a deep breath and decided to wait for Roland to make the move. When he did, she was almost shocked by the amount of grace he exhibited. Her eyes had never fully comprehended the exact movements he made. They had seemed fast and smooth, but now she could see just how his muscles bunched and how each step was deliberate.

Snapping back to reality, she raised her sword and deflected his first thrust. Spinning, he brought the sword around and toward her neck. She leaned backward and managed to miss the sweeping edge of his blade. Sliding around him, she brought her elbow toward his back, causing him to stumble once. He dropped to the ground and swept his leg through her feet. She fell onto her back and grunted. He stood up and raised his sword to bring it down for a killing blow. She rolled to the side and jumped to her feet. As she gained her footing, she brought her sword in down low and clipped his leg before he got out of the way.

He dove out of the way, ducking and rolling, his sword carefully held out to the side. He dropped into a ready stance, his sword held low. Ree stepped back so one foot was in front of the other and held her sword with two hands at waist height.

"First blood to you." Roland's expression was amused. He snapped a quick salute to her and lowered his blade to his side.

Ree grinned and lowered her own sword. Weylin let out a loud whoop and Paden smiled at her proudly.

Ree gave a quick bow and went to the wall to return the sword. "I guess Sophie passed on a lot more than we thought."

"Seems that way. I wonder if she had gotten things from Tria." Roland frowned and his face tightened with a pained expression.

"She did know how to use the power, so it's likely she had gotten that knowledge from Tria." Paden's voice was thoughtful. "Didn't she say it didn't work quite the same way for her that it did for you? Because the power wasn't intended for her to use?"

"I know she couldn't sense everything I could. I could pick out a lot more information than she was able to." Ree sat down on the mat and leaned over one of her legs to stretch the muscles.

"What if the Death Gift acts the same way for you?" Paden looked at Ree, and she could feel him fighting to control his worry.

"Well, we already know I didn't get the fangs." Ree took a deep breath and leaned back on the mat.

"Your body wasn't genetically set up to have fangs. The Guardians were bred so their bodies would be ready for the change. They always had the prospect open to them the same way the Alastriana line was bred to be able to use the power." Roland sat down across from Ree and looked at her thoughtfully.

"So you think this might have affected Ree negatively?" Paden sat down next to Ree, his knee brushing hers.

"I'm not sure. Have you gotten anything else from the gift? Other than speed and strength?" Roland leaned forward, resting his arms on his crossed legs.

"I heal." Ree glanced at Paden, curious about what he was thinking.

"It seems to be slower than we heal, though." Paden frowned in her direction, obviously still unhappy about testing her theory.

"Well, that is probably a side effect of not having the same genealogical make up again. I would think if you heal at all, that is a good sign. I'm willing to bet you may have stopped aging as well."

"Stopped aging or just slowed down?" Paden's voice was quiet, obviously worried.

"If she is healing at any rate at all, I believe that would mean her cells are constantly repairing themselves the way yours do." Roland looked from Ree to Paden. "That's why you guys are always so hungry. Your body is constantly working."

"So, I've stopped aging then." Ree felt relieved to hear someone else second her hypothesis.

Roland nodded his head and smiled. "Looks like we're going to have to learn to put up with you after all."

Ree laughed and looked at Paden, relieved. She could

feel Roland's stab of jealousy, but she pushed it away and tried to focus on the good news. Something in her clicked in that moment. With all of the bad things that had happened in the last few weeks, all of the scary moments and death that had plagued her and her friends, she needed to enjoy the good things. And to know she had one more weapon in her arsenal and a chance at a long life with Paden meant she had something to be happy about.

Chapter 12

"So, do you think that being immortal is breaking the rules?" Melanie sat next to Ree in the kitchen, her empty plate in front of her.

"I was born to human parents with no immortal lineage. That was the rule, and it hasn't been broken." Ree took a bite out of her sandwich and chewed thoughtfully. "I mean, that's what should count."

"You're right. I just can't help but think the dark gods will cause trouble when you win." Melanie cocked her head to the side.

"If I win." Ree sat her lunch down and frowned at her friend. "Even with this, there is no guarantee. "

"No. When you win. You can't think any other way." Melanie closed her eyes and touched her middle finger to her thumb as if meditating. "You must visualize the outcome you want."

Ree rolled her eyes at Melanie. "Okay. I will visualize everyone kicking Dark One butt."

"Good." Melanie's face fell for a moment. "I really

feel the need to kick some Dark One butt."

"Hm." Ree picked up her sandwich and feigned interest in the crust. "Does this need have anything to do with Roland?"

Melanie's cheeks turned bright pink. "What makes you think that?"

"Just some things I've noticed." Ree took a bite out of her sandwich and tried to pick her words carefully. "You know, I wouldn't be upset."

"Upset about what?" Melanie stared at the crumbs on her plate studiously.

"If you have feelings for Roland. I get it. He's an awesome guy and deserves a great girl like you. Just barely though. You're pretty incredible and it would take a lot for someone to be worthy of you." Ree set her food back down and turned to look at Melanie's shocked face. "Close your mouth. I'm serious."

"But... I thought... I know how difficult this has been on you..."

"It's been difficult on everyone. Melanie, Tria was never Roland's soul mate. That job belongs to someone else." Ree raised an eyebrow and looked at her friend pointedly.

"I thought I had been doing a good job of hiding my feelings." Melanie gave Ree a small smile.

"Uh, yeah." Ree pointed at her head. "Emotion radar built in, remember? Once I got my head out of my own butt, it kind of became apparent."

"It's just all so confusing. I mean, he's a Dark One. A Dark One killed my dad. And then there's you and the whole Tria thing. I must have some kind of sadistic need to torture myself." Melanie met Ree's eyes openly. "But, I can't help it. When we're alone, there is something there."

"Have you told him?" Ree leaned forward on the counter, bracing her head on her hand.

"What would I tell him? Um, hey, Roland. I know you're in love with my best friend and all, but why don't we go out for a movie? Grab some popcorn and kick Dark One ass during the previews?"

"Well, I can see where you might have some trouble with that." Ree frowned. "The gods really did a number on us, didn't they?"

"You could say that." Melanie sighed and looked back at her plate. "It just feels so hopeless."

"Don't give up, okay?" Ree reached out and grabbed Melanie's hand. "Just keep working at it."

"I hear you, I just don't know how. He's been in love with you for so long." Melanie looked at Ree and winced.

"No, he hasn't." Ree shook her head adamantly. "He's been in love with the idea of me. That's not the same thing. You just need to make him realize how awesome you are."

"Okay." Melanie smiled. "Seems kind of silly to be worried about this type of thing with everything else going on."

"Not really. This is exactly the type of thing we're fighting for." Ree stood up and took her plate to the sink. "And speaking of fighting. I think it's time we started calling the shots."

"Oh, I like that." Melanie dumped her plate in the sink too. "I like a woman in charge."

"Then let's round up everyone else and come up with

some strategy." Ree headed out the door, calling for everyone to meet up in Sophie's office. She decided to turn the fireplace on so it wouldn't feel so empty and lifeless. She looked around the room, not sure where to sit and decided to take a place on the hearth. It felt wrong to sit at Sophie's desk and she wanted everyone to feel equal. She had been given more Guardians than usual and she planned on picking their brains today.

Melanie took a seat on the couch and Paden sat next to Ree on the edge of the large fireplace. He touched her knee, making her smile. She laced her fingers with his and tried to soak up his presence through the contact. Weylin and Roland were the next in the room. Weylin threw himself onto the couch and put his head in Melanie's lap. Roland looked at them for a moment, before grabbing a chair and dragging it toward their small group. He turned it backward and straddled the seat, his arms resting on the back.

Juliet and Bryce were the last to show up, holding hands and giggling. Ree blushed and tried to look anywhere but at them. The emotions and giddiness were rolling off of them in waves and she didn't want to think about what must have brought that about. Juliet sat on the floor in front of the couch and Bryce knocked Weylin's feet off of the couch's armrest and sat there. Everyone looked at Ree, and she had to swallow to clear her throat before talking.

"We have to stop running. No more letting the bad guys decide the circumstances. They keep getting the home court advantage, and I think things need to be evened up a bit." Ree leaned forward. "I'm ready to start kicking ass, and I don't want to wait."

"What do you have in mind?" Paden leaned forward to match her, his face taking on a glint of eagerness.

"I was thinking about the attack on my parents' house. They had Dark Ones stationed nearby to take advantage of the false dark. They must have safe houses of their own to stay in during the day."

"Yes. There are often nests in abandoned buildings, or in houses where the owners had been turned." Roland frowned. "They are guarded by darklings, of course. That's one of the main reasons Dark Ones create darklings."

"In other words, we would likely have to kill the darklings." Bryce looked at Ree speculatively. "And I have a feeling you will not be okay with that."

"Actually, I have an alternative." Ree looked at Paden before continuing. She knew he would worry about her using too much power, but she was sure she could handle it. "If we capture the darklings, I can remove the taint from them."

"No." Paden stood up and paced the room. "That's too dangerous."

"Paden, I can do it. You saw me do it at the park." Ree tried to stay calm, knowing he was just worried for her.

"You would be too worried about saving them to protect yourself. It's not the same when you're fighting." Paden looked at her and frowned. She hated seeing him frown so often; she missed his relaxed smile.

"Paden is right. It's much more expedient to kill them." Roland nodded toward Paden. "You have to remember that many of them wanted to be darklings."

"Isn't it possible some of them didn't ask to be changed? Or didn't understand what was really happening?" Ree knew some of the people wanted it, craved it, like the guy from the square.

"I've heard of some Dark Ones creating darklings for convenient meals and there were Dark Ones with harems." Roland shrugged at Ree's sharp intake of breath. "Remember how they can make you feel. It's part of it all."

"That's disgusting." Juliette said.

"It's just like crack addicts who prostitute themselves out for drug money. Only with this, they get a dose of blood that makes them faster and stronger." Bryce squeezed Juliette's shoulder.

"That's disgusting, too." Juliette shook her head. "I don't know why anyone would ever want to be dependent on something like that."

"Did you have a harem?" Melanie looked at Roland suspiciously. Everyone in the room turned to look at Roland in curiosity. Ree remembered bits and pieces from when she was Tria, but for the most part it was a blank.

"I did things I am not proud of before Tria restored my humanity, but having a harem was not one of them." Roland looked at Melanie, his eyes clear and fierce. "Don't forget I was changed against my will. I think it gave me a distaste for it even when my morals were not to be seen."

Melanie nodded her understanding. Ree looked at Roland and tried to distinguish his emotions. They were tumbling through the room in a flurry of confusion. Anger, guilt, and surprise were the strongest feelings, though she also felt something bright that he kept trying to smother. She couldn't help but hope it was something to do with Mel.

"Okay. We go to these places, wherever they are, and what? Run in and take out as many Dark Ones as possible?" Paden sat back down next to Ree and took her hand once more.

"No. We take them all out. Then there will be no one

left to tell Tristan anything." Ree looked back at her friends. "And if I can't take the taint out of the darklings, then we do what we have to." Standing up, Ree walked toward the map of Savannah that Sophie had on her desk. She didn't want to think about killing darklings; she would deal with that when the time came. "Roland, do you have any ideas about where the darklings might be?"

"It's fair to say they are spread throughout the city, not just the Historic District. Our best bet is to scout the abandoned buildings." He stood up and walked over to look at the map. He tapped his finger on a street. "I'm pretty sure there is a nest here in the abandoned house on the corner."

"It might not be a bad idea to watch the night clubs for activity. We could try to follow them back to their hidey holes." Bryce walked over to look at the map where Roland was pointing.

"We should split up and try to cover a bunch of places." Ree looked at each of her friends. "We don't engage unless we have to. We need to take out as many Dark Ones as possible. The less they have at the final battle, the better our chances."

"Don't engage?" Melanie stood up, dropping Weylin's head onto the sofa.

"Hey! I was comfortable." Weylin sat up and ran a hand through his hair.

"What if they attack a human?" Melanie stood across the desk and frowned at Ree.

"We can't let them kill innocent people." Ree frowned. "If you have to intervene, make sure no one escapes."

"So, when do we leave?" Weylin stood up and cracked his knuckles.

***

The cold wind was almost painful as they crossed the water, and the choppy waves made Ree's teeth slam together. Low clouds took away any light the stars might have offered, leaving the group to find their way in the dark. Ree gripped the railing next to the boat console as they crashed down.

Paden moved to stand behind Ree, his hands settling on her waist and offering his warmth and support. She leaned back into him and sighed when he wrapped his arms all the way around her. She was worried about their plan, scared she was making the wrong move. The fact was, the more information they had, the better off their group would be. She just wished she had been able to run her plan past Sophie.

"It's going to be okay." Paden leaned forward, his lips touching her ear.

She shook her head and tried to not be surprised at how well he read her. "I'm scared something will go wrong."

"Something will go wrong." There was a note of amusement in Paden's voice.

"What?" Ree jerked around to look at Paden in surprise.

"No plan is fail proof. All we can do is out best." He leaned down to kiss her forehead, but a large wave sent them both stumbling into the railing they had originally been holding onto. Paden caught hold of the bar and scooped Ree against his chest. He chuckled and looked down at her. "See? Nothing goes as planned. You just do your best." With that, he leaned down and caught her mouth in a sweet kiss.

When he pulled back from her, his eyebrows pulled

together in worry. Confused, she blinked and realized her eyes were casting a soft glow on his face. She looked over her shoulder and realized they were close to the dock of the dilapidated safe house.

"Don't dock! Keep going!" Ree hollered at Roland. He slammed the boat into gear and, as they tore away from the dock, Dark Ones poured out of the shadows. Ree threw her hands out toward the bank and let the energy flow out of her hands. The Dark Ones at the front shattered into a wave of ashes. Before the dust of the dead had even started to settle, more Dark Ones had taken their place and this time Ree realized they were holding weapons.

Ree called for everyone to get down and flung the power at the remaining Dark Ones. She threw the power again, this time toward the trees near the house. Loud cracking cut through the roar of the boat engine as the trees fell across the path to the dock, keeping any other Dark Ones from having easy access. She was seething inside when she turned back around to look at Roland.

"Where are we going to go? They know we're headed for the city." She gripped the edge of the console and took a deep breath. "Do we scrap our plan?"

"No. We pretend to run back to the island and hit another dock." Roland headed for the island and they all grew quiet.

"So, we pretend to run because that's what they are used to us doing." Ree spit the words out in disgust. There was a soft groaning and the metal under her fingers bent under the pressure. She moved her hand and sighed.

"Yes, but we aren't really running this time." Roland smiled at her. "We're letting them assume."

"And you know what that means!" Weylin shouted over the motor and crash of waves.

"No, what's that?" Melanie looked at Weylin with wide innocent eyes.

"Oh, you know! It makes an ass out of you and me. I mean, them and us." Weylin looked at Melanie in shock. "Get it?"

"No. How does it make an ass out of them and us?" Melanie hollered.

"Assume. It's spelled A-S-S, then U, then M-E. So it makes an ass out of U and me." Weylin leaned toward Melanie and pointed at his chest.

"It makes an ass out of M-E?" Melanie shook her head in confusion.

"Me! It makes an ass out of ME!" Weylin pointed at his chest again. Everyone died laughing and Weylin looked around the boat in frustration. "What? Oh. I see, you're so funny, Melanie." He sat down on the bench next to Mel and crossed his arms.

"Ah, c'mon, Wey. You know it was funny!" She threw a friendly arm around his shoulder.

"Well, it would've been funny if it hadn't been me." Weylin looked at her from the corner of his eyes and smiled.

"And that's exactly why it is funny." Juliet laughed from the other side of the boat.

Chapter 13

After circling Sanctus Island once, Roland had set course for Savannah again. After what felt like a torturous eternity, they arrived at a dock behind a local restaurant. Roland shut the motor off and expertly coasted into a spot before Paden hopped out and used the rope to secure the boat. Ree jumped lightly to the wooden dock and looked at the building in front of them. It was an old house that had been extended to include other buildings, and was currently a very popular themed restaurant.

"Does anyone else find it ironic that we just parked behind a pirate restaurant?" Jules stepped onto the dock and tilted her head.

"Argh, matey." Weylin stepped up behind her. "Let's go a-raiding!"

"Will they mind that we docked here? Our boat isn't going to be towed, right?" Ree looked at Roland, her eyebrows pulled together. "This is a really busy place, and they might need the space."

"No. I know the owners and the managers. We will be fine. Plus, it's better to leave the boat somewhere there are a lot of people. We're less likely to be attacked in front of so many witnesses." Roland lifted one of the seat cushions on the boat bench and pulled out weapons for the group. "Take what you can conceal and let's go. We're getting a much later start than we planned."

"Bryce and Juliette, take River Street. Weylin, you come with me and Paden. Melanie and Roland can check out the abandoned houses." Ree had been thinking about the groups on the way over. Melanie raised an eyebrow at Ree and shot a look at Roland. His expression was completely neutral, but she could sense his worry. "We meet back here just after dawn. No reason to be out in the daylight with the cops looking for us everywhere."

"We all have our cell phones. If something happens or we're running late, we need to let each other know." Bryce piped in.

"And make sure your cell is on silent, not vibrate. Dark Ones will be able to hear it otherwise." Roland grinned, baring his wicked fangs.

"So, we have to compulsively check our cell phone throughout the night. Got'cha." Weylin picked up his phone and glanced at the screen. "Just making sure."

Ree rolled her eyes and checked the clasp on her short sword hilt. The others all drifted into their groups and headed in the directions of their tasks. Ree looked back up at Paden and Weylin. "Well, let's go."

"Do you want to set the pace?" Paden cocked his head to the side.

"Human pace. There are some secrets that should only be shared at the right time." Ree headed toward the busiest nightclub in town, the boys a half-step behind her.

The streets weren't very crowded. There were the usual groups near popular tourist spots and restaurants, but the cold, wet weather seemed to have sent most people home. Ree kept her head down as they walked past people. Paden and Weylin clustered on either side of her as they hustled down the sidewalk. Ree cut her eyes at Paden and studied his profile. His green eyes watched the people they passed; his hard expression enhanced by the stubble along his jaw. On the rare instances they came across other pedestrians, the people quickly moved to the opposite side of the road.

Paden looked down at her and winked before returning his attention to the street. Ree let the power search ahead of her for any signs of Dark Ones or darklings. As she scanned an alley, her eyes fell on Weylin and she was shocked to see Paden's deadly expression repeated. Weylin had always been attractive, not that she would tell him that, but to see his usual relaxed face turned into something so serious was unnatural. If she was being very honest with herself, she had wanted Weylin with her and Paden so she could keep an eye on him. Ever since her talk with Aphrodite, she had been worried about her friend. What if he was an acceptable loss? She didn't trust the gods as far as she could see them; and that wasn't very far.

Turning onto a side road, they headed for the nearest nightclub. Loud music boomed along the walls and Ree winced. It sounded like thunder in a can, thankfully she could still pick out the lower voices of her friends and the people closest to the inside wall of the club.

"There are Dark Ones here. We need a good vantage point until they leave. Somewhere nearby, where they hopefully won't sense my presence." Ree looked back out at the buildings across the street. She pointed at the tallest building from City Market. "There. We wait on the roof."

Weylin took point as they made their way to the

building. Paden slid his arm around Ree's shoulders, but kept his intense expression as they dodged people. Pedestrian traffic increased closer to all of the shops and restaurants. Weylin ducked into the alley behind the old, three-story restaurant. They were busy as usual, but no one was near the back door. Paden looked from side to side before jumping and grabbing an old rickety ladder. It slid down the wall, making a loud racket. Ree glanced over her shoulder, sure someone would have heard the noise, but no one came to investigate.

They made quick work of the ladder and hopped onto the roof. The concrete was cracked but sturdy. They slid through the maze of metal vents and generators to the perimeter where they could watch the club. Ree could still hear the booming music from their perch, but focused on the cold spots that mingled with all of the bright lights of humans.

"Can you still sense them from here?" Paden knelt next to the short wall at the edge of the building.

"Yeah. My range seemed to grow after Sophie gave me her power." It still hurt to think about Sophie and her sacrifice.

"So, you don't think they will be able to sense you here?" Weylin leaned against a large brick pillar and crossed his arms.

"I don't think so. They would have to move in this direction for them to get a whiff of me and the power, and even then we would probably still be far enough away that they wouldn't be sure where we are." Ree sat next to Paden, her back against the wall, and closed her eyes. She didn't need to see to know where the Dark Ones were at that point.

"Best to not let them sense you if we can help it. We want them to think you're on the island, right?" Weylin's voice was eerily calm.

"You're right. We should keep our distance at this point." Ree felt Paden reach into his pocket for something. She assumed it was his cell phone, because he didn't say anything and returned whatever it was pretty quickly.

Ree let them discuss things between themselves while she concentrated on the Dark Ones. There were more in the area than she would have liked. One was lingering outside a bar at the other side of the market, another was leaving the area and she was pretty sure they were headed to River Street. Part of her wanted to chase them all and kill them. While she had always wanted to keep them from killing innocent people, the unexpected feeling was almost bloodthirsty. She wondered if this was the new part of being immortal. No wonder the others had been so ready to go hunting that first day. They were programmed for it.

She felt one of the Dark One's cold spots flash brightly, and she gasped out loud. She clenched her fists and ground her teeth. She knew they were feeding, and there was nothing she could do about it at this point. By the time Ree and her friends busted into the club it would be over and they would have blown their cover. Paden's hand closed on her shoulder, and she felt his sympathy. He must have picked up from her emotions what was happening.

"They're feeding?" Weylin's voice was quiet and rough.

"There isn't anything we do can at this point." Paden's voice was slow and calm. She knew he was telling her as much as answering Weylin.

"They will head out once they feed. No reason to stay where they might be caught." She stood up and turned to look at the club. She grabbed her cell phone to check for missed calls and shoved it back into her pocket. Her hands shook from the rage that gripped her heart. She wanted to kill. Narrowing her eyes, she placed her hands on the top of the wall and spread her fingers as wide as they would go. Her hands itched to grab a weapon and to run for the building.

She took a deep breath and turned to look at the guys. They were both waiting on her signal to move. Paden stood with his hands hanging limply beside him. Weylin held the short pommel of a collapsed sword in one hand, his eyes bright with determination. As soon as she felt the Dark Ones gather, she nodded at the guys and walked back near the brick pillar Weylin had been leaning against. She flashed Paden a wicked smile and ran toward the edge. With one large push, she leapt from the wall to the next building. Air pushed against her face and her stomach twisted with adrenaline. When she landed on the flat top across the street she couldn't help the small laugh that escaped her mouth.

Paden landed two seconds after her, his eyes glinted with amusement. Ree turned to watch as Weylin cleared the space smoothly. He obviously enjoyed it as much as Ree had, because his eyes were bright and excited. Taking a moment to decide which way the Dark Ones were headed, Ree turned and raced for the next rooftop.

The Dark Ones eventually ended up in a less-than-savory neighborhood. Chipped paint and a sagging porch greeted them as they walked into the house. A darkling sat on an old couch beside the front door. He was a large man with squinty eyes and a foul expression. The tattoos on his left arm indicated he was part of a gang, his whiskered face and dirty clothes showed a lack of concern for cleanliness.

Ree crouched down on the roof of an old store a block away. Paden took out his two long knives and held them loosely in his hands. A snap-hiss announced Weylin's sword as he released it from the sheath. Ree could see the shine of her eyes reflect off of the long blade and smiled. She pulled out her cell phone and typed a quick message to everyone else.

"I think it's time to make a statement." She took off her jacket and pulled her short sword from the sheath on her back.

"Here." Weylin pulled something out of his pocket and tossed it to Ree. She caught it, pressed the small button, and swung the blade as it released.

"No one leaves." Ree looked from Paden to Weylin so they knew she was serious.

Ree moved to the edge and dropped to the ground. She landed in a crouch, her swords held out at either side. Paden and Weylin landed silently beside her. She took off running, the houses passing in a blur. She came to a stop on the front porch, her sword sweeping up and around as she decapitated the darkling on the dilapidated porch. Dark, tainted blood splattered from his neck, but his eyes registered only shock as his head bounced along the broken floorboards. A Dark One arrived at the porch just as quickly and threw himself at Paden. He held two wicked, curved, short swords and was obviously well-trained. Weylin didn't stop to help; instead he dodged the flurry of their movements and headed straight to the back of the house.

Ree followed suit, not ready to unleash her magic yet. She didn't want to accidently be sensed by Dark Ones that might be nearby. The house was lit by two small lamps and the stink of grime and marijuana instantly filled Ree's nose. She sensed that Weylin was engaged near the back door, so she checked the rooms along the hallway. She kicked in two doors that were locked and felt her anger flare. There were dirty beds with chains and straps. The dead body of a beautiful black woman lay discarded near the closet. Welts and raw markings along her wrists and ankles testified to her last hours on Earth, the gaping wounds on her neck examples of the violence she suffered. Her sightless eyes burned a hole in Ree's soul.

The power flowed around Ree's feet, sending dirt scattering along the floor. Turning from the room, she ran for the last bedroom and the Dark One that hid there. She pushed the door open with the power and flew at the man with blood dripping from his mouth.

"Too late. I already called them." He laughed at her and pointed at a small fire in the corner of the room.

Ree didn't stop to decipher what he was talking about. Instead she came at him with all of her strength. He met her strikes with his own, whirling to dodge her slashes and thrusts. She dropped to her knees and spun her swords at his legs. He didn't see it coming and fell to the ground with a roar. His hands reached for her, but she was already gone. She stood behind him and severed his head with a quick scissor move. She watched as his body disintegrated slowly. Her shoulders moved with her angry breaths.

Paden crashed through the wall and landed on his back, his fangs bared in a feral smile as a Dark One followed him through the man-sized hole. The Dark One couldn't have been any older than a high school freshman, but his eyes were purely animal. He fell on Paden with a hiss, his hands scraping at the godling with speed and precision. Paden laughed before grabbing the boy's face and savagely twisting. The stunned Dark One fell to his side, but he wasn't dead. Breaking his neck had only slowed him down. With blood dripping from his face, Paden knelt next to the kid and thrust his long knife into the Dark One's chest.

He stood and looked at Ree, his eyes lingering on her cheek and blood-soaked pants. She reached up to touch her face, not registering the wound until that moment.

A loud crack of energy sent Ree's heart plummeting. They ran for the back of the house and skidded to a halt as they watched Dark Ones pour through a glowing slash in the wall. Weylin backed in their direction and held his sword ready.

"I think it's time for a dramatic exit, Ree." Her friend turned and winked at her before pushing them all toward the front door.

As they exited the house, Ree turned to look over her shoulder. Dark Ones followed them out into the streets. She couldn't risk her secret being exposed yet, so made a quick decision.

"Get behind me." She spun on her heel and felt Paden and Weylin skid to a halt. She let go of the power leashed inside of her and threw all of it at the house and the Dark Ones spilling out. The ground shook under her feet before her shoes left the ground in a wash of power.

She pulled energy from her friends and from the trees along the street. Raising her arms she directed it all at the drug house and the evil monsters inside. Wave after wave of energy flew across the space to crash into the house. Dark Ones burst into ash and the house itself shook with each burst. The porch splintered into flying wood and the front wall collapsed. The house seemed to fall into itself, nothing left but a large cloud of dust and dead Dark Ones. The old homes on either side of the rubble shook as if frightened. Glass from their windows littered the road, and she could hear screams from inside.

Ree fell to the ground, landing on one knee, and used

her hands to catch herself. She looked up at the destruction and felt hollow. She had killed the trees along the street. The plants sitting on porches were wilted and brown. Dead bodies of birds littered the ground under drooping limbs and she prayed she hadn't killed anyone's pet.

Strong hands slid over her shoulders and helped her stand. Paden turned her to face him, his green eyes searching hers. She nodded her head, letting him know she was okay.

"Jesus Christ, Ree. You're one scary chick, you know that?" Weylin stood with his sword at his side, his eyes wide with amazement.

Paden glared at him, but Ree felt her lips turn up into a small smile. She was okay with being scary. As long as it meant they won.

Chapter 14

Sirens filled the night air and Weylin cursed. Ree wanted to make sure no one had escaped, but they couldn't risk being caught by the cops. She knew they had connections in the department, but that wasn't an obstacle they needed to deal with right now. Paden pulled her with him, his hand clamped firmly on hers until she seemed to be moving on her own. They scaled the old store to retrieve their coats and made a quick getaway along the other roofs. Paden didn't want to leave any evidence if it was at all possible.

Ree pulled her phone out of her pocket to check for messages as they ran. The first one was from Juliette telling her to be careful and that they had tagged several Dark Ones on River Street. The next message was also from Juliette. They had decided to take out a safe house of their own. The Dark Ones had taken in a young couple. Her next message was to let them know they were okay. The next message was from Roland. They had seen Ree's blast and were worried. Next message was from Melanie saying Roland wanted to meet back at the boat.

"Roland wants to head back." Ree looked at the others and nodded in the direction of the restaurant.

"Have they found any other houses?" Paden asked as they scaled another roof.

"Jules and Bryce took one out. Apparently the Dark Ones had kidnapped a young couple/" Ree shook her head. In reality, they were still young too. She just didn't feel like it anymore.

"What about Mel and Roland?" Weylin hopped onto a metal box that covered the air conditioner for the store.

"She didn't say. Just that he wanted to leave." Ree looked over the edge of the roof and watched as some pedestrians made their drunken way from City Market.

"Maybe he found something." Paden suggested. "They're gone." He nodded toward the ground before using one arm to push off and over the concrete wall. He landed smoothly on the ground in an alley beside the building. Ree stepped off the wall and landed next to him. Once Weylin was with them, they ran through the streets, aware the sun wasn't far from rising. It would be harder to hide from the police looking for them in the daylight.

"Maybe. Or he could just be trying to avoid being here during the day." Ree jumped a pothole. It didn't take them long to get to the other side of town. They stood back in the shadows as they scanned the restaurant.

"Any Dark Ones?" Paden's eyes swept the area intently.

"No. They're probably holed up somewhere." Ree frowned at the empty parking lot. Her gut kept telling her something was wrong. "I think I sense the others nearby."

"I guess we should go then." Paden grabbed Ree's hand and they crossed the road quickly. They stayed close to the building to try and not to attract any attention from the few passing cars. Weylin seemed to be feeling something odd too, because he had the pommel of his sword in his hand. Juliette and Bryce appeared seconds behind them. Juliette had a huge slash along the chest of her shirt and she was wearing Bryce's jacket.

"Are you okay?" Ree asked. Her stomach clenched at the thought of what could have happened.

"Meh. I'm fine. Mostly caught my shirt." Juliette looked down at the tattered ends of her shirt. "Jerk."

Bryce frowned but didn't say anything. Ree knew it had probably scared him to death.

"Have you seen Roland or Melanie?" Weylin asked Bryce, his eyes sweeping the empty parking lot.

"Not yet." Bryce looked at everyone. "We should go to the boat."

"I'll text them." Ree pulled her phone out and sent a quick message. Hopefully they were just avoiding people and would be back soon. Almost immediately a text came back. "Start boat. Got company."

"Start the boat!" Ree ran for the whaler and hopped over the edge. Bryce grabbed the helm and the boat roared to life. Paden and Weylin untied the boat from the dock and stood holding the ropes.

"Pay! Turn the boat so we're facing out!" Bryce looked over his shoulder at his friend. Paden and Weylin pulled on the ropes until they had the boat facing the direction they wanted.

"Dark Ones or cops?" Juliette asked.

"No idea." Ree shook her head, but didn't take her eyes off of the parking lot. The sound of sirens reached her ears, and her gut clenched.

"Shit. It's the po-po." Weylin looked over his shoulder just as Roland and Melanie tore across the parking lot.

"Get in!" Bryce revved the engine. Paden and Weylin jumped in with the ropes. The boat took off, but Roland and Melanie jumped at the last moment, both landing in heaps on the floor of the boat. Roland rolled over to his back and looked up at the sky, while Melanie laughed.

Ree felt her eyebrows raise in surprise, but was relieved to see they were both okay. She reached down and grabbed Melanie's hand to help her stand. Roland stayed where he was for a moment longer, before standing and moving to take the controls from Bryce.

"What happened?" Paden asked.

"A cop saw us walking from between two crack houses. He shined a light on us and then did a double take. He obviously recognized us, because he turned the car around and hit the lights." Melanie pushed her hair out of her eyes and looked at her friends. Ree noticed there was a happy glint to her expression, and she wondered what had happened while they were out searching.

"That area is patrolled heavily, so we were constantly ducking cops. Thankfully, we're a little faster than their cars." Roland threw a smile over his shoulder at Melanie. For a split second, Ree's stomach clenched in jealousy, but it was gone so fast it might as well have not happened.

"Did you find any Dark Ones?" Bryce asked.

"Two of the houses are used as safe houses, but they all disappeared. Roland thinks there was a portal or something." Melanie sat down on a bench next to Juliette.

Paden looked at Ree, obviously thinking along the

same lines. Now they knew where their mystery Dark Ones had come from.

"Was this after we told you what we were going to do?" Ree frowned at Melanie.

"Yeah. Why?" Melanie redid her ponytail while watching Ree's face.

"I think I know where they ended up." Ree sat down on the opposite side of the boat.

"Ah, that's where they came from!" Weylin moved to stand on the other side of the console from Paden. "But, how?"

"A god can open a portal between places." Roland glanced at Ree. "You mean to tell me all of those Dark Ones showed up where you were? What happened?"

"The Dark One started a fire, but I don't know what he actually did with it." Ree shook her head. At this point, she didn't really care how it worked.

"A summoning spell. They would have contacted whoever is helping them and asked for help." Roland narrowed his eyes at Ree. "What did you do when they showed up?"

She shrugged and looked out over the water. "We took care of it."

"Damn right! Ree lit up the whole street like Christmas! That house is complete rubble!" Weylin held his hand out to Ree for a high-five. She returned it weakly, but didn't meet anyone else's eyes.

"That was that flash? You destroyed the house?" Melanie looked at her with big eyes. "But, that would have taken a lot of power, right?" She looked at Paden and Weylin as if checking for wounds.

"Not just the house, Mel. She took out all of the Dark Ones that showed up." Paden kept his voice steady, but she could feel him trying to send her support. "It was the right decision." She nodded her head but still didn't look at anyone. She hated knowing she had killed all of the earth on that block. She worried nothing would ever grow there again.

"You did the right thing." Roland seemed to understand she had taken energy from things around her, and his voice was firm.

As they left Savannah behind them, the sick feeling in her stomach didn't go away. The closer they got to the island, the worse she felt. She wrapped her arms around her stomach and stood up from her seat. She went to the front of the boat and watched as the sun came up. Paden moved to wrap her in his arms.

"You saved hundreds of people by doing what you did." He rested his forehead against the top of her head, obviously thinking she was dwelling on the destruction she had caused.

"No, something's wrong. Don't you feel it?" She looked at him over her shoulder.

"I do." Bryce stepped up to take the spot Paden had left. "Roland, can you call the island?"

"We might be heard on scanners." Roland shook his head.

"Man, something isn't right." Bryce leaned toward Roland. "You've got to have a private band."

"I do, but someone could still happen on it."

"Do it anyways." Ree turned to look at Roland. She knew her face was set into grim lines and, apparently, he understood something was very wrong.

Roland picked up the receiver and spoke into it several times. He held it with one hand while steering the boat. No one answered. He tried again. Still no reply. Ree turned back to the front of the boat and prayed everyone on the island was safe.

Once the island was in sight, so was the large plume of smoke. There were muttered curses from everyone on the boat. Ree took off her jacket and threw it onto one of the benches. By the time they were near the dock, everyone was prepping for trouble. One of the boats next to the dock had been sunk, only the very top visible from the dock. Ree leapt from the boat as soon as they were close. She drew her swords in quick movements and flew down the path. She couldn't feel any Dark Ones, but it was obvious they had been there. An ash pile was still steaming near the wall around the house, and Ree wanted to be sick. This was supposed to be their safe place, guarded by the gods, a sanctuary for the people who had already been hurt by the Dark Ones.

The house was a smoking shack. The walls had crumbled, smoke still curling into the air.

"Ellie! Kay! Pam!" Ree shouted as she leapt over piles of debris. Melanie was right behind her, her voice panicked as she called for her mom. "Pam!" Ree crawled over smoking furniture and charred walls to get to the kitchen. When she got there, her power flared out in an angry wave. Pam was lying on the counter, her throat torn out. Blood pooled under the woman's head, her kind eyes blank.

She looked up at the sky and hollered. "Where the fuck are you? You let someone step into our home and snub your power, yet you do nothing?" She spit the words out, barely able to keep from sending the rest of the house down on everyone. She reached down and closed Pam's eyes.

"Ree." Paden stood in what remained of the doorway. "We need to look for everyone else. Can you feel any humans on the island? Any at all?" He held his hand out to her, but she brushed past him, too angry to take the comfort he offered. She took a deep breath and closed her eyes. She searched for anything. After a moment, she opened her eyes and headed toward the back of the house. There was a very faint spark, but she hoped whoever it was could be healed by Paden.

Ree kicked through ash piles and frowned, realizing they were dead Dark Ones. By the time she reached the room where the dwindling spark remained, she was ready to kill something. Using her anger to add to her strength, Ree threw a couch out of the way and pushed her way into a back bedroom. She almost tripped on Ellie's lifeless body and couldn't help the gasp of anguish that slid out of her throat. She didn't stop though, desperately wishing there would still be someone alive.

"Oh, please, please, please." Ree mumbled under her breath as she fought through the debris. Between a large dresser and a corner, Melanie's mother was curled into a tight ball. "Melanie! Paden, help me! I found Kay."

Ree moved the dresser as carefully as she could and Paden slid in next to the dying woman. He started to lift her, but paused. He ran his hands over the woman gently, the green glow highlighting her battered form.

"Don't let Melanie see Ellie like that, Ree." Paden didn't take his eyes off of the woman in front of him, but his words seemed to snap Ree into motion. She turned and walked over to the dead woman blocking the doorway.

Kneeling down, Ree scooped Ellie into her arms and moved her from the doorway. Carefully she placed her in a clear space out of the way. Yanking the blanket off the bed, she placed it over Ellie. She didn't linger, not wanting Melanie to see the dead body right away. With slow steps she moved back to Paden and watched as he worked on Mel's mom.

The sound of furious gasps and fear announced Melanie's arrival. She stopped in the doorway for just a moment, fear and pain clouding her features as she looked from the covered form to her mother. Ree stood up and moved so her friend could take her spot but Paden shook his head.

"Help me move her to the bed now." Kay's eyes were clenched in pain, tears mingling with the blood on her face. "Gently, I've got to concentrate on her back."

Ree helped lift the older woman, and carefully placed her on the bed. It was clean of ash and that struck Ree as weird, until she realized she had taken the top blanket to cover Ellie. Melanie moved next to Ree, her eyes on her mother's face.

"Mommy?" Melanie moved to kneel next to the head of the bed, her hands shaking as she brushed the hair out of her mother's eyes. "Paden?"

"She's hurt, Mel, but I think I can help." Paden never looked at anyone else. His eyes stayed on his patient as he worked. Ree looked up when the others slid into the room. Weylin shook his head no, letting Ree know they hadn't found anyone else alive. When Juliette saw the shrouded body near the closet, she covered her mouth and turned into Bryce's chest. Ree watched numbly as her friend's shoulders shook with quiet sobs. Weylin moved to sit next to Melanie, his arm sliding around her shoulders. Ree felt her breathing hitch when she saw the tears on her normally chipper friend's cheeks. Kay had had been like a second mother to Weylin.

Unable to take sitting there and doing nothing, Ree

walked past her friends and left the room. She walked through the house, staring at the odd bits and pieces that had survived. There was blood splattering the walls near the kitchen and she felt her stomach quiver. She tightened her resolve and pushed her way back out the front door. She stood staring up at the sky, her hands clenched at her sides. The soft sound of footsteps made her turn around and she looked up at Roland.

"How could this happen?"

"There is a god-strike near the dock. Someone blasted through the enchantments." He frowned and looked toward the house. "They had help."

"Melanie needs you." Ree turned to the side and the statue of Brigid caught her attention.

"I doubt she would want to see me right now." Roland shoved his hands into his pockets and looked away from Ree.

"You'd be wrong." Ree looked at him, her face blank. She wanted to be alone, but she knew Melanie needed someone to be there for her right now. Roland looked torn for just a moment, but ducked into the house without another word.

Ree marched over to the statue of the goddess and stared at it for a minute. She wanted to know how this could happen and she planned on getting some answers. She picked up the statue and headed for the large tree along the pathway.

Chapter 15

Ree set the sculpture down next to the tree and sat down on a large root. Her anger hadn't dampened while carrying the marble statue through the woods and she still wanted answers. She looked at Brigid's white face and then placed her hand on the tree trunk. Taking a deep breath, Ree tried to calm the anger in her heart before addressing the goddess.

"I don't know if you're listening, Brigid, but something has gone very, very wrong. Where are you? Why weren't you here to protect your island?" Ree waited for a minute, but there was no answer. She stood up and looked down at the statue. "Where the hell are you? You've screwed us left and right and don't even bother to show up when another god gives you the finger?" Ree threw her head back and screamed at the top of her lungs. The power flew out of her and the statue shattered into a million pieces.

"Throwing a tantrum is not the best way to get my attention." The silky voice caught Ree off guard.

"Where have you been?" She whirled to glare at the tall red-headed god.

"I was busy." Brigid walked past Ree and looked down at the remaining bits of her statue. "I kind of liked that one. So many of the others look nothing like me."

"Why didn't you protect the people on this island?" Ree spit the words out, barely able to keep from teetering over the edge of rage.

"We were preoccupied." Brigid narrowed her eyes and Ree felt very small.

"Preoccupied?" Ree asked. "Too busy to come down and save the people that put their trust in you?"

"Preoccupied," Brigid asserted. Loki and Ares made sure we couldn't come to the island when we felt the warning." Brigid's eyes flashed with fire. "Once the Council of Gods is called, we cannot leave. Not for anything."

"Then how did Loki and Ares rip down the shield?" Ree tried to keep hold of her anger, but it wouldn't listen to reason. "Why is some council more important than the people of this planet?"

"You're assuming it was Loki or Ares that caused the shield to collapse." Brigid placed her hands on her hips. "It is not your place to question how the council is run." She turned and leaned over to brush some of the shattered statue off of the tree roots before taking a seat. She folded her long legs in front of her and still managed to look dignified. "But considering your position, I can understand your frustration."

Ree felt a sliver of relief at her last sentence. Maybe she would finally get some much needed answers. "If it wasn't Loki and Ares then who else could it have been? Could it have been another god that has joined them?"

"The dark gods could just as easily have attacked this island while we were in Council. However, I cannot rule out Loki. He has many talents and being in more than one place at a time is among his skill set."

"You want to keep this planet, right?" Ree looked at Brigid, her mind focused on forcing them to get more involved.

"Yes." Brigid looked at Ree with guarded eyes.

"Then you need to forget all of the rules you have in place for gods. No one else is paying attention to them. You need to start being more invested in the outcome." Ree stared at Brigid, not showing a reaction when a heated wind ripped through the clearing, causing the goddess's hair to whip angrily.

"Do you know how hard it is to keep all of the gods from fighting? To keep them from destroying the Earth themselves? There is a reason we have rules." Brigid stood up and walked toward Ree, her eyes flashing with lightning. "You may be immortal now, little Alastriana, but you are not a god. You have no right to tell me and my brethren how to do things."

"I'm the Alastriana." Ree embraced the power and let it wash out of her. The green energy clashed with the smooth blue glow of the goddess. "You made me to protect your planet. To protect the people of this world." She took a step forward and felt her energy melt into and over the goddesses' power. "You created me to protect all of you." The green energy crept along, devouring and absorbing the goddess's power. The green energy began to pull at the goddess's feet, feeding on the substance that made Brigid a god.

Brigid looked at Ree with narrowed eyes. "You were created by us. You are ours." Suddenly, Brigid's power disappeared and her eyes softened. "Because we need you." She sighed and brushed away some of the dirt on the root next to her and motioned for Ree to sit. Ree hesitated, still angry, furious with everything that had happened in the last few weeks, she could barely keep from exploding. After a moment, she let go of the power and tried to swallow some of her anger. Taking slow steps, she claimed the seat next to Brigid and rested her head against the trunk of the tree.

"Then why aren't you helping me?" Ree cut her eyes at the goddess.

"I know it doesn't seem that way, but we are helping you, Ree. We're doing everything we can to make sure you win." Brigid leaned back next to Ree and folded her hands in her lap. For just a moment, the goddess lost some of the otherworldly sheen and looked like a tired woman who'd been working too many jobs.

"You're right. It doesn't seem that way." Ree picked up a twig and ran it through her fingers. "It feels like you guys are set on making me your puppet. Trying to take away and kill everything that makes me human."

"You aren't human anymore, Ree. But I know what you mean." Brigid looked at her and frowned. "Many of the gods only see you as a tool. But a few of us are working to make sure you have everything you need. Try to understand that for a long time, the gods thought nothing was on their same level. They will always think they do not need humans."

Ree bit her lip to keep from bringing up the mess with Roland and Paden; to not point out all of the times they could have helped or intervened but hadn't. Thankfully, Brigid kept speaking, so there was no empty silence for Ree to fill with her angry thoughts.

"The fact is, we can't be seen intervening. We can't do anything the dark gods could use to try and overthrow the final verdict. We have to maintain our stance that the battle remains between the chosen warriors."

"Looks like the bad guys are getting an awful lot of help. From both sides." Ree threw the stick down on the ground and turned to face the goddess. "I'm not losing any more people. You guys need to step up and start working to protect the innocent. I have enough on my hands that and I shouldn't have to worry about the safe zones not being safe. I'm going to fight my brother. To the death. And I'm going to fight with everything I have in me. But you guys need to start making sure I have someone backing me up. My team isn't going to be able to function if you keep letting our families be murdered. On your land." She stood up and rubbed her hands on her jeans. "Step up and fight back. You ask that of me, and now I'm telling you. Show them you're not letting them break the rules either. They are laughing at you. At your laws and the lack of conviction you are showing. If you want to keep this planet and its people the way it is, then you need to act like you care."

Brigid stood up and looked down the trail leading to the house. "I will work to keep the island protected. Leave it to me. For now, you need to get your head on straight and focus on your plan."

"You know what our plan is?" Ree let her hands hang limply at her side. "You think it will work?"

"I think it's smart. Of course, Athena wouldn't have been so set on making you her kin if you didn't have a brain for strategy." Brigid looked back at Ree with an amused smile. "I'm going. Don't break any more statues if you need me. Just call. I'll be listening." With that, the goddess snapped out of existence. Ree sat back down on the root and looked at her boots. The soft sound of feet running down the path brought her attention away from the dirt on her shoes.

Paden rounded the bend with a frantic look on his face. As soon as his eyes landed on her, relief washed over him. He slowed down when he took in her expression and came to sit next her. He braced his elbows on his knees and leaned forward, turning slightly so he could look at her.

"I felt Brigid come to the island." His voice was steady and even, but she could feel the worry just underneath the surface. "Looks like you made an impression." He nodded with head toward the gritty residue of the statue.

"You could say that." Ree snorted and leaned back against the tree. "We... had words."

"Ah." Paden looked down for a minute. "Are you okay?"

"I'm fine. How is Melanie's mom?" Ree sat up and looked at Paden. She wasn't fine, but she didn't want to talk about herself.

"She's going to be fine." Creases deepened near his eyes and mouth for a minute. "They are really upset about Ellie."

"We all are." Ree looked back at her feet and fought the sudden onslaught of tears.

"It isn't your fault, Ree." Paden's warm hand cupped her chin and forced her to meet his eyes.

"It definitely feels that way." Ree shook her hand and stood up, out of Paden's reach. "I should have left someone to guard the island. It was stupid to put my trust in the gods that keep screwing us over."

Paden stood up and walked to Ree. He turned her gently so he could see her face. Slowly, he reached up and wiped an escaped tear away. "They should have been paying attention. What did Brigid say?"

"That they had been in a council meeting and by the time she was able to leave, it was too late." Ree shook her head, but Paden didn't let her walk away from him again. "A council meeting kept them from protecting the island. Protecting the people that had put their trust in them. Ellie…" Ree choked up and stopped, unable to finish her sentence for a minute. "God, Ellie had already given so much."

"She saved her daughter. Ellie did some kind of magic that kept the Dark Ones from entering the room, even after they busted down the door." Paden leaned down and touched his forehead to Ree's. "She died doing exactly what she wanted to do. Ellie would never have wanted to live if it meant Kay and Mel were hurt instead."

Ree nodded her head and sniffed. Paden wrapped his arms around her and pulled her closer. Rain began to fall from the sky, but they didn't move. It matched how Ree felt in her heart, it was right that the sky would cry over the death of Ellie. The world would be a sadder place for the loss.

"Let's go back to the house." Paden leaned down and kissed her head.

"Why? We'll just get rained on there too." Ree snuggled closer to his chest, wanting to soak up his warmth.

"The gods rebuilt the house. I was just finishing up healing Melanie's mom when the house righted itself. One minute it was destroyed and the next it was just as we left it." Paden squeezed her a little tighter. "We need to figure out what to do with the… to make arrangements for the ones that didn't make it."

"I don't want to go to the house. Anywhere but the house." Ree shook her head against his chest. She didn't want to face the dead bodies waiting for them. She didn't want to look at their blank expressions.

"Okay." Paden let go of her, but slid his hand down her arm and twined his fingers around hers.

Chapter 16

Ree didn't question him when he started down the path, heading away from the house. She didn't care where they went as long as she didn't have to face everyone. She tucked her wet hair behind her ears and blindly followed Paden while tears fell down her face. Had her brother been here? Killed Ellie? Someone who had baked him pies and cookies as a kid? She hadn't been drained. Ree hadn't noticed any teeth marks when she had moved Ellie's body.

Paden pulled her with him down the trail, before veering off the path and heading toward a small pond. Just past the trees were tiny stone houses. He opened the door to the first one and led her inside. They were small, but cozy, and had obviously been used not that long ago.

Paden took her to a chair before going to the fireplace and arranging the logs. She watched him quietly as he built a comfortable fire. When it was blazing nicely, he came back to her and picked her up before sitting back down with her in his lap.

"What are these?" Ree laid her head against his chest.

"Groundskeepers stay here." Paden's voice rumbled out of his chest and she nuzzled closer to him.

"It's funny, you know?"

"What?" Paden moved so he could see her face.

"That there are groundskeepers. Why would the gods need groundskeepers?" Ree shivered and Paden pulled her closer.

"I suppose it was their way of giving victims a place to be productive while they were protected."

"Huh. I told Brigid she needed to care more about the victims." Ree stared into the fire, but didn't really see the flames.

"What else did you tell her?" Paden's voice was quiet, barely more than a whisper.

"That someone had made her look like a fool and she needed to step up and prove them wrong."

Paden's heart stuttered for a minute against Ree's back, and his mouth opened in a frustrated groan. He didn't move though. He kept her firmly pressed against his chest. "Ree. She could've killed you."

"No. She won't kill me. Not yet, anyway. I pointed out they made me because they needed me. They better start listening to what I have to say or things aren't going to go the way they want." Ree sat up so she could look at Paden. "I'm done being their tool. If they want me to do what they couldn't, then they need to start respecting me."

Paden's eyes were bright with something Ree couldn't quite understand. It was warm, whatever it was; pride and something else. He touched her cheek and pulled her face to his. Very gently he kissed her, his lips a whisper of a touch, before drawing back, just enough to speak.

"You are so incredibly brave. You're right, they should respect you." He kissed her before pulling back slightly one more time. "But please, don't piss off any other gods unless I'm there with you. Promise."

Ree turned so she was straddling his lap and ran her hands over his chest, before raising them to wrap around the back of his neck. "No more pissing off gods unless you are there with me." She leaned forward and pressed her mouth to his. His warm, soft lips parted immediately and she slid her tongue in to find his. The smell and taste of him were intoxicating. His hands ran down her back to cup her bottom, gently squeezing before shifting her on his lap. She groaned into his mouth, enjoying the warm sensation of him pressed against her body. She shifted gently, moving her hips so she could feel his response, and he groaned deep in his throat.

"Promise me, Ree." Paden's voice was a low growl. "I can't think of you being hurt."   His hands moved to bunch in her shirt and she was overwhelmed by the need to feel his hands on her skin. Ree leaned back and looked into his hooded eyes while she slowly pulled her shirt over her head. Her cheeks burned slightly in excitement; she felt bold and daring, but the look on his face was worth it.

"I promise."

She threw her top on the floor and leaned forward to kiss him again. Paden's hands skimmed up from the edge of her jeans to and trailed lightly over her back, finally stopping on her shoulders. Their kiss deepened, and it was as if, suddenly, all the careful barriers they had in place crashed down around them. She couldn't get enough of him; she wanted all of him.

His mouth trailed hot kisses down her neck and stopped at the hollow of her collar bone, where his tongue flicked out gently to taste her skin. His fangs descended and gently scraped along the skin, but she didn't care, because everywhere his fangs touched, his mouth did too.

"Sorry." He pulled back and looked at her sheepishly. She was vaguely aware of her power swirling around them, stirring the material of her shirt on the floor. He couldn't help his body's response any more than she could help hers.

"It's okay." Ree tilted her head at the spinning power along the floor. Paden chuckled softly before returning his attention to her throat.

She arched her back as his mouth continued its downward trek. When his hot lips moved over the wet material of her bra she sighed in pleasure and tangled her fingers in his hair. He slid his hands back down to cup her bottom, and moved her gently against him before standing. She wrapped her arms around his neck and held on tightly while he moved across the floor.

Paden set her down carefully before pulling his own shirt off. Ree's breath quickened and her eyes roamed over his chest, down to the white skin where his jeans hung loosely on his hips. Paden looked down at himself, as if not sure what she was looking at so raptly, which made Ree want to giggle. Shrugging, he crawled onto the bed and slowly covered her body with his.

Ree could feel his desire, his need, and it was overpowering when mixed with her own. She ran her hands over his chest and greedily returned his kisses. When his fingers moved to slide the straps of her bra off her shoulders, she shifted so he could reach the clasp in the back. Paden threw the bra away from the bed and looked down. Intense heat washed over her body everywhere his eyes touched.

He lowered himself so his mouth could touch hers in delicate kisses that made her heart pump harder. When his hand slid between them to undo the button of her jeans, she thought her heart would explode. Her breathing became ragged, and her fingers dug into his shoulders.

"Is this okay?" He pulled back a little, his hand splayed on her bare stomach and looked down at her. His eyes bored into hers, wanting her to be honest, wanting her to want him. She didn't trust herself to speak, so she only nodded and pulled his head back down to hers. When his fingers slid into her pants to touch her, she gasped loudly.

"I can stop. Just tell me." His hand stilled, and he kissed her neck gently.

"No. Don't stop. Please." Ree shook her head to make her point before turning to kiss him again. Through her eyelids she could see the green current of her power running through the little cottage. The glow seemed to intensify with each stroke of Paden's hand.

As he explored, Ree let her hands explore his body as well. She traced the contours of his back, before running her hands over his chest. When she hit the edge of his jeans she hesitated for only a moment before cupping him through his clothes. He groaned into her mouth, and that was all the encouragement she needed. She pulled at his pants until she had freed him, and her hands surveyed this new territory. After a moment, he pulled her hands away from him and held them above her head.

"Too much." He kissed her soundly. "I want you too much for that."

Slowly, he leaned back and pulled at her jeans until

they slid off of her hips. He threw them on the floor next to her bra. He lay back down next to her, kissing her again while his fingers traced the lines of her panties.

"Off," Ree whispered against his mouth and tugged at his pants.

"Are you sure?" Paden looked at her with serious eyes. The sun from the window glinted along the stubble on his chin, and she wondered why it had taken them so long to get to this point. Her heart swelled with love and the need to be closer to him was unbearable.

"Very." Ree watched as his mouth turned up in a slow smile. He kissed her gently before standing and shrugging out of his jeans. His boxers landed next to the growing pile of clothing. Paden's cheeks turned a soft pink as she stared at him, and it was nice to know she had that effect on him as well. She sat up on her knees and held her hand out to him. He slid onto the bed, pulling her to lay down with him. When his mouth covered hers, his fingers pulled at her panties until they were down by her ankles and she was able to kick them off. Their hands slid over each other, touching and stroking places that had always been off-limits. When he rolled over to dig through the clothes on the floor, she kissed along his neck and curved her body to fit against his.

She kissed him while he carefully put on protection, her fingers running up and down his chest. She was grateful he had brought something with him. Now there were no worries to hold them back, no chance of an unplanned family. He rolled her over so he was holding himself above her, his mouth closing on her neck, where his tongue flicked slowly over her pulse point. Her back arched and she pressed against the length of his body.

"Please," she whispered. She wasn't really sure what she expected, or just what she was asking for, but he looked at her with heavy eyes.

"I can stop, anytime. Just tell me." With that, he slowly joined their bodies. There was a sharp jerk of pain, but it didn't last long. Whether it was her own body healing herself, or Paden working his own healing magic, she would never know. The only important thing was that they were there, together, and she had never been so full of love in her life.

"Ree. Ree." He whispered her name like a prayer as he moved against her. As their bodies twined together, her power whipped through the room. She couldn't control it any more than she could control her response to Paden. As their bodies peaked, she gasped his name, and clutched at his back. He shuddered, his breath washing out of him in hot waves. Carefully, he lay down to the side and cradled her in his arms.

He buried his face in her hair. "I love you, Ree."

"I love you, Paden." She snuggled closer to him and turned so her face pressed into the crook of his neck. Her heart felt lighter than it had in a very long time. Even with the world falling apart around them, they had each other.

Paden shifted so he could wrap the blanket from the bed around them both. Ree listened to his heartbeat and felt her own match pace. It wasn't long before she couldn't hold her eyes open any longer.

Chapter 17

The cold woke Ree up, and she snuggled closer to Paden's warmth. He shifted so he could pull her onto his chest and still keep them covered with the blanket. She laid her head on his chest and smiled to herself when he ran his fingers through her hair.

The snap and hiss of the dying fire was the only sound in the room, and Ree felt incredibly relaxed and peaceful. She could tell Paden was happy too. His emotions were calm and joyful.

"Why are you so happy?" Ree tilted her head and smiled up at Paden.

"I just realized I don't have to worry about homework." He narrowed his eyes, a small smile playing along his mouth.

Ree sat up, pulling the blanket with her. She punched his arm and mock-glared at him. "Oh, that's all?"

"Hey! It's cold! Get back down here." Paden tugged her back down to his chest and chuckled when she pretended to be upset. "Or maybe it's just that I really like waking up with you in my arms. Especially when you aren't wearing anything."

Heat flooded Ree's face, but she couldn't help but grin. He wasn't the only one happy with this new experience. They grew quiet again, simply enjoying their time together. Paden ran his fingers through her hair while she lay there and listened to his heartbeat and breathing. It wasn't until Ree noticed that the sun was down that everything came crashing back.

"We need to go back." Paden sighed, obviously sensing her change in mood.

"Yes." Guilt made Ree cringe. She had spent hours in Paden's arms while her friends dealt with death and sadness.

"Don't." Paden sat up in bed and pulled her into his lap. "You needed a break. We both needed something happy, for just a little while. Something to remind us what we're fighting for."

"Ellie is dead. And while our friend grieved we…" Ree motioned between them.

"Do you think this was a mistake?" Paden looked at her with a neutral expression.

"No! No. I just… I don't know." Ree shook her head.

"Ree." Paden cupped her face in his hands so Ree couldn't look away. "People deal with grief in different ways. We've had so much sadness, so much anger lately, that I'm glad we spent the time together."

"I am too." Ree sighed softly and leaned forward to kiss him softly. "I just hope they won't hate us for leaving them to deal with it all."

"When I left, Melanie and Kay asked to be left alone for a while. They probably didn't even notice we weren't there. The others aren't going to care where we were." Paden leaned forward and touched his head to hers.

"I wish we didn't have to leave." Ree whispered.

"Me too." Paden kissed her softly. "I wish I could keep you here, naked, for years." Ree couldn't help the giggle that escaped at his words.

"That would be nice."

"Oh, nice? That's it?" Paden pulled back and frowned.

"Perfect. Fabulous. Amazing."

"Much better." Paden leaned down to kiss her neck. "When this is all over, we'll go away together. Somewhere peaceful, somewhere no one will bother us."

Ree tilted her head so he had better access to her throat. "Hmmm. That sounds perfect."

"It will be sunny, with crystal clear water, and you can wear little bikinis." Paden moved Ree a little closer on his lap.

"And you can wear some of those little swim briefs guys wear in Europe." Paden sputtered against Ree and she burst into laughter. She wrapped her arms around his neck and pulled him tightly to her. "I love you, Paden."

"Love you, too."

Ree pulled back from him and looked mournfully at their clothes on the floor. "Time to face the music."

Paden kissed her one more time before playfully pushing her toward her clothes. "Get to it." He leaned back on the bed and folded his arms behind his head.

Ree looked at Paden and raised an eyebrow. Grinning, she pulled the blanket with her as she stood up.

Laughter bubbled out of her throat when she looked back at him and his bottom lip was sticking out. She searched through their clothes until she found her panties and bra, quickly pulling them on while he pouted.

"No fair." Paden stood up and stretched. Ree felt her eyes glaze over as she stared at the perfection of his chest and shoulders. He smirked broadly as he took his time pulling his boxers on and shook out his jeans. Shaking her head, she dropped the blanket and reached for her own clothes.

Once they were dressed and the fire had been put out, they headed back to the house to see what the others were doing. Tonight they needed to say goodbye to the people they had lost, but tomorrow Ree intended to hit back. And hit back big.

The house was exactly the way it was before they had left for Savannah. As Ree walked through the halls she felt odd and out of place. Just a few hours ago, the entire place had been destroyed. A complete mess of rubble and charred furniture. She stopped in the kitchen and leaned against the doorframe. It felt empty somehow, as if the loss of Pam took away the homey feeling that once permeated the room.

Something glinted on the window frame above the sink. Ree walked over slowly and let her fingers dance gently over the plaque. Her heart tightened as she looked out the window at the beautiful Magnolia tree that was blooming at the wrong time of the year.

"For Pam, a woman that bled Southern hospitality. You shall be missed." Paden read over Ree's shoulder softly.

"Do you think they truly cared?" Ree didn't look away from the large tree with its beautiful white flowers.

"I think that they wouldn't have done this, had they not cared at least a little." Paden looked at the tree with clouded eyes. He squeezed her shoulder and pulled her away from the kitchen.

The house was quiet, but Ree could feel where everyone was located. She headed for Weylin's room. Paden knocked once before opening the door slowly. Juliette and Bryce were curled on the floor in front of the fireplace. Weylin sat in a tall wingback chair. His hands were lying on the armrests, his face taught with grief. Ree went to him and made him scoot over. She sat next to him, pulling his hand into hers, just offering strength and love quietly. She would turn the world around if it meant saving those she loved from the pain of the last few weeks.

He squeezed her fingers. No one said anything for a little while, just finding a little peace in each other's company. The last few weeks had been so hard for all of them, and Ree knew they would never go back to normal. How had the other Alastrianas returned to normal lives? Hadn't they felt the need to pay back all the hurt that had been inflicted upon them? Had they hunted Dark Ones for the rest of their lives?

"We should go to Melanie." Weylin's voice was hoarse, his eyes red-rimmed.

"Okay." Ree stood up and pulled Weylin into a hug.

"What do we do?" Juliette asked quietly. Bryce stood, holding her hand, his eyes dark with compassion. Only Ree could feel the anger bubbling under the surface of her friend's expression. He wanted revenge. Ree nodded her head in Bryce's direction to let him know she understood. She wanted it too.

"We need to find them a final resting place." Paden answered Juliette's question, but kept his eyes on Weylin.

He nodded his head once and they all headed toward Melanie's room.

Roland sat on the floor next to Melanie's door, his head tilted forward, his confused emotions swirling through the hallway. Ree wished she could make him understand what he was feeling, to point out the obvious, but she knew he had to figure it out on his own.

"They wouldn't let me in." He looked up when they got closer, his eyes bleak. He studied Ree and Paden for a minute before looking away. Ree wanted to help wipe the despair from his face, but knew only time could do that.

Paden held his hand out to help Roland up. Ree squeezed his arm before she walked to the door. Taking a deep breath, she knocked twice softly. The door came open slowly and Melanie looked at Ree with sad eyes. Ree stepped forward and wrapped her friend in a hug. The pain from the two women in the room was like drowning in hot water. It was thick, suffocating, and stifling. The others slowly came in the room behind Ree. Weylin went straight to his aunt and wrapped her in his arms. Kay looked fragile next to Weylin's tall frame, her eyes closed as he whispered something quietly to her. She reopened her eyes and grabbed Weylin's face.

"This is no one's fault. No one but the Dark Ones that came here." She looked around the room, meeting each set of eyes. "Do you hear me? This is not any of your faults. My mother went doing what she loved." She looked at the body covered on the bed and her lip trembled softly. "She would never have wanted us to find blame in ourselves."

A knock on the door made everyone in the room jump—which was a surprising occurrence. Ree felt the power just out of sight and immediately went to open the door. Just past the arched doorframe stood Brigid, Hecate,

Athena, Aphrodite, and several other gods and goddesses Ree didn't recognize. Brigid stepped into the room, and nodded to Kay. Instead of her normal jeans and sweater, she was wearing a long green dress, with a dark blue cloak that trailed on the ground. The dark red hair around her face had been pulled back in braids that swung gently when she knelt next to the bed. She bowed her head and placed a hand on Ellie's limp form. Hecate went straight to Kay and pulled her into a motherly hug. Her weathered hands stroked Kay's hair, and she placed a soft kiss on the woman's cheek. She stepped back to look at Melanie, her eyes full of tears.

"Because Kay is the remaining human on the island, and from my line, I will speak for the gods tonight, as I say that we are terribly sorry for your loss. We cannot bring back the dead, but I can promise to take good care of the woman you called mother." Hecate turned to look at Ree with compassionate eyes. "We would celebrate their lives with you tonight."

Ree nodded her head. Hecate walked to the bed and gently lifted Ellie. Turning carefully, she walked out the door and headed for the front door. As they walked, other gods joined them, each carrying a limp form in their arms. The hairs on Ree's arms rose, the power making her senses tingle. To see these immortal creatures carrying the dead, was one of the most surreal moments of her life.

There along the beach stood eight pyres. Hecate gently laid Ellie's form on the first pyre and unwrapped the sheet. Once she had Ellie free, she kissed her forehead once. Each of the gods and goddesses did the same thing. Pam's battered form was hard to look at, but Ree refused to turn her eyes. Paden pulled her against his chest and wrapped his arms around her. Hecate motioned for Melanie and Kay to say goodbye to Ellie.

Kay stepped up and whispered quietly to her mother.

She adjusted Ellie's shirt and kissed her on the cheek. She stood up and turned to look at the gods and goddesses. "Make it worth it. Make all of this worth the cost."

Melanie stepped up to stand in her mother's place. She leaned down and gently kissed Ellie before brushing some of the hair away from her face. She didn't say anything, just walked back to stand next to her mother and Weylin. The gods and goddesses formed a half circle, enclosing the group so that they were closest to the pyres.

Hecate's voice rose in a haunting tune that made Ree's heart clench. As the goddess sang of love and death, Brigid went to each pyre and, with the touch of her hand, lit the wood. The flames grew until they heated the tears running down Ree's cheeks. She tried to think good things for the dead, to focus on the bright moments she had shared with Ellie, but her mind tripped over the image of the older woman's dead body and stuttered when she thought of Pam and her suffering. She hadn't known Pam long, but she had been a kind woman. Someone who had felt real and normal in the middle of a crazy sea.

When Hecate finished her song, she turned to look at Ree. "Go and do what you need to. We shall stay with the pyres until they are gone. No one shall set foot on this island who is not welcome."

Ree nodded her head and looked at her friends. They all wore the same expression. It wasn't the fire that had once filled them at the thought of hunting. Instead it was cold and serious.

Chapter 18

As she turned to leave, Ree caught Athena's hard stare. The goddess's face was partially blocked by the hood of her white cloak, but her intent was obvious. Ree jerked her chin up and left without a second thought. The goddess obviously wanted the same thing Ree did—to make the ones who did this pay.

Ree didn't stop walking until she got into the armory near the practice room. She shrugged out of her jacket and grabbed sheaths that went along her back. Once she had her swords in place, she loaded herself down with throwing knives and daggers. She wasn't sure she would need them for what she had planned, but she wasn't going to be caught without them, either.

The only sound in the room was that of clinking metal and the whisper of leather as everyone "suited up". Ree pulled her hair over her shoulder and quickly worked it into a braid. Her eyes traveled over her friends, taking in their expressions and intense feelings. She knew they were ready to go kill, to take out as many Dark Ones as possible, but she wanted to make sure their heads were in the right place. She waited until everyone was done, waiting around the room with deadly expressions.

"We're going out tonight to take out as many Dark Ones as possible. That means that if we see Tristan and I have the opportunity, I'm going after him. But we need to be focused on our task first and foremost. We need to take all of his back-up, his help from him. Don't go looking for trouble." Ree pulled her jacket back on and zipped it up carefully.

"What if trouble finds us?" Weylin's knuckles creaked around the pommel of the collapsible sword he was holding.

"Then make them regret it." Ree turned and led the way to the boat at the dock. She slowed once they got near the water and looked for Melanie. She turned to her friend. "Melanie, I think you should stay with your mom."

"I'm fine, Ree. Don't try to keep me away from this." Melanie started to walk past her, but Ree grabbed her arm. She looked at Melanie and absorbed her emotions for a minute. She fought with her instincts but finally nodded her head. Maybe this would help Melanie, to keep busy and have an immediate goal.

As they hopped onto the boat, Ree felt the tugging presence of a god nearby. She looked over her shoulder to see Athena and Brigid standing next to each other near the trees. They were both looking out at the water, so Ree followed suit. As she watched, a slight shimmer seemed to appear in front of the boat before fading away. She looked back at the goddesses and nodded in understanding. They were consciously shielding the island now. Nothing would get through at this point.

"I guess you made an impression." Paden whispered. He was looking at Ree with gleaming eyes.

"What did you do?" Roland asked. He glanced briefly at Ree before turning back to the console.

"We had words." Ree sat down on the bench next to Melanie. She didn't touch her friend, worried Melanie's careful façade would fall apart.

"Must've been some words." Bryce muttered from the other side of the boat. Ree just shrugged and thought about what they were going to do when they hit the mainland.

Roland took them to a shipping company and carefully motored the boat into a slot between two large freighters. Once everyone was ready, they headed downtown. They had to walk through an unsavory area to get to the historic district, but Ree wasn't worried. If someone didn't sense the danger that followed her friends like a dense smoke, they could deal with it quickly. As they came to a crosswalk, the two men standing there quickly left. Each of the humans eyed Roland and Paden with suspicion as they quickly walked down the block.

"We hit the furthest safe house from here and work our way back to the boat." Ree started off on a jog, heading for the side of a building that had a broken fire escape. She jumped and grabbed the highest rung, before quickly scaling the rattling metal to the roof. Roland seized the lead, taking them to the house that had portals in it the night before. They all crouched on the top of a building across the street and decided on the best plan of action.

"Fire?" Weylin licked his lips and narrowed his gaze at the dilapidated house.

"Could spread," Bryce said. "Is there anyone in the surrounding houses?"

"No." Ree bit her lip and knew she had to make a decision. "I can blow up the house, but we should save that for an emergency for now. It saps me, even with the new healing stuff." She sat back on her heels and looked over at Paden. "It will be dawn soon. We hit once they're in the house. No one to help them from the sunlight."

"Should we split up? Hit two houses at once?" Melanie was staring at the house, her mouth pressed into a line so tight her lips were white.

"You're right. That way if the others get news of it, they won't be able to portal out before we get two houses down." Ree nodded her head.

"I'm staying with you." Melanie looked at Ree with determined eyes. "I want to watch these jerks burn."

Ree appraised her friend for a long minute before nodding her head. She turned to look at the rest of the group. Paden starred at her intently, and she knew he was worried she would send him with Weylin and the others. There was no doubt in her mind it would only cause a fight, and that was the last thing they needed.

"Who brought explosives?"

"That would be me. I'm demo." Weylin reached into the bag he had looped over one shoulder. Drawing out two small devices, he held them up for everyone to see. "Stick it to the wall and press the button in the center. You've got twenty seconds to get the hell out of the way."

"Roland, can you, Bryce, and Juliette handle the other house?" Ree looked at Roland steadily. She was worried about the conflicting emotions that rolled off of him any time he looked at her or Melanie. Frustration, confusion, and pain tore at him, and it made Ree beyond nervous to see Roland—the rock—so mixed up. He bowed his head in understanding and moved toward the next rooftop. Ree turned her gaze to Juliette. "I want you with them because you can use your gift if everything goes wrong." Juliette nodded her head and silently followed Roland and Bryce.

"Okay." Ree sat down with her back against the wall. "Now we wait." She closed her eyes and blocked all of the emotions around her. She waited for the cold trickle that signaled approaching Dark Ones.

It wasn't long before she had a tingle of warning. She opened her eyes to see the purple and light pink of sunrise brightening the sky. Her eyes went to Paden's first, and he looked at Ree with a calm that made her even more relieved to have him with her. Weylin was running his thumb over the leather wrapped around the handle of his dagger. Ree turned and peeked over the edge of the wall just in time to see the Dark Ones turn the corner. The one in the center was laughing, his hands miming something in front of him. Melanie shifted next to Ree and growled low in her throat.

The female Dark One closest to the building stopped and sniffed the air. She said something quietly to the others and they all looked around. Ree ducked down, pulling Melanie with her. She forced Melanie to look her in the eyes and raised her eyebrows. Ree needed to know if Melanie could handle this, because she was fairly sure Mel couldn't. Melanie nodded her head and looked at Paden over Ree's shoulder. Apparently he was telling her to get herself together. Ree hoped she hadn't been wrong about bringing Melanie.

Ree closed her eyes and listened to see if she could hear anything from the Dark Ones. They were arguing, but apparently the leader thought she'd heard a human. The rising sun made the decision moot. There wasn't enough time for the Dark Ones to check out the situation, and the big guy from the center wasn't willing to send the darklings away from the house to investigate. Ree opened her eyes when she heard them enter the house and slam the door.

"They're in." Paden barely breathed the words,

knowing if they could hear the Dark One's whispered argument, the Dark Ones could hear them.

"Sun all the way up." Ree pointed at the shadows along the roof before pointing to the ground in front of them. "Stay." She looked at Melanie and Weylin and held her finger to her lips. At the rate their attempted arson was progressing, they'd have done more damage throwing flaming dog poo at the front door.

Weylin crouched down next to Melanie and put a hand on her shoulder. She looked at him and nodded her head in some unspoken conversation. They seemed to understand each other's grief more than anyone else could. Deciding she would let them comfort each other, Ree sat back down on the wall and concentrated on their surroundings.

Once she could see the pink glow of the sun through her eyelids, she opened her eyes and looked at the others. Standing up, she ran for the edge of the building and jumped to the next roof. They all climbed over the railing on the back side and made their way for the house. Paden leaned around the corner and checked out the area before they headed to the empty house next to the Dark Ones'.

Ree noted the darkling loitering in the living room, along with a darkling on the front and back porch. The emotions they exuded made her want to take a long, hot shower. She didn't know what they were doing in there, but she didn't want anything to do with it. In fact, she was starting to wonder if any of them were worth saving. Weylin wanted the explosive as close to the center as they could get. Ree could feel the cold, dead spots congregated in the center as far from windows as possible. She knew they were out, literally, so her friends only needed to deal with the darklings.

Ree shrugged out of her jacket and pulled the rubber

band out of her ponytail. If she could tempt the darklings away from the house, it would be easier for Weylin to slip in unnoticed.

"Melanie, take your sweater off." Ree pulled her shirt down so it hung as low as possible and looked at her friend. "We'll tempt the ones on the front porch away. Weylin, slip inside and set up the explosive. Paden, watch for more trouble."

Melanie pulled her sweater off, revealing a little tank top. Carefully, she tied the sweater around her hips to conceal the knives she shoved in her pockets. She ran a hand through her hair and nodded at Ree.

"I don't like this." Paden stared at Ree and she could feel his lust mixed with his concern. It made her shiver, but she knew this was the best way.

"We'll be fine." She stood on her tiptoes and kissed his cheek. "Let's go." She stepped away and grabbed Melanie's hand, laughing loudly. On their way out of the little alley, Melanie swooped down and grabbed an empty beer can.

"Nah-ah!" Melanie leaned on Ree's shoulder and grinned up at her friend. It was spooky to see the loopy expression on Mel's face, combined with the seething emotions underneath.

"He did! He totally did!" Ree laughed again and pretended to trip a little on the broken sidewalk. "Stupid piece of crap."

"Naughty!" Melanie laughed. She held up the beer can but frowned before turning it upside down and shaking it. "Oh no!"

"You are so drunk!" Ree cackled.

"Not drunk enough." Melanie threw the empty can

and pretended to be shocked when it hit the porch in front of the darklings. "Oh my gosh. My bad!" She covered her mouth and giggled.

One of the darklings leaned down and picked up the can before leering at Melanie and Ree. "Looks like you two had a fun night."

"The bestest!" Ree shook her head so her hair fell over her shoulders and she smiled up at the men. She had never tried to be coy, but she had a feeling it wasn't going to take much to entice the goons.

"Why let it end? I think we've got some drinks." The larger one sat down on the edge of the porch and patted a spot next to him.

"Mom says we aren't supposed to talk to strangers." Melanie giggled.

"What kind of drinks?" Ree hollered.

"Oh, a bunch of different kinds. Why don't you come up here and pick something out." The big darkling leaned forward and gave a nasty grin. Ree could see the red welts on his neck and wrist where he had recently been bitten.

"I don't know. Your friend doesn't look like he's much fun." Melanie pointed at the other darkling, who was leaning against the house as if bored. He looked at Melanie and smiled. Ree traced the collar of her shirt with her fingers and winked at the thin darkling. She felt his eyes run over her body and his lustful response. It disgusted her, but she needed them distracted. Walking forward, she swayed her hips as much as possible and licked her lips.

"I think he looks like fun." Ree stepped onto the bottom step.

"Looks like you found a friend." The other darkling laughed loudly and turned toward his accomplice.

The thin darkling stepped into the light and smiled down at Ree. He was missing a bottom tooth and smelled like a sewer. He grabbed Ree's hand and pulled her close to him. She giggled and squirmed when he leaned his head closer and sniffed.

"You smell like sex." He didn't let go of her hand but looked down at her with a new intensity.

Ree gasped, partly in an honest response and partly because she needed to keep up the charade. She pretended to try to pull out of his grasp but he held tight. He leaned down close to her face, and she tried to not gag at his terrible breath.

"That would be okay with me. If you didn't also smell like a godling." He tried to throw her against the wall, but she held on to his arm.

"That's because I am one." Ree deftly freed the dagger strapped under her shirt and held it to his neck.

"This didn't go quite like we hoped." Melanie was standing over the other darkling, who was unconscious and drooling on the dirty floor boards.

The darkling hissed at Ree and tried to break her hold. She pushed him against the house so no one would be able to see her knife from the street. Weylin ran toward them, his pack strap clutched in his hand so it wouldn't make any noise. He jumped onto the porch and looked at the two darklings.

"Better get them out of here." He ducked through the front door without another word.

"Let's go." Ree pushed the darkling toward the street. He turned to fight her, his eyes crazed.

"What is he doing?" He fought Ree with all of his might and she had a hard time not stabbing him with her knife.

"Quit it. Or you'll die too."

"What do you think he's doing?" Melanie hefted the unconscious darkling onto her shoulders and glared at the one Ree was holding on to.

"My wife. My wife is in there." His voice was frantic and his eyes had turned to the angry black a darkling wore when ready to attack.

Chapter 19

"There are no humans in there." Ree said. For a moment she felt sorry for the disgusting creature in her arms as she fought him down the steps.

"She's a Dark One! You're trying to kill my wife!"

Ree's heart stopped and she looked at Melanie. Her friends' face was a frozen mask of horror, matching the cold sensation in Ree's stomach. Weylin barreled out of the door, grabbed the guy Ree was fighting, and helped drag him away. They pulled the incensed man down the road and into the shadow of the alley. Paden was only a few seconds behind them. Blood was splattered on his shirt and his face was grim. As soon as he cleared the entrance to the alley, the house exploded. Dust, debris, and smoke filled the street. Weylin let go of the darkling and ducked back out to make sure all of the Dark Ones were destroyed.

The darkling howled in fury and fought free of Ree's grip. He tried to run out into the alley, but Paden caught hold of his shirt and threw him to the ground. "What is his problem?"

"His wife was a Dark One." Melanie looked down at

the darkling starting to stir by her feet.

"Oh, shit." Paden looked at Ree, his eyes a little wide.

"Let me go to her!" The darkling pulled himself up.

"It's done." Weylin walked into the alley and covered his ears when the darkling howled in pain. "Dude, you were hitting on teenage girls. It can't be that serious."

"I was getting her dinner." The darkling snarled and tried to run at Weylin. "You killed her. You killed my wife."

"No, I didn't. Someone else did that a while ago." Weylin grabbed the guys' arms and penned him to the wall. In the distance, another explosion sounded, and their group looked at one another. They needed to get back to the boat before the place was crawling with cops.

"You have a choice." Paden looked at the darkling over Weylin's shoulder. You can let Ree take your taint away, or we end this all now. We don't have time to fight."

"Don't touch me. We chose this! This was our way out." The madman fought harder and managed to pull one of the knives out of the sheath of Weylin's waist. He stabbed Weylin in the gut and tried to slash at his neck, but Weylin reacted quickly. Using both hands, he grabbed the darklings' head and snapped his neck.

"Weylin!" Melanie rushed over and pulled his shirt up. The wound was puckered and angry, but starting to heal. Paden walked over and placed his hand over the red slash for just a moment.

"We've got to go. I can hear the sirens." Paden nodded his head at Weylin and turned to look at Ree. She let her gaze fall on the dead darkling and felt hollow inside. She looked at the larger darkling that had finally woken up.

"It's your turn to decide." Ree looked down into his eyes and knew the moment he made his decision. As he launched himself from the pavement, Ree raised her hand and sent him careening into the wall. The crunching sound of his skull meeting brick made Ree angry. Angry she had been put in a position to hear it. Angry she had been put in a position to cause it. Turning on her heel, she sprinted out of the alley and toward the boat. She didn't want to think about it anymore. She just wanted to get out of that alley and make sure her friends were all safe. The soft sounds of her friends' feet following closely behind her was reassuring.

Paden slid next to her and laced his fingers with hers as they ran. He was offering the only assurance he could, and Ree was willing to take it. She felt the other group of her friends nearing them as they ran. Eventually, she caught sight of Roland as he slipped into their group. When they neared the edge of the city Ree slowed down to a walk.

"I think we should hit one more." She squeezed Paden's hand, because she knew it was going to bother him.

"The city is crawling with cops. And very likely gods now too." Paden looked down at Ree, his eyes serious.

"The cops will be paying attention to the two houses we already destroyed and the gods will be waiting for us to run back to the island." Ree stopped and looked at all of them. "We hit one more house. I'm tired of running. I'm ready for a little payback."

"Ree, this is dangerous." Roland stood behind Paden, his eyes intense. "There are a lot of things that could go wrong."

"It's all dangerous. There are always things that could go wrong." Ree narrowed her eyes at him. "It's time to start working toward ending all of this. I'm not going to run away or hide behind you guys. Let's take them out while we can."

"She's right." Melanie moved so she was standing behind Ree. "Even if we win and kill Tristan, we're going to have to clean up all of the leftover Dark Ones anyways. Might as well take them out now so we don't have to worry about them later."

Ree kept her face expressionless and debated the merits of having Melanie side with her. On one hand it was nice to have someone backing her up, and on the other, it was kind of worrisome that it was the girl out for blood. Paden seemed to know what she was thinking because he just raised an eyebrow and looked at her.

"Look. It's the right thing to do. The Dark Ones are sitting ducks right now." Ree put her hands on her hips.

"I'm sure they know, Ree." Paden glared at her. "They're safe because they know we don't want to draw attention to them or ourselves. Especially with the cops looking for us everywhere."

"And we just created a giant distraction. They won't be expecting us." Ree wasn't about to back down. If there was one thing she was certain of, it was that less enemies was better for their side. This was war, and she was going to treat it that way. No more trying to figure things out. It was time for action.

Paden's eyes bored into hers, but he didn't say anything. Ree felt a small amount of relief. It was easier to deal with silence than an outright fight.

"Where is the closest house?" Ree asked Roland.

"About five blocks north of here." Roland jerked his

chin away from the river, and Ree looked down the street. That would put the Dark Ones in the nicer neighborhood. She hoped it wouldn't make it harder for her friends to go unnoticed.

"Okay. Then we hit them fast and get out quickly." Ree headed down the sidewalk and felt the anger bubbling under her skin. She was tired of waiting. Tired of having things happen to them. Tired of seeing people dead or hurt because of the evil roaming the streets. The faster she walked, the more power swirled in her chest.

Knowing they couldn't afford to be seen, she eventually took her group down a dark alley and came at the house from a small back street that people used to get to their garage or carports. She held up her hand so they wouldn't get too close. She could feel a large group of Dark Ones and darklings in the tall Victorian house. Paden cussed under his breath behind Ree, and she agreed with him wholeheartedly. Looking at the large green and brown house in front of them, her eyes strayed to the sign on the sidewalk. It was one of the most prestigious bed and breakfasts in the city.

Ree turned to look at Roland. "So, you didn't think to mention it was a hotel?"

"It's not a hotel. It's a bed and breakfast." Roland replied evenly. "Would it have mattered?"

Ree looked back at the building and frowned. "Probably not." Paden sighed behind her, but she ignored him. "Weylin, how many explosives do you have left?"

"More than enough." The sound of things being moved around in his canvas bag floated up to Ree's ears. She looked back in time to see him pull out two handfuls of little black devices. Weylin held them out for everyone to see. "There were a ton at the house, so I brought as many as I could grab."

"What do you think? Do we need to get them in the house again?" Ree bit her lip, trying to make her decision.

"If we put these outside of the house, the explosion would destroy everything around it. They need to go inside to minimize the collateral damage and to make sure they destroy the Dark Ones. If you put the explosives on the outside, you run the risk of the Dark Ones not being destroyed. They might just be covered up with debris. No. For this to work, we need to know they have been exposed to the sunlight or ripped apart." Weylin held one of the devices between his fingers and narrowed his eyes. "These babies need to be as close to where they're sleeping as possible."

The thud of someone jumping down from the roof sent everyone into action. Two darklings threw themselves at Ree and Paden while the others jumped back to give them room.

"Go!" Ree shouted at Weylin. He took off almost instantly with Melanie and Roland on his heels.

Darklings seemed to pour from the house, filling the little back alley with bodies and angry energy. Bryce and Juliette fought their share, giving Ree glimpses of their spinning and ducking, moving together like one person instead of two. Paden lifted one of the darklings from the ground and threw him down the alley with a growl. The sound of the darkling skidding across the road to slam into a dumpster made Ree look down the alley.

A sharp stinging sensation made Ree suck in her breath. She looked down at her stomach and saw the point of a sword jutting out from her shirt. Ree felt her eyes widen in shock and would have tumbled forward if the darkling who had snuck up behind her had not grabbed her shoulder so she could twist the blade in Ree's back.

A ferocious roar filled the alley, so loud Ree thought the walls shook. Something flashed past Ree and she stumbled to keep from falling over. The sound of flesh meeting flesh filled the air, confusing Ree. Cool hands touched her shoulders and she looked up into Juliette's calm eyes. Her mouth moved, but Ree wasn't sure what she was saying. The only sound she could make out was the blood rushing in her ears.

A sharp sensation made Ree wince, but was quickly replaced with a feeling of emptiness that made her want to vomit. Juliette pressed a hand to Ree's stomach, her long fingers trying to staunch the flow of blood that poured from the wound. Bryce was moving behind Ree, obviously keeping the darklings at bay. As her hearing came back, Ree could make out someone hollering her name over and over again. The anguish in Paden's voice brought tears to her eyes. She looked up at Juliette in fear.

"You're going to be fine. You're already healing." Juliette moved her hand a little so Ree could see the wound was starting to knit itself back together, slowly growing smaller.

"Help them." Ree nodded her head and tried to move toward the wall out of the way. She tripped on the curb, but was able to walk herself. She leaned against the brick and covered her stomach with her own hand before weakly pushing Juliette away.

The amount of broken bodies littering the ground was astounding, but Ree only had eyes for Paden. He was cutting through the darklings as if they were butter. All darklings that came at him were brutally removed from existence. By the time he reached Ree, she was starting to feel better, but his hands immediately went to her wound. The healing glow of his magic worked and sped the process along.

After a few seconds, he pulled his hands away to look at the scar across her stomach. His fingers traced it gently as he examined what wouldn't have been there had she been born to an immortal line. The clatter of the demo team coming down the alley was the only sound other than Paden swallowing convulsively, as if he couldn't get himself under control.

"Never again." With his fingers still tracing the scar, Paden leaned down to kiss Ree. His mouth touching hers the moment the explosives ignited. The ground shook under their feet, but Ree couldn't tell if that was from the explosion or Paden's touch. He pulled her against him, his hand moving up to cup her head while he kissed her passionately. As the dust floated down to land on their shoulders, Paden leaned back to look at her before placing a soft kiss on her swollen lips.

"Never again, Ree. I can't live without you. Do you hear me?" Paden cupped her face with his hands, lifting her eyes to meet his. His voice cracked with emotion. "Do you hear me?"

"I hear you." Ree stood on her toes and kissed him back quickly. She tried to reign in the tears that threatened to spill at the look on Paden's face. "We have to go."

Chapter 20

They made it about a block before someone spotted them. The little old woman with her giant hat and knit shawl stopped walked by and openly stared at them. Ree groaned and Paden squeezed her hand. To be fair, they were covered in blood and dirt. Unfortunately, the little old woman's face lit with recognition as she stared at them, and Ree felt her spike of fear.

"She knows who we are." Ree whispered quietly.

"We look like we just fought in the battle of Gettysburg. Of course she recognized us." Weylin shook his head. "We look like the vagrant punks the news has been making us out to be. Weaving destruction everywhere we go."

Sirens sounded in the distance and Ree felt her heart plummet. No one said anything else, just ran. Ree was tempted to throw in some extra speed, but she worried about the humans that might see them. Paden pulled her towards an alley, where he solved their problem. The group flew through the witness-free alleys and dark streets, only slowing down to cross roads, or where the buildings opened up. The sound of sirens filled the air no matter how fast they ran. The cops were out to find the culprits.

Ree wished she had just let them leave the first time, but they had managed to kill a large group of Dark Ones. She could smell the water and knew they didn't have much further to go before they were back to the boat. When they neared the shipping yards, Ree skidded to a stop. Power pulsed from the area and she knew what that meant. There was a god waiting for them somewhere amongst the freight containers. To make it worse, she could also hear the crackle of police scanners and the sound of dogs sniffing.

"This day is really starting to suck." Juliette ran a hand through her hair.

"Tell me about it." Weylin shook his head.

"What do we do?" Melanie asked.

"There are other ways to the island. We have other boats." Roland stepped up to take charge. "We just need to get out of here without them spotting us."

Ree opened her mouth to tell them there was a god with the humans, but didn't have the chance. Loki appeared behind Roland and smiled.

"Now, that would ruin all of the fun." Smiling, he pushed his sunglasses back on his head. "I went through all of this trouble to arrange a welcoming committee and you're just going to skip out?"

"So, you're just going to come out and admit you're a traitor?" Melanie pushed around Ree and growled at the god. Ree's eyes widened, surprised by Melanie's candor. She reached out to touch her friends arm, but it did no good.

"What's gotten under your skin, godling? You're too

pretty to be so angry." Loki's eyes flashed dangerously and Ree's stomach tightened.

"You killed my grandmother, you bastard." Melanie pulled her dagger from the sheath on her hip.

"I haven't killed anyone." Loki smiled at Melanie, his perfect teeth glinting in the sun. "Yet."

"Fuck you! You killed my grandmother! You killed all of those people on the island! You want to kill all the humans. Because you're a sick bastard and you think it's fun!" Melanie threw her dagger and it stopped just short of Loki's face. Something seemed to shift under his skin, making him look far more dangerous than a well-dressed surfer.

The dagger clanked to the ground and Melanie was lifted into the air by an invisible force. Her eyes spit fire at Loki, hate rolling off of her in waves.

"Watch how you speak to me, little girl. I've killed better than you in my day for far less." Loki looked at Ree and smiled. "Alastriana, you're not doing such a good job of controlling your little ragtag team of godlings." One of the dogs howled in the distance, obviously smelling something. Loki's eyes lit up with excitement. "Oh good. The fun is about to start."

"Put her down, Loki." Ree moved so she could see the god clearly.

"You're a spoilsport." Loki looked at Melanie, and she flew across the parking lot they were standing in. Ree grabbed the power and flung it at Melanie, trying to shield her from the brunt of the impact. Her friend smacked into one of the shipping containers, but was on her feet immediately.

Ree looked at Loki, her own anger getting the better of her. "You need to leave, before you blow your thin cover."

"Don't think you can order me around, Alastriana. Besides, the others will assume I was only here to have a little fun. It's in my nature to make things difficult. I just can't seem to help myself." Loki smiled indulgently, his eyes taking on a wild edge.

Ree felt Loki's magic reach for her, trying to wrap around them all, pinning them in place. Even Melanie had been halted in her progress to get back to them. Ree tried to move, straining muscles she hadn't even realized she had, but to no avail. He held them tighter than quicksand.

"BRIG—" Paden's voice cut off.

"Nah ah ah. No calling your grandparents." Loki slid his sunglasses back down onto his nose. "That's just sad."

Ree tried to say something, but couldn't get any words to form. Her mind raced, the only thing still free, trying to find a way out. Rage filled her and the power responded. Green energy flooded out of her body, in no way hindered by Loki's magic. The shell she had been trapped in shattered, the little pieces of his power dropping into the greening swirl of energy to become part of her own.

Loki growled deep in his throat, the sound reminiscent of an angry wolf being challenged. Lightning scored through the sky, thunder rumbled in angry fits. Ree pushed at his power, shoving it away from her friends, sending it flying in thousands of little pieces. Loki raised his hands in Ree's direction and she felt the hairs on her arms and neck stand up straight. Knowing he was about to strike at her, Ree did the first thing that came naturally. She pulled as much power in as she could and threw a shield between her and the god. She pulled and pulled until the inside of her skull felt raw.

Suddenly the thunder stopped, and Loki's eyes looked surprised. The sound of running feet echoed off the walls of the surrounding warehouses. Loki dropped his arms and disappeared, but not before winking at Ree.

"Shit, shit, shit." Weylin's voice seemed to bounce around in Ree's tender head. She was holding more power than she had ever pulled before and for a second she thought it might cause her to burst apart.

Ree raised her hands and looked at the empty freight containers. She threw the energy at them, wrapping them in tight bands of power. She jerked her arms towards the alleyway, just in time to see the first of the humans. The containers slammed down with an almighty sound, shaking the ground under everyone's feet.

Paden wrapped an arm around her shoulders and pulled her in the direction Roland was leading. Ree's head was still buzzing from all of the energy, but despair smacked into her at the thought of what she might have killed. Roland took them down the back streets of the scarier parts of the city, and Ree was forced to focus on their surroundings. The amount of hate and anger in that area was overwhelming to Ree while she was brimming with so much power. She squeezed Paden's hand and tried to focus on him and her friends. Melanie's anger hit her like shrapnel every time she thought of her friend, which made Ree do her utmost to block everything.

The group jumped over a small wall that surrounded an apartment complex and dodged into the parking lot of a doctor's office. Roland pulled his cell phone out and quickly dialed a number.

"We need some help." He paused for a minute and listened to the other end. "That would work. We're at Dr. Paulsen's office." Roland paused again, the corners of his mouth lifting at something the other person said. "That's the one. See you in a bit."

"Who was that?" Ree moved closer to where Roland was crouched.

"Nick." Roland looked down at the hole in her shirt. "Are you okay?"

Ree jerked her head in answer, not wanting to really talk about it.

"You scarred." Roland hooked one finger in the hole on her shirt and peered closer. His worry hit Ree like a ton of bricks, and she realized he must've been working very hard to contain it. Unfortunately, she could also sense the overwhelming feeling of despair from Melanie and the ping of jealousy from Paden.

"I'm okay." Ree looked Roland in the eyes. "I guess my human genes aren't going to work exactly like all of yours." Very gently, she moved his hand away from her abdomen. "So, why were you laughing?"

"Nick and I met here. Holy water and a cross was involved." Roland looked away from Ree and sat back on his heels. An amused grin pulled at his mouth. "I don't think he will ever really like me, but I can't say I blame him on that account."

"Holy water, huh?" Ree couldn't fight the smile that came with that thought.

"Yeah. Needless to say, we were both surprised. And wet." Roland smiled at her, and Ree felt her stomach unclench a little. With time, she thought, they could be friends. Real friends, not the uneasy truce they seemed to be walking around.

It wasn't long before Ree saw the flashing lights on top of the ambulance. The large vehicle rumbled into the small parking lot, turning so it could back up toward the building, not far from where her friends were sitting. The red-haired young man Ree had met the first night her group tracked Dark Ones popped out of the driver side. He walked to the back and opened the door before making a small bow in their direction.

"Your chariot awaits." His voice was calm, an amused smile causing small wrinkly lines around his mouth and between his eyebrows.

"Thank you." Ree stood up and smiled at the red-head.

"Are you okay?" Nick's smile dropped and he pointed at her bloody shirt. "Or are you trying to make a statement?"

"I'm fine, thank you." Ree wished she could change the shirt, but at this point it didn't really matter.

"Fashion continues to elude me." Nick held his hand out to help her into the back of the ambulance. She didn't need the help, but appreciated his offer. Once everyone was in, he closed the doors and the ambulance pulled out of the parking lot. There wasn't a lot of room for everyone, so it wasn't the most comfortable ride. Ree sat on a chair that was facing the back doors, while everyone else squeezed onto the tiny bench on one side, sat on the bed, or folded themselves into an uncomfortable space on the floor.

Roland sat on the floor next to Ree and held onto the black net that hung from the ceiling to the floor. He gave directions to Nick, and they barreled off through the city. When Nick turned onto a major interstate, Ree looked at Roland with curiosity.

"Just going a little further away. I don't want to risk any of the closer spaces." Roland stared out the front windshield, his eyebrows pulled together.

"Where is Sophie?" Nick asked.

Ree turned in her seat to look at Roland. Her heart clenched at the memory of holding Sophie's dead body. Roland's hands clenched convulsively on the black straps and his jaw flexed. Sophie had been his family for centuries. She had been his sister for far longer than Tria had been alive.

"She's no longer with us." Roland didn't look at Nick, and his eyes stayed glued to the street.

"She's gone?" Nick didn't take his attention from the road, but Ree felt his shock and sadness.

"Yes."

"I'm sorry." Nicks eyes flicked to Roland in the rearview mirror. "She will be missed."

"Yes." Roland swallowed. "She will be missed."

The rest of the ride was quiet, except for the occasional direction that Roland gave to Nick. Eventually, the ambulance ended up on a long dirt road that dead-ended at a shack with an old pier. Nick opened the rear doors for them to exit and looked around at their surroundings.

"Will that ancient bucket get you to where you need to go?" His eyes lingered on the rusty old boat tied at the end of the pier.

"It's much sounder than it looks." Roland held his hand out to Nick, who shook it. "Thank you for saving our tails."

"Happy to return the favor." Nick smiled sadly at Roland. He waved a hand at the others before hopping back into the ambulance and heading down the old road.

"Are you sure, that thing isn't going to sink?"

Weylin looked down the pier and frowned. "Because, I'm pretty sure it isn't going to make it very far."

"Well, I guess we'll just have to swim then." Roland smiled at Weylin. He walked over to the time-worn shack and pulled some keys out of his pocket. The rusted old lock fought it, but eventually opened. Roland threw the doors open and stepped inside.

Everyone peered into the door, wondering what Roland was doing. There were boat parts, an old car, and weapons lining the walls. Somewhere just out of sight, soft sounds of scurrying critters had Ree wondering how long it had been since someone had visited this outpost. There wasn't a floor, just hard-packed dirt and only a single light hanging from the ceiling.

"What was this used for?" Weylin looked around the room and grimaced.

"I believe it was a smugglers' drop point. Why?" Roland dug through some boxes in the back.

"This place is as old as dirt!" Weylin pointed at the car. "That thing has to have been here for forty years or more."

"Try sixty." Roland stood up and tossed something to Weylin. "Seems like just yesterday."

Weylin caught the small thing in his hands. "A starter?"

"Yeah. Check the box on the table. There should be a wrench in there that will work." Roland dug through another box and came up with a small pouch.

"You mean we have to fix the boat before we can use it?" Weylin dug through the tools until he found what he was looking for.

"It's not broken. It just needs a couple of parts." Roland walked out of the building and headed for the boat.

"Isn't that the definition of broken?" Melanie piped in from the back of the group.

"Not if the parts are missing on purpose." Roland jumped into the boat and dropped to his knees near the console.

Ree looked down at the boat and felt herself frown. The leather seats looked much newer than she would have expected, and the console had shiny knobs and dials. Her eyes slid over the boat to rest on the covered motor. She watched as Paden walked over and unzipped the plastic cover to reveal a large gleaming motor.

"Now, that is a motor." Paden whistled softly.

"The best I could find out here." Roland looked at the motor with pride. "This boat has been my project for a few years now."

"Nice." Paden folded up the cover and stuck it in a cubbyhole. It didn't take long for them to get the motor put back together. They were on their way not long after locking up the shed, and it only took a little longer to reach the island than it would have from the other landings.

When they neared the island, Ree watched as the shield shimmered for a moment before dropping away. There were no waiting gods Ree could see, but she felt their presence anyway. They were keeping their word and protecting the island, but not offering any other help or interference. It was all Ree could hope for.

Chapter 21

Ree trudged into her bedroom and threw her coat onto the chair. She sat down on the bed, pulled her boots off, and peeled off her socks. It had been a long night and day. Standing up, she shed the rest of her clothes on the way to the shower and sighed as soon as she stepped into the warm spray of water. The water ran over her head and down her body, relaxing her shoulders and the pressure in her head. She knew it was a headache from stress, because her body wouldn't be hurt by allergies or migraines. Grabbing the soap, she started to clean away the grime, but paused when her fingers hit the ridge of the scar on her stomach. She hadn't really looked yet, but knew it had to be bad. It was almost three inches wide, a shiny ribbon of scar tissue. Reaching around behind her, she felt along her back for the scar she knew had to be there as well. When she found it, she closed her eyes and took a deep breath. It was wider than the one on her stomach, but, thankfully, smooth and not puckered.

The sound of someone opening the door to her bedroom made her freeze. Carefully, she reached out with her power to see who had come in her room. Instead of relaxing, her heart thumped a little harder. Paden stopped outside of the bathroom and tapped on the door.

"Come in." Ree swallowed and hoped he didn't hear the slight squeak in her voice. She knew it was unlikely he missed it though, because she could hear him swallow before opening the door. "I'll be out in a minute."

Paden didn't say anything. He just walked in and closed the door behind him. She grabbed the shampoo and tried to work out the knots in her hair. She heard rustling from the other side of the shower door, but couldn't see anything through the frosted glass. Closing her eyes, she ducked under the showerhead and tried to get all of the shampoo out of her hair. She was debating the merits of cutting her hair when she heard the door open.

"I thought maybe we would conserve water." Her eyes opened wide and she looked up at Paden's amused expression. He reached past her for the soap on the ledge above her head. Her heartbeat picked up as she watched him rub the soapy lather over his body.

"Hm." Ree reached for the bottle of conditioner and tried to keep from knocking everything off the shelf in her nervousness. "Well, we might as well protect the planet in every way."

"Right." Stepping around her, Paden ducked under the water and rinsed the soap from his body. She watched as the soapy water ran down his chest. He peeked one eye open and chuckled. "Ree, you're pouring conditioner on the floor."

She looked down and realized that she was holding the bottle upside down. She snapped her mouth shut and cursed under her breath. Using her foot, she pushed the mess toward the drain. Paden slid an arm around her waist and pulled her against his chest. He pressed his chin to her shoulder and looked down at her stomach. With soft fingers, he traced the scar, making her stomach twitch. A warm glow grew from her center as she watched his hands trail over her skin.

"I'm so sorry, Ree." His lips brushed against her temple as he leaned back and traced the scar next to her spine. "I should have stayed closer to you."

"It wasn't your fault, Pay. I should have been paying better attention." The tips of his fingers felt electric, running over her skin. She turned around so that she was facing him and put her hands on his chest. The water from the shower trailed down his shoulders, over her hands and cascaded off of her arms. Very gently, he brushed the wet hair out of her face and tilted her face up so he could see her eyes.

"It won't happen again." Slowly, he brought his lips down to hers in a soft kiss. She twined her hands around his neck, melting against his body. It turned out to not be such a quick shower, and Ree was sure that they hadn't conserved much water. However, it was the best shower she had ever experienced.

Later, they lay on her bed, their towels discarded on the floor. Ree propped her chin on his chest and looked up at Paden. He twirled some of her hair around his finger, a small smile playing along the edges of his content expression. She watched him, memorizing his face as if she didn't already know it perfectly. The sounds of the others moving around the house, mingled with the sounds of the wind outside, made things seem almost peaceful for a little while. Paden chuckled, making her chin bounce.

"What?" Ree wrinkled her nose.

"I can't believe you didn't kill me when I got in the shower." He tugged gently on her hair. "I was a little nervous."

"Well, I thought about it." Ree narrowed her eyes at him.

"Oh yeah?" Paden's grin grew even more.

"Yeah. But I figured that we were supposed to be saving the planet and all, so you had a good case." Ree smiled.

"You know, I don't think it worked out the way I planned." Paden smirked.

"Are you sure about that? Because I'm pretty sure it worked out just the way you planned." Ree looked around at the messy room pointedly. She still couldn't control her power when she was with Paden.

He rolled her over, so he was leaning over her. "Well, maybe some of it worked out the way I planned."

"And what was that?" Ree stared up at him, enjoying the way the low light from the table on her nightstand played on the planes of his face.

"Did you forget already?" Paden nuzzled her neck, trailing kisses along her collar bone.

"I might need a reminder." Ree sucked in a breath as his hands slid over her body.

"Well, I might be able to help with that."

The wave of alarm that washed through the house had Ree scrambling to sit up before someone pounded on her door. Paden didn't ask any questions, just rolled off the bed and pulled his pants on.

"Ree!" Juliette's voice was loud through the door.

"I'm coming! Hold on!" Paden threw her a shirt from her closet and pulled on a white T-shirt of his own. Ree scrambled into the long sleeved black shirt and ran to her dresser. Once she was decent, she pulled open the door and looked at Juliette's white face.

"They're striking back." Juliette's words sent a chill through Ree's body. Paden placed a hand on her shoulder and pushed her into the hall.

"What's happening?" Ree followed Jules as she headed toward one of the large sitting rooms. She could hear the sound of the TV and feel the anger and apprehension from her friends. Stopping in the doorway, Ree stood, staring at the large flat screen. The breaking news banner was scrolling at the bottom, listing the names of missing or dead people: Fourteen dead, six still missing. Pictures of burning houses and wrecked cars flashed before her eyes.

"The police fear that the escalating gang violence is to blame for all of the recent destruction. It was originally thought the missing teenagers involved in the downtown antique store fire were responsible, but now it seems they may have been the ones that were targeted. They are still wanted for questioning. If you have any information concerning these individuals, please contact the Savannah Metropolitan Police Department." The reporter on the screen looked up into the camera with a serious expression. "The police are warning people to stay in their homes, to avoid answering the door for strangers, and to call them if you see anything suspicious."

Ree's stomach churned with anger and her fingers tingled with power. She didn't realize she was leaking any energy until Paden moved next to her and slid his fingers between hers. She looked up into his angry eyes. He wanted to offer her assurances, but he was just as angry as she was. As they all were.

Roland came walking swiftly into the room, his cold fury radiating through the around the enclosed space. He hung up the cell phone he had been using and shoved it into his pocket. "I'm getting calls from all of the safe houses. There have been attacks on all of them. Thankfully, the shields seem to be holding, even the one that was made by Ares."

Roland looked at Ree and Paden, but for once, she didn't feel any of the jealousy that typically followed. Instead, anger permeated his entire body. "I've called some of the people we've marked from immortal lines. I can't reach some of them."

"I've pulled a list of all the missing people and the dead." Melanie walked into the room, looking over the papers in her hands. "They are definitely going after the magical lines." Mel looked up at them and grimaced. "Some of the people on the news aren't on our list, but I think it's fair to assume they must have been people we hadn't come across yet."

"They are doing to us what we did to them." Ree clenched her hands into fists. "We have to get the rest of them out of town."

"Ree, we can't do that." Roland looked at her worriedly.

"Why not, Roland?" Ree narrowed her eyes. "They need to be taken out of harm's way. Other than the fact that I'm not okay with innocent people being killed by my monster-brother, it doesn't make any sense to let him have more magical blood to fuel his chances against us."

"Ree, you're risking starting a city-wide panic!" Roland looked at her, shocked.

"So what? Damn it! We have to do something! Let the people get the hell out of here! Who cares if they know about—" Roland was across the room in an instant, his hand pressed to her mouth.

"Ree, you cannot say that. You do not understand how much they will do to protect their secrets." Roland leaned close and whispered in Ree's ear. Paden growled deep in his throat before pulling Ree back away from Roland.

"Fine. Then we do it as quietly as possible." Ree looked at Roland, wondering what had happened to make him so scared of the gods.

"Ree, there aren't enough of us to get all of those people out of here safely." Melanie was looking at Roland and Ree worriedly.

"Then call in backup." Kay's voice trailed across the room. Ree looked over at the couch where the older woman had been sitting. Such an obvious solution, that Ree wasn't sure why it hadn't occurred to her before now.

"Yes! Backup!" Ree looked at Roland and nodded her head as if to emphasize the rightness of the solution.

"That could bring unwanted attention." Roland rubbed a hand over the scruff on his chin.

"If this is the only way we can do it, then you need to make it happen." Ree looked at him pleadingly. "We can't just let them be hunted down, Roland."

"What about the other humans?" Weylin looked over at everyone.

"They aren't in any more jeopardy than before, it would seem. The Dark Ones seem to be targeting those with something extra in their blood." Roland looked at the TV for a minute. "Weylin. Pause that!"

Weylin hit the pause button on the remote and looked at the screen. "Holy shit."

Ree looked at the screen and froze. Standing in the

shadows was a grinning blond young man who made Ree want to scream in horror. Tristan stood in the shadows, surrounded by a bunch of bystanders, the flames from a burning car sending wicked shadows over his smiling face.

"When did all of this start?" Ree moved to the couch, her eyes glued to the frozen image on the TV screen.

"Looks like it's been going on for almost an hour or so." Weylin looked from Ree to the TV. He reached over and grabbed her hand. "We'll get him, Ree."

She squeezed Weylin's hand. He seemed to understand the hurt she felt at the evil her brother was committing. "That means he was out and doing this just after sundown."

"He has become very strong." Roland looked at the screen with a frown. "The blood from immortals is speeding his growth."

"What do you mean?" Ree looked back at Roland. "How long does it normally take before the battle happens?"

"Sometimes months. Sometimes weeks or a year. But, this is much faster than I have seen before."

"Months? A year?" Ree felt her mouth hang open for a minute. "Holy crap! It's barely been a month!"

"Yes." Roland looked at her steadily. "When do you think the battle will happen, Ree?"

Ree looked from Roland to everyone else in the room. She looked back to the flat-screen TV and frowned. Her thoughts raced over the people that had died, her parents hiding, the missing people. Her heart squeezed. Her brother had been turned into a monster. "Soon."

Chapter 22

Ree sat at Sophie's desk and looked through all the paperwork she had been able to find. Melanie had already looked through the lists of known immortal lines, but Ree felt like there must be something they were missing. She was still working on finding backup to get the rest of the targets out of the city. Frustrated, she ran a hand through her hair and stared at the fire. Roland was insistent they not alert the general public to the actual trouble. He argued for hours with her that calling in other Guardians would send the Gods into a panic. Ree just couldn't understand what the big deal was, but she was certain she couldn't leave all of those people to be killed by Tristan. It was just bad strategy, anyway.

She sat up straight in her chair. Looking around the room, she narrowed her eyes.

"Athena, I would like to talk to you." Ree didn't raise her voice, just waited patiently to see if the goddess was listening.

"I was wondering how long you were going to avoid me." Athena appeared next the fireplace. The goddess was tall, much taller than Ree or even Brigid. She was wearing a dark suit, her white, button -down shirt tucked around her narrow waist. Ree found herself staring at the small square glasses that perched on her nose. "You certainly have bad timing. I was in the middle of business negotiations."

"Thank you for answering." Ree stayed at the desk, not wanting to give up her spot of power.

"Well, some things are a little more important." Athena's mouth pulled to the side in a small smile. Ree was certain the goddess knew just why she wasn't vacating the large desk chair. "Besides, it was getting a little boring. I have them right where I want them, and they are barely squirming."

Athena pulled her glasses off and tucked them into her shirt pocket. She walked over to the table in the corner and poured an amber liquid from the decanter into a small glass. Ree knew it was alcohol, but had no idea what kind. The goddess sat down in one of the chairs facing the desk and crossed her legs. She took a sip of the drink and sighed happily.

"Sophie always did stock the best whiskey. A weakness of mine." Athena toasted Ree before taking another sip. "So, you look at home behind that desk."

"You mean I look frazzled and frustrated." Ree narrowed her eyes, not sure if the goddess was teasing her or not.

"Exactly." Athena kicked off her shoes and looked at Ree with narrowed eyes. "We should have had this talk sooner."

"Possibly. I've been a little busy, however." Ree laced her fingers together and rested her hands on the desk. "I'd like to talk to you about something important."

"I see. So, this isn't about you thanking me for giving

you immortality?" Athena took another sip of her drink, smiling at Ree around the cup.

"Let's be honest, Athena. You would have turned me into a toad if you thought it would have helped the situation." Ree's heart beat a little faster, wondering if what she was planning would blow up in her face. "I want to bring in the other Guardians."

"I take it you do not mean your friends."

"No. I want to call in backup." Ree watched as Athena frowned.

"What for?" Athena stayed in the chair and gazed at Ree with bright eyes.

"I want to remove the source of Tristan's growing strength." Ree chose her words carefully.

"I see." Athena continued to stare at Ree, but didn't offer anything else.

"The more blood he ingests from the immortal lines, the stronger he becomes. He's already wreaking havoc in the city. The more he gets, the harder he will be to beat." Ree took a deep breath and hoped she was playing her cards right. "However, I've been informed the gods would not take kindly to having their existence exposed. Not even by the immortals that carry their blood."

"So, you appeal to me to see reason." Athena smiled slowly at Ree. "You are hoping I will see the merits of removing his food source."

"When in war, you block a country's trade routes. You take out its resources. This is simple strategy." Ree tried to keep her face blank, but knew the goddess understood just how much she needed her help.

"And how do you propose we remove the humans?"

"If we can have the Guardians from other locations come help, we may be able to take them and hide them ourselves. There are houses in the center of the island. We could bring them there to stay until after the battle." Unclenching her hands, Ree picked up the pen on the desk in front of her. "There are six more families on this list. I'd like to bring them here for safekeeping. We could settle them in the small houses easily."

"And what will you feed those that you bring to the island?" Athena twirled the whiskey in her cup.

"Well, there is plenty of food in the kitchen…"

"Not enough to feed the twenty-two people you are suggesting bringing over."

Ree looked down at the list in front of her and frowned. The six families remaining did add up to twenty-two people. "Perhaps you could help provide food for them the same way you do for us."

"So, you ask me to help win over the other gods to this plan. Then you ask me to grant you a favor, by providing for the refugees." Athena narrowed her eyes over the drink.

"Providing for your family and extended family is not a favor to me. It's what families do for one another." Ree narrowed her eyes at the goddess. "But, yes, I do ask that you help me convince the other gods that it would be in their best interest to remove those that are in harm's way."

"And what would you do for me in return?" Athena smiled when Ree's shoulders jerked in surprise. "Is that not how favors work? I help you and you help me?"

"I've already given you everything with nothing in return. You could say that was advanced payment." Ree took a deep, slow breath.

"That's not how negotiations work, Alastriana. You want something, you must offer something in return." Athena set the glass down on the table next to her before leaning her head back against the chair.

"You've already asked something of me. Now I want something in return." Ree gnashed her teeth together.

"Then, no. I will not help." Athena pulled out her glasses and slipped them back on. "Now, I have a business meeting to get back to."

"What would you ask for?" Ree's fury was quickly accelerating.

"What do you plan on doing with yourself after the final battle?" Athena looked over her glasses at Ree, her eyes dancing with something that made Ree squirm.

"A vacation. A long vacation somewhere pretty."

"After the vacation. What then? You can't spend all of eternity on a beach." Athena tilted her head to the side. "Trust me. It would be great for a little while, but you will end up bored stiff. Even with the godling to keep you company."

"What do you have in mind?" Ree leaned back in her chair, trying to mimic the ease the goddess exuded.

"There will be clean up, of course, but we might need you again someday." Athena narrowed her eyes at Ree. "You might need to help with a different project."

"What type of project?"

Athena shrugged delicately. "That would have to be determined. There are lots of things going on in the world. Not just the battle you are involved in."

"So, in other words, you want to be able to call me in for something later." Ree rubbed the arm of her chair with her thumb as she thought it over.

"No. I want to be able to call you in anytime I need you." Athena narrowed her eyes at Ree.

"I will not spend the rest of my life as a soldier. I deserve some happiness, just like everyone else."

"Of course. I'm sure there would be time in between situations when you might be able to de-stress." Athena's grin grew a little and Ree felt as if she was standing in quicksand.

"I will give you three times to call on me." Ree leaned forward and put her arms on the desk. "I will not do anything that will hurt a human for you. I will not put my family in jeopardy. I will not kill an innocent being. And I will not do something I know will get me killed."

Athena smiled. "Five times. And I will abide by your restrictions."

"Three times and you will abide by my restrictions." Ree narrowed her eyes at Athena. "You need me. You don't like it, and I don't like it. That doesn't mean we can't help each other. There are two families on Sophie's list that are linked to your line. You should be doing this without me asking."

"Three times and my terms." Athena narrowed her eyes at Ree, but her smile stayed in place.

"No." Ree stood up. "Thank you for taking the time to meet with me."

"That's it, then?" Athena stood up and looked down at Ree. "You will just give up that easily?"

"I never said I would give up. I will find another way." Ree met Athena's stare with her own.

"I knew I chose right with you, Ree." Athena nodded

her head, her face relaxing. Ree was surprised to hear her nickname used by the goddess. "Very well. Three times, with your restrictions."

"You will talk to the others?" Ree tried to keep her voice smooth, not wanting to show her relief.

"I don't need to. They will accept my word that it was necessary." Athena took a step toward Ree. "The extra Guardians will be here before sunrise."

"Aren't they spread around the world?" Ree asked.

"I'm a goddess, Ree. They will come through the portal near the large tree." Athena held out her hand to Ree. Reluctantly, Ree returned the gesture and shook the goddesses' hand. Light wrapped around their fingers, and Ree felt something tighten for just a moment.

"What was that?" Ree jerked her hand back.

"Our deal has been struck. There is no backing out now." Athena smiled at Ree.

"You do realize I might not win, right?" Ree looked at her fingers.

"I believe in you." Athena walked over to the fireplace. "More importantly, I believe in my ability to choose well."

"Thank you?" Ree raised an eyebrow, not certain how she should take that statement.

"Thank you. This was much more entertaining than arguing with fat men in suits." Athena disappeared, her laugh lingering in the quiet office.

Ree flopped down into her chair and took a deep breath. The office door banged open, and Paden flew into the room.

"What happened? Are you okay?" Paden walked straight to Ree, pulling her up to stand. "We've been trying to get in this room for half an hour."

Ree looked past Paden to see her friends all standing in the entrance to the office. "I'm sorry. I didn't know you guys were out there."

"We've been beating on that door forever." Paden glared at Ree. "I thought you were dead. I couldn't feel you."

"You'd think you would have heard Paden trying to beat his way through the wall." Weylin looked at Ree in question.

"I'm sorry, Paden. I didn't know." Ree looked at the cuts that were healing on his hands. "Athena must have done something to the room."

"Athena?" Paden's voice dropped an octave in anger.

"Don't worry. I didn't piss her off." Ree tried smiling at Paden, hoping it would smooth things over.

"You promised me, Ree." Paden stared at her, his eyes tight.

"I promised to not piss off any gods if you weren't with me." Ree looked at him seriously. "And I didn't. We made a deal."

"Deal?" Roland's voice cut through the room like a knife. "What have you done, Ree?"

"We're expecting company before dawn."

Chapter 23

Paden looked like he was going to murder someone. When she told him what she had agreed to, she thought his hair was going to catch on fire. She knew he wasn't mad at her, so much as worried about what she had agreed to. Ree didn't really blame him. She would be upset and worried if he had been the one to strike that deal. She walked over to where he was standing and slid her arms around his waist. He didn't move for a minute, his eyes watching Roland as he left to go wait at the tree for the arrival of the new Guardians.

"Don't be mad, Paden." She pressed her cheek against his back.

Paden grunted, but turned so he could pull her in front of him. His arms wrapped around her waist, and he rested his chin on top of her head. She let him hold her for a minute before moving so she could look up at him.

"I did what I had to." She watched as his jaw tightened.

"I know, Ree. I'm not mad at you. You did what you thought best for everyone." Paden's eyes snapped with green fire. "But you shouldn't have to ask them to do what's right. You shouldn't have to barter your life to get them to save people they put in harm's way!"

"I didn't barter my life. I just agreed to do three things for them."

"Ree. You're not stupid. You know they aren't going to call on you for anything that isn't dangerous." Paden stared at Ree until she sighed. "It's like they want to do everything they can to get you killed!"

"Yes, I know that." Ree started to step away, but he wouldn't let her move. "I don't think they want me dead exactly, but they like to have an ace in the hole. Just in case."

"You save aces for when you really need them. If they need you, it's going to be bad, Ree." Paden's lips pressed together.

"Well, we need to get through this battle first. One thing at a time, okay?" Ree pulled on the collar of his shirt so that his head came closer to hers. Pressing her lips to his, she kissed him softly until she felt him loosen up. Pulling back, she smiled up at him. "Besides you'll be with me. How much trouble can I get into?"

"Lots." Paden groaned and closed his eyes. He touched his forehead to hers and sighed. "Okay. We focus on this first and go from there."

"Right." Ree closed her eyes and took a deep breath, enjoying his smell. Enjoying how their smells mingled together. Suddenly her heart stopped and she looked up at him with wide eyes. "Oh my God. They all know, don't they?"

"Who? Knows what?" Confusion clouded Paden's face.

"The others. They all know that we… when… and

oh my God! The power! They probably heard us too!" Ree covered her face with her hands, but Paden laughed.

"You just thought about that?" Paden tried to peel her hands away from her face.

"The darkling said I smelled like sex. I didn't even think about everyone else smelling us on each other! And the power! I knocked a bunch of stuff over in our room." Ree groaned and squeezed her eyes shut. "I'm so embarrassed."

"I'm not." Ree looked at him exasperated. Paden smiled again and touched her cheek. "Our room, huh?"

Ree looked up into his eyes. His happiness at her words mingled with a swift sense of possessiveness.

"Well, yeah. You didn't think you were going to run away every night, did you?" Ree smiled at him for just a minute, but her embarrassment snatched her back. "Why didn't I think about them hearing us?"

"Ree, they probably knew the first time." He tapped his head.

"Oh no. The baby monitor! They knew what we were doing." Ree closed her eyes again.

"Are you upset we were together or upset they know about it?" Paden's smile turned serious.

"Paden, you know how I feel about us." She placed her hand over his heart. "But, that doesn't mean I want everyone else listening in to us when we… do that!"

"They won't bother us, Ree." Paden smiled at her.

"Speak for yourself, Paden!" Weylin's voice drifted up from the back of the house. "I need brain-bleach! No way I'm letting you slide on this!"

The sound of scuffling made Ree laugh. She heard Melanie whispering something to Weylin and knew her friend was trying to whip him into line. "No! If I have to suffer, they do to!"

"Can it, Weylin! Or I'll tell them what you said while you were drunk." Melanie's voice rose threateningly. The only other sound that came from the room was scuffling and then maniacal laughter. Ree looked up at Paden, eyes wide and her mouth hanging open. She wasn't sure if she wanted to laugh or scream in embarrassment. Thankfully, Paden made up her mind for her and took the opportunity to kiss her. His hand slid up to cup the back of her head, and she felt her embarrassment wash away.

"Seriously! Cut it out!" Weylin hollered.

Paden and Ree broke apart before laughing. Paden's eyes drifted over her shoulder and back to the path. Ree sighed and turned around to face the window. The sky was starting to take on the purple tones of dawn, the subtle black of the trees started to turn green, and the bubbling water in the fountain sparkled delicately. The soft mist that had blanketed the ground was slowly fading away. It wouldn't be long before the other Guardians were on the island and then it would be a long day of organizing the rescue plans.

Bryce and Juliette would be back on the island soon too. They had left to try and guard some of the families without calling attention to them. Ree hated sending them out there without backup, but Melanie had been scouring the computer for more information about the missing people and looking for links to any that may have not made the news. Weylin had been on the phone with the golems at the safe houses, working to get them ready for the pick-up of the community members who had known to go and hide.

Roland had talked to Nick on the phone before leaving for the gateway. He didn't trust the news stations to portray all of the details they may need. Since Nick was, in fact, a first responder, he could give Roland more details about the fatality rate, what the wounds had looked like, or if there were survivors Ree needed to be concerned about.

When the first jolt of energy washed over Ree, she grasped the windowsill in anticipation. She wasn't sure what to expect from the new Guardians, but hoped they would work together to save those they could. Paden looked down at Ree, his eyes asking the question. She nodded her head to let him know they were starting to arrive. She looked back over her shoulder when she saw Melanie and Weylin walk into the room. They must have sensed her eagerness for the new people. Weylin ruffled her hair and Melanie stood at the French doors, her arms crossed while her eyes stared seriously at the shadows along the path.

"Did she say how many she was sending?" Weylin looked at Ree from the corner of his eyes.

"No." Ree frowned. "I should've asked her."

"Any help is better than none." Weylin elbowed her gently.

"True," Ree whispered. She sucked her bottom lip into her mouth and chewed. When the first dark shapes started to make their way out of the trees, she stood on her tiptoes as if that would help her see better.

"Where do you think they are from?" Melanie asked quietly.

"I guess we'll find out." Ree moved to the door so she could greet the new people. Paden shadowed her, staying close enough that she could feel his heat radiating on her back. "They're on our side, Pay."

"Can't be too careful," Paden replied.

"Look at that," Weylin said from his vantage point at the window. "There must be twenty of them." Roland was at the front of the group. It was hard to miss his characteristic swagger. Ree felt Melanie's heartbeat pick up a little and tried to tune out the emotions radiating from her friend. Subtly, she bumped Melanie with her elbow and smiled. Melanie blushed furiously but gave her a small smile in return.

Ree felt her heart pick up in excitement. This could really turn the tables in their favor. When the new group neared the house, Ree opened the door and stepped out. She wasn't sure that many bodies would fit in the living room. Roland raised an eyebrow at Ree and flashed his trademark grin. It warmed Ree's heart to see him a little happier. The Guardians arranged themselves around the little clearing, while Ree's friends stood behind her. There were women and men, some older than Ree and some that looked even younger. All ethnicities, some in clothing that seemed too old for them, others in clothing that looked entirely too hip to be worn while fighting.

A young girl with large brown eyes and loose, wild hair smiled at Ree from where she stood. Her hands were planted on her hips, large army boots strapped to her legs, and so many knives strapped to her body Ree figured she couldn't go out in public. Letting the power reach out, Ree sensed the mood of the arriving group and found about what she expected. Eagerness, frustration, interest, and excitement seemed to emanate off of every person.

"Thank you for coming." Ree looked around at everyone, keenly aware that they were all waiting for her to speak. "I'm not sure what you've been told, but we need your help."

"We had to do it all ourselves. Why do you get help?" A bored looking man from the back frowned at Ree. The rolling of his Scottish accent seemed to accentuate his disgust. "A few Dark Ones too much for you to handle?"

Roland laughed, a deep, dark sound that filled the area. He turned to look at the Guardian and unleashed his fangs. "Niall, do you really think we would need your help with a few Dark Ones? You're only here to play babysitter for some humans."

Ree stared at the opinionated Guardian, he looked like he was no more than fifteen years old. He was wearing dark jeans and a T-shirt that had nothing but a hand holding up its middle finger. Charming. Paden tensed behind Ree, his temper snapping at the young man.

"We don't need you to take care of any Dark Ones. We need you to ride herd on some humans. The Dark Ones are targeting any human from an immortal line, anyone that has something extra in their veins." Ree was looking at Niall, but she spoke to everyone. "We've been given permission to bring them to the island."

Some of the Guardians were muttering under their breath a few of them out-and-out shocked by the news. The girl with the dark eyes stepped forward and held out her hand to Ree.

"What do you go by, Alastriana?"

"Ree." She reached out and shook the Guardians' hand.

"Sakhmet." The girl smiled at Ree. "Call me, Met. I'm used to it."

"It's nice to meet you." Ree returned the girl's smile. "Thank you for coming." She turned to look at everyone else. "Thank you all for coming."

"The Dark Ones are really hunting down the immortal lines?" A woman who looked to be in her late twenties asked.

"It's more than that, Magda." Roland turned to look at the Guardian. "They are doing it so it's making headlines. It started out slow and methodical, but has escalated. Last night they attacked four homes, caused several car accidents, and there are a many dead and missing people."

"What about the civilians? The cops and military?" A tall man with a deep voice asked. He stood next to Magda, his arm brushing against hers.

"The police are blaming it on gangs. There is no military involvement yet, but this could blow up into a terrible mess any minute." Ree looked over her shoulder at Paden. He nodded his head in encouragement. "I'm not asking for you to fight my battle. I'm not asking for you to clear out the city. We just need help rounding up the people that are in most danger and getting them to safety. To the island."

"Well, that's disappointing." Met frowned. "I was kind of hoping to kick some ass while I was here."

"For now, we just need to get organized and start bringing the humans over." Roland looked at Met, the corners of his mouth twitching.

"Well, tell us what we need to do, then." Met walked toward the house and made her way into the living room. She winked at Weylin, who was openly staring at the woman. Ree caught his eye and pointed to her head. Very carefully she mouthed the words, brain-bleach. He smiled widely and sauntered into the house after Met. Melanie followed, shaking her head. Ree stood by the door, greeting everyone that entered the house. When Niall neared her, Roland stepped behind Ree, mirroring Paden's protective stance. The young man peered at Ree through the hair that lay on his forehead as if weighing her. His inspection moved to Paden before slipping to Roland.

"So, you have a Guardian and Roland already working with you." His voice was dripping with condescension.

"Yes." Ree nodded her head.

"And the other two who were standing up here? You seem to know them." His eyes slid over Roland and lingered on Paden.

"They are my Guardians as well." Ree wondered what Niall was getting at. She could feel that he was working to keep his emotions to himself, and he was doing a good job.

"You have three Guardians." Niall narrowed his eyes at Ree. She could feel something bubbling under the surface, but she wasn't sure what he was hiding.

"Five. She has five Guardians." Paden's voice was calm, but the warning under the surface was obvious to everyone.

"What makes you so special?" Niall's face twisted in a sneer.

"Because she is the last Alastriana. The last to fight for Earth." Paden moved even closer to Ree. "Because she is special."

"They're all special, aren't they?" Niall moved without a sound. Spinning in spot, he brought out a dagger and swiped at Ree. She moved backward to avoid his strike, her hand raising automatically and glowing with power. Paden and Roland acted in unison in a move that must've been choreographed. Niall was lying on the ground in a matter of seconds, his blade lying on the other side of the clearing, his face amused. He looked up into Paden's eyes and began to chuckle.

"You should find someone else, godling. Loving an Alastriana will leave you broken-hearted. If she makes it through the battle you will have to watch her waste away." Niall's voice cracked and his grip on his emotions slipped for just long enough for Ree to understand.

"Sophie Diakos made a death gift to Ree." Paden hissed down at the Guardian on the ground. "The only thing I have to worry about is a Dark One stealing her away. Or an idiot making me kill him."

Putting a hand on Paden's shoulder she held her hand out to Niall to help him up. "I'm sorry for your loss, Niall."

The Guardian looked up at Ree, his eyes lost in memory as he stared at her hand. "I'm glad to know your Guardian will not have to watch you fade away."

Roland looked down at the godling and frowned. "How long has it been, Niall?"

"Sixteen years, eleven months, and twelve days." Niall's eyes finally fixed on Ree's. He accepted her hand before bowing over her hand. "My apologies, Alastriana."

"You do not get off with an apology." Paden moved between Niall and Ree, his body pushing a barrier between the two. "If you attack Ree again, I will kill you."

Niall nodded his head in understanding. "Yes, I figured as much." Without another look, he walked into the house and claimed a corner for his own. Ree walked into the house and smiled in relief when she saw Bryce and Juliette walking through the masses. Juliette looked around the room, her eyes taking in everyone's faces. Bryce, however, ignored everyone as he walked up to Ree.

"The Dark Ones have run to their caves for the night, but the darklings are looting. It seems to be limited to the historic district, which makes me think the Dark Ones are holed up somewhere nearby. It's going to be difficult to get past all of the cops that have been called in to help." Bryce frowned. "I'm pretty sure that was their plan."

Chapter 24

"We can give them the information and let them get the humans out of Dodge." Roland's voice was louder than necessary and Ree frowned. She looked once again at the text message her mother had sent and felt a pang of pain. She'd received it just a little while ago, and it had made her heart hurt. She missed them more than she thought she would. They were safe, that was the most important thing at the moment.

"They don't know the area." Melanie pointed out.

"Actually, I've been to Savannah before." Met looked up from the map on the desk. "It's pretty easy to find your way around once you know the key streets. If the cops find us, we can play the tourist card."

"We can't go, Melanie." Ree looked at her friend. It pained her to say that. She wanted to make sure all of those people were safe, just as much as her friend did.

"Look, the longer we argue about this, the more daylight we waste." Met leaned forward on the desk, her eyes trained on Melanie's. "I will take care of your people, Guardian. The Dark Ones have broken the agreement by going after the lines. It is our responsibility to protect those that cannot do it for themselves."

The Guardians that had squeezed into the office all grunted their agreement. Niall sat on the edge of the fireplace, flipping a blade over his knuckles.

"Melanie?" His accent-heavy voice seemed to catch everyone's attention. "This isn't our first rodeo." He smiled at Melanie, his face transforming into something much more attractive. "We will be fine. Besides, your Alastriana has spoken. Her plan is solid or Athena would not have sent us to help."

Melanie stared at Niall for a minute. "Fine. Put the addresses into the GPS on your phones. It may not get you there as quickly as we would be able to, but you'll get there eventually."

"How do you plan on us convincing the humans we are safe? Your television is telling everyone to not answer the door." Magda was perched on the edge of Ree's desk opposite of Met.

"I'm open to suggestions." Ree looked at the Guardian. "Because, short of having them grow fangs of their own, I don't know how to convince them."

"I have an idea." Roland said quietly. "We can knock out the less cooperative ones."

"You want to hit them?" Weylin asked from behind Met.

"We can dose them with a sleeping agent." Roland shrugged. "We have it in stock in case one of you had not taken well to the change."

Ree closed her eyes for a minute and resisted the urge to rub her temples. She was pretty sure she was the only one they had been worried about freaking out. "Okay. Break up into teams. No less than two people in a team." Her eyes shifted toward Niall, who didn't look up but smiled. She wasn't willing to have him go on a suicide binge while she was on watch.

Roland stood and quickly slipped out of the room. Everyone started talking amongst themselves, deciding who would work together. Ree got up from the desk and headed for the kitchen, Paden following closely behind. She couldn't remember the last time she had eaten. People moved out of her way respectfully, and it made her want to cringe. They nodded in her direction or watched her warily, and Ree fought the urge to shiver. She was grateful her friends hadn't treated her like that.

Kay was in the kitchen, busy making sandwiches for everyone. She offered a small, tired smile to Ree and Paden. "You look hungry."

"Starved." Ree took the plate Kay handed her and smiled. "Thank you, thank you, thank you." She sat at the long island and dug into the food.

"You too, Paden." Kay handed him a plate.

"Thanks, Kay." He gave her a one-armed hug and kissed her temple.

"No problem. I was going to cook something, but don't know where anything is in this kitchen." Kay looked over the counters and shrugged. "I guess I'll figure it out."

"You don't need to cook for us." Ree finished off her sandwich and eyed the one sitting on the cutting board. Kay smiled, scooped it up, and deposited it on Ree's plate. "Thanks."

"I don't mind and, to be honest, sitting around doing nothing was killing me." Kay wiped her hands on a dish towel and leaned against the edge of the sink. "So, you guys are going to back to the city?"

"Not yet. The new Guardians are going to pick up the people in danger." Ree looked out the window, her thoughts back on the people that needed to be brought to the island. "I guess I should go make sure those houses are all in good shape before they get here."

"You need to sleep, Ree." Paden grabbed her hand and squeezed. "You might be immortal now, but no one can go without sleep forever. It's been two days since you rested for more than an hour."

"I can do it." Kay set the rag down and looked at Ree. "Shouldn't be much to it."

"No, Ms. Kay. You've done more than you need to." Ree shook her head.

"Paden, take her to bed." Kay made a shooing motion. She smiled at their interlaced fingers. "To sleep, you two. Don't make me call your parents."

"Um…" Paden's cheeks turned a bit pink and Ree almost laughed as he squirmed.

Kay narrowed her eyes at Paden. "I said sleep! Do we need to have a talk? I could draw a chart and go on about condo—"

"No! I mean, no. I'll just go tuck Ree in and make sure she gets some sleep." Paden tugged Ree to her feet.

"Good. I may not have super sensitive hearing, but I'm not stupid." Kay turned her back on them and set their plates in the sink.

Paden practically ran from the kitchen, his cheeks still pink when they got to Ree's room. He opened the door and ushered her in, not sparing a glance at the Guardians they passed. Ree turned to look at him and couldn't help the snicker that fell from her lips.

"I've never seen you so embarrassed before in my life." Ree threw herself on the bed and kicked off her tennis shoes.

"Our friends knowing is one thing, but Ms. Kay knows my mom. She knows your mom." Paden lay down on the bed next to her and pulled her into his arms. "She knows your dad." He shuddered, making Ree laugh even more.

"C'mon. It's not that bad." Ree dug her finger into his side.

"You didn't see the glare your dad gave me before he left." Paden nuzzled her neck.

"Dad gave you a bad look?" Ree's eyes widened. She would have thought that Paden would be someone her parents would approve of.

"Not bad, just warning." He sighed. "I'm in deep shit."

"We've got other things to worry about." Ree rolled over on her back and stared at the ceiling. "I need to go check that everyone has everything they need." Sitting up, she ran a hand over her eyes and fought the yawn that came out of nowhere. "We need to plan. I feel like Tristan is going to up the ante."

Paden pulled her back down on the bed. "Sleep. A few hours, that's all I'm asking for."

"There is so much to do…"

"Trust in your friends. Trust the Guardians that are here to help. I doubt Athena would pick anyone she didn't think was capable." Paden pulled Ree against his side.

"Niall—" Ree started.

"Niall is hurting, but he isn't the only one who lost

someone he loved." Something in Paden's tone pulled at Ree's heart. She could feel his empathy for Niall, but it mixed with his anger at Niall having threatened her.

"What would have happened, Pay? If I hadn't been given the Death Gift?" She whispered the words.

"Sophie talked to me about it in the beginning. I think she was trying to prepare me or something. It was hard to think about and made me so angry." Paden ran his fingers over her hair. "But, now I don't have to worry. You're not going anywhere."

"You really want to stick with me forever?" Ree looked up at him. "Most marriages only last twenty years at most. Eternity is a long time." Her cheeks colored at the word "marriage", shocked she had used it to describe them. He had asked her for forever, but nothing with a title.

"Forever." Paden moved so they were lying on their sides looking at each other. He traced the palm of her hand with his fingertip before running over her ring finger and stopping. "I want all of you, all of life with you and everything that entails. We may not have regular day jobs or a house with a picket fence, but I'd like to call you my wife one day. See you carrying our child."

Ree's heart bucked in her chest, her stomach fluttered with butterflies, and a warm glow suffused her body. "Have you thought about that before now?"

"Maybe not in so many words, before everything went crazy. More like I wouldn't let myself think about that sort of stuff. But now? With the good and bad things in life in sharp contrast? Yeah. I want to grab the good and fight the bad." His full lips curved into a breath-stealing smile. He placed his palm on her chest, just over her heart. "I like being able to make your heart race."

Ree reached out and mirrored the touch on his chest. He covered her hand with his and leaned forward to kiss her. His lips glided over hers before moving up to kiss her head. He pulled back and lay down on the pillow, his hand still covering hers while they looked at each other.

"Sleep tight. Don't let the Dark Ones bite."

Ree rolled her eyes but listened to his heartbeat, his soft breathing, and let sleep claim her.

***

"Sleeping with the godling will not protect you." Ares's voice was like a knife between her ribs. "Neither will the shield that's erected around the island. Dreams are a funny thing."

Ree looked around the white room she was standing in and tried to gain her bearings. The god of war stood behind her, his feet spread wide, a whip in his hand. Immediately she looked around her for a weapon and mentally cursed the white toga she was wearing. It wouldn't offer her any defense against that whip.

"We use these on slaves." Ares snapped the whip. The sound echoed through the room. "That's all you are. A slave. A tool to be used by the gods as we see fit."

"You're only going to get yourself in trouble, Ares." Ree took a step back. Trying to keep her distance from the approaching maniac.

"Do not speak, slave!" Ares snapped the whip. Ree scarcely dodged the stinging lick across her chest. "What foul trickery is this?"

Ree crouched low, waiting for the next strike. Ares swung the whip over his head, before bringing it toward Ree. It cracked next to her ear, barely missing her after she moved.

"You do not move like a human, slave." Ares moved the whip so it traced circles on the floor between them. "What have you done?"

"I don't know what you're talking about." Ree watched his every step, waiting for a twitch to alert her to his next move.

His eyes seemed to rake her body, lingering on her chest and the skin exposed by the toga. It was like slime crawling over her body, and she couldn't help the shudder. He smiled, showing his perfect teeth.

"Do you know what we use slaves for, slave?" His whip caught Ree around the ankle and she gasped in pain. She ducked to the side and almost sighed in relief when his whip loosened. She risked a glance at her leg and noticed the bleeding stripe of skin that wrapped around her ankle. Every time she moved it felt like she had put her foot in a fire.

"We use them." Ares answered his own question. "For whatever we want." His voice oozed with menace. A loud crack filled the room, and the god disappeared. Ree looked around the room wildly. She needed to get out of there, but the hallway she used last time was nowhere to be seen. There were no doors, no windows, nothing she could escape through. Only white, shining stone everywhere she looked.

"Please, wake up. Wake up, Ree." She chanted the words, hoping something would snatch her out of the dream.

The loud sound of Ares returning filled her ears. She spun around to find herself face to face with the god. He grabbed her around her waist and pulled her against his body. "Slaves are required to do whatever we want them to do. And I want you to please me." He leaned down and sniffed at her hair.

Rees' heart stuttered and fear pushed her into action. She brought her knee up to his groin and shoved away from him as hard as she could. She landed in a heap ten feet away and scrambled to her feet while he howled in rage. Ree grabbed the power and threw it at him as hard as she could. He flew across the room and hit the wall. When he lifted his head to look at her, his eyes had turned an evil red. He opened his mouth in a primal roar, a double set of fangs sliding into sight.

He battered at Ree's shield, gaining a few inches each time he struck out. Ree could feel her energy dropping. There were no Guardians for her to pull from, she couldn't feel any plants or animals. As he fought against her shield, the bits of their magic fell to the ground and mingled together. Ree fell to her knees, exhaustion taking her breath away. Desperately, she stared at the shimmering fragments of power. Barely feeling strong enough to pull another breath, Ree grabbed at the only other power source in the room.

Latching onto Ares's energy, she sucked in as much as she could, feeding it back into her shield. His roars of rage seemed to grow, but Ree could barely hear anything but the sound of blood rushing in her ears. The god's progress stopped, but his temper grew.

The sound of a loud banging drew Ree's attention, but she didn't dare look away from Ares. Chunks of white stone exploded into the room. Ree slid across the floor, her head hitting the wall with a loud thunk. She covered her face as gravel and stone fell from the ceiling. When she opened her eyes, Brigid, Athena, and a smaller goddess were striding into the room. The red-haired goddess had a bow and arrow pointed at Ares. Her face was frightening, her eyes flashing with lightning, similar to the way Ree's glowed silver. She was wearing brown leather pants and a white top that made her red hair look even redder.

"Drop the shield, Alastriana. I shall handle this from here." Brigid's words were thick with a Gaelic accent. Ree obeyed immediately, scrambling to get even farther away from the gods.

The small goddess standing next to Brigid held her own bow and arrow, a crescent moon hanging from chain braided through her hair to lie on her forehead. Athena was carrying a spear and wearing modern-day combat clothing, complete with large, black boots.

"Go home, Alastriana. This animal will not threaten you again." Brigid did not look at her, but Ree could feel the goddess's fiery anger.

Ree stood up and limped for the hole they had blasted in the wall. Her ankle wasn't healing the way it would have in the real world, but she didn't have time to figure out why. Hecate appeared at the opening and motioned for Ree to hurry. The twang of bow strings sounded behind her, but Ree didn't look back. As Ares roared, she scrambled over the rubble and grabbed the outstretched hand of Hecate.

"Go home, love."

***

Ree woke immediately, sitting up in bed and scaring Paden. He immediately wrapped his arms around her.

"Ree! What happened? I couldn't wake you." Paden turned her face toward him and frowned.

"Paden, she's bleeding." Juliette was standing at the edge of the bed and pulled the bloody sheet away from Ree's leg. "What the hell caused that?"

Chapter 25

"Whip." Ree muttered.

Paden shook with rage, his fangs sliding out to press into his bottom lip. He closed his eyes and tried to reign himself in. As gently as possible he ripped her jeans from the ankle to the knee. Moving so he could inspect her leg, he cussed when he saw the damage. He pressed his glowing hands to her wound and stared at the blood surrounding her leg. Ree could feel the wound knitting back together, but it hurt more than any of the other wounds he had healed. She hissed through her teeth and looked away from her foot.

There were five people crowded into her room, not including Ree and Paden. All of them looking worried and angry. Roland's fangs were down, his fists clenched at his sides. He was standing in the doorway, where her splintered door hung from one hinge.

"What happened?" Roland looked at Ree, and she was glad for the distraction. "When we got in here, no one could wake you."

"Ares took me." Ree gasped in relief when Paden finished. She looked down at her ankle and couldn't help the frown that came at the sight of the scar wrapping around her leg.

"Took you how? You were here the whole time, Ree." Paden looked up at her with haunted eyes.

"In a dream. I've crossed over before, but never really understood how it happened. I guess this time, he took me once I fell asleep." Ree shook her head. "I really don't understand. If Brigid and the other goddesses hadn't shown up, I don't know if I would have escaped." She looked at Paden and thought about all she had to lose. "I don't know how they found me, but they got there just in time."

"Paden called for Brigid." Melanie moved closer to Ree, reaching over to grab her hand. Paden's despair had scared all of them. She could see the relief in their eyes battling the worry over what they had just gone through.

"She was… fierce." Ree told them, remembering the goddesses' ire. Ree took a deep breath, remembering how rude she had been to Brigid not that long ago.

"She wasn't here long. Just enough time to touch your forehead and tell Paden she would take care of you." Melanie squeezed Ree's fingers. "There was nothing for us to fight, no way to protect you."

"I fought. I'm not sure what else anyone could have done." Ree couldn't help the shiver that slid down her spine when she remembered Ares's red eyes and fangs. "Fangs. He had fangs." Ree went to jump out of bed, but her leg got caught in the sheets.

"What are you talking about?" Paden steadied her with a hand on her arm.

"Ares had fangs. Not just fangs, but two sets!" Ree spun around looking at them. "He had four upper fangs! Just like Della!"

"Ree, the gods don't have fangs." Roland looked at her worriedly.

"He did. At the time, I was just trying to get away, but now I remember it clearly. He growled at me when I threw him across the room." Ree looked around the floor for her shoes.

"You threw the god of war across the room?" Paden's face was blank.

"There were no doors, so I couldn't run." Ree turned to look at him, confused by his tone.

"How did you throw the god of war across a room?" Roland moved closer, his eyes trained on her face.

"When he told me what they do to slaves… I—I panicked." Ree swallowed. She didn't want to relive the moment. Being pressed against Ares had been vile enough. And if Paden knew, he was likely to go into a rage. "So, I grabbed the power and shoved it at him. Well, actually, I kneed him between the legs and then shoved him across the room."

Juliette held her hand up and Ree reached out to return the high-five. Roland narrowed his eyes at Ree and she was pretty certain he knew something of what had happened. Thankfully, he didn't say anything, understanding it would only make things tougher for her to deal with.

"So, you were able to use the power against a god." Roland stated the fact with surprise.

"At first." Ree saw the toe of her shoe sticking out from under the bed and reached down to grab it. As she bent to put it on her foot, she stopped. Her white sock was now blood red and her jeans hung in tatters. "He started to beat down my shield, but I was able to get enough strength to last until Brigid and some other goddesses showed up. Hecate and I think Artemis. Not sure who the other one was. She sort of looked like Brigid; long red hair and scary expression."

Standing up, Ree went to her closet and pulled out some new clothes and socks. She ducked into her bathroom and pushed the door closed. She would be able to hear them through the door no matter what.

"You were in a room with no doors or windows with nothing but a very angry god for company." Roland moved closer to the bathroom. "Where did you find the strength to fight him off? I'm assuming you were most likely on Olympus and the room you were in was one of the detaining rooms. You can't sense anything through those walls."

Ree bit her lip while she slipped on her jeans. She had found more than enough power, but she wasn't sure who might be listening in on their conversation. If Brigid and the others hadn't noticed that she had been taking power from Ares, she'd rather not call attention to the fact. Many of the gods already acted like she was some type of threat and she was just beginning to understand why.

"I'm not sure." She sat down on the edge of the toilet to pull on her fresh socks and stopped. The smooth, shiny scar on her leg curled up from her ankle and around her calf muscle like a snake. She traced it with her pointer finger and frowned. At the rate she was going, she was going to be a side-show freak by this time next year.

Shaking it off, she put her shoes on and stepped out of the bathroom. Roland was leaning against the wall next to the door, his eyes narrowed on her face when she stepped out. Paden had put on a new shirt and was pulling on combat boots. His eyes flickered to hers and she could feel his frustration at having not been able to protect her.

"You aren't sure?" Roland's voice pulled her eyes back to him and she could almost hear him asking, Or you don't want to say?

"Maybe a burst of adrenaline?" Ree looked at him, not sure how to respond.

"Or desperation." Roland jerked his chin once and Ree was certain he understood she couldn't say. She didn't put it past him to have come to the right conclusion.

"Right. She was backed against a wall and did what she had to." Juliette nodded her head as if that ended the discussion and in many ways it did. No one else asked about it, whether they understood she couldn't say or didn't care, she didn't know.

She headed out of her bedroom and went straight to her office. If napping wasn't an option, she'd use her time planning. Someone had taken a map and circled spots in different colors. She leaned over to study it, trying to figure out what the colors all meant.

"The blue ones are the homes of people we know are of immortal lines. Green are the offices of jobs of people we know have immortal blood." Melanie stepped next to Ree and looked at the map. "The purple circles are the people we suspect of having some kind of extra in their blood. The red circles are houses we know have hidden Dark Ones in the past and the orange circles are places the Dark Ones have been known to frequent."

"Do you guys see what I see?" Ree stared at the map, her eyes trailing over the circles. There were clusters of orange circles along the busy areas like River Street and Broughton. Red circles strategically placed in each neighborhood area, near apartment complexes. More importantly, they were all arranged in a pattern.

"Yes. Looks like they are protecting something." Melanie frowned down at the map.

"The college." Paden put his hand on the small of Ree's back. She could feel his need to be near her, and she was glad to have him close by.

"Melanie?" Ree looked up at her friend. "When was that special effect conference being held?"

"Um, not for another week or so." Melanie looked down at the map. "You think that is when they are planning the final showdown?"

"That's when they were planning the final showdown." Ree narrowed her eyes at the map. "But, we're going to move the show up a little bit."

"What are you thinking, Ree?" Paden circled the college with his finger. "That they were going to go after you with all of those people there?"

"That's exactly what I'm thinking." Ree shook her head. "But I'm not planning on waiting for them to decide when it's time. And I'm certainly not going to let them choose a time where they have hundreds of potential casualties."

"So when are you thinking?" Roland's voice was quiet, but serious.

Ree looked over her shoulder to where Roland was standing, his hands tucked into the back pockets of his jeans. "Tonight."

The energy in the room shifted dramatically with that one word. Roland's eyes gleamed and Ree could feel Paden behind her stand up taller. Melanie's eyes narrowed for a minute, taking on a grim look. Shifting her eyes around the room, she looked at her friends and tried to gauge their thoughts. There was a sense excitement, but under that was nervousness. This was a huge moment for their group. In a few hours they would be facing destiny and Ree hoped they could claim it for themselves.

"What about the Guardians in the town?" Bryce asked.

"When did you hear from them last?" Ree looked back to look at the map, her mind running over different strategies.

"Met and Niall called an hour before we realized there was something wrong with you. They had gotten two families and were heading back to their boat." Bryce came over to look over the map.

"Hm. Did they have any trouble?" Ree tapped her finger on the college and then traced a line to City Market and River Street.

"They had trouble with one set of parents." Bryce frowned. "Not that I blame them. Any parent would be freaked out if people with fangs showed up and demanded they bring their kids and go with them."

Ree grunted in agreement. "What did they do?"

"Well, Met said that Niall was pretty good at convincing them to go along." Ree saw Bryce shake his head out of the corner of her eye. "I think he liked knocking the father out a little more than he should have."

"What about the others?"

"We've had contact off and on, but not a lot of chatter. There have been run-ins with darklings, but nothing they couldn't handle." Bryce shrugged.

"What about the cops?" Ree moved her fingers back to the college, her eyes moving over the surrounding squares and houses.

"Magda had a run-in with some cops. Thankfully, she was able to get out of it. Very diplomatic, that one." Roland smiled. "Makes a nice balance, considering her partner."

"Tall guy? Very military?" Ree looked at Roland surprised. "I thought relationships were forbidden between godlings."

"The gods tend to overlook things when the godlings have already completed their battle." Roland frowned. "Most do not form permanent attachments, though. I think they feel they must be battle ready at all times. Considering the current situation, I can see their reasoning."

Ree looked at Roland for a moment, remembering her barter with Athena. She couldn't help but wonder if those godlings had also found themselves in a position to be on call in the future. It felt as if the gods planned on keeping them all for future purposes. Sighing, she turned back to her map. There were other things that required her attention.

"How do we know Tristan will be at the college tonight?" Juliette drew everyone's attention to where she was sitting.

"Do you see the way these houses are set up? There is a pattern, a strategy to where they set up the Dark One's bases. They are protecting the school." Ree tapped the spot on the map that stood for the college.

"You're saying Tristan has been hanging out on the college grounds this whole time?" Juliette stood up and looked at the map. "Why there?"

"Home court advantage." Paden put his hands on the desk and leaned forward. "He always liked playing on our soccer field better than anywhere else. He would go on and on about the dips and where rain water pooled."

"Then even if we attack tonight, he's going to know the area much better than we do," Bryce pointed out.

"Yes. And he will no matter when we attack. If we wait for him to lure us in, then not only are we playing on his court, but on his schedule." Ree shook her head. "We have to take any advantage we might have."

"We could wait another day or two and study the layout of the buildings. The school isn't set up like a regular campus. It's spread throughout the historic district." Melanie chewed on her thumbnail. "And if he is there, then it's a sure bet that some of the teachers and staff are darklings or worse. There are a lot of night classes."

"No. We do it tonight. We can't wait any longer. We focus on the buildings in the center of their circle." Ree shook her head. If, for some reason, the other gods found out what she had done to Ares, it would likely end up with her dead. If Tristan found out she was no longer human, she would lose her secret weapon. Time was of the essence and she wasn't going to waste it. Explaining all of her reasons wasn't an option, either. Everyone was just going to have to follow her lead on this. Thankfully, she didn't feel much opposition to her plan; it was more like they wanted to be prepared as much as possible.

"This is it. We can't wait for Tristan to have a giant supply of convention-goers to use as leverage. We can't let the darklings continue to tear apart our city. Tonight we do what we were made to do. Tonight, we go to war and send the dark gods packing." Ree looked at everyone, her eyes lingered for just a moment on each of them. "I don't know how this is going to go. I don't know if we will all make it out of this alive. But, I do know I wouldn't want anyone else at my side, and I will do everything in my power to make sure we win."

Chapter 26

Ree checked her watch one more time before looking at the dock again. They still had a couple of hours before dusk, but she wanted to be headed for the city before full dark. If things went as she hoped, they would be scouting the college before the Dark Ones even woke up. She was only waiting for the refugees to show up and somehow the waiting was the worst part. Frowning, she batted away a piece of pine straw that had landed on her shoulder. So much to do. So little time to kill her brother.

"You've been staring at the water for the last ten minutes." Melanie's soft footfalls made the pine straw whisper.

"I'm worried." Ree didn't look at her friend.

"About what?" Melanie stood next to Ree and watched the water.

"Everything." Ree took a deep breath. "I'm worried about the people on their way here. I'm worried about you guys." She stopped and took another breath. "I'm really worried something is going to happen to one of you. I try to not think about it, because we don't really have a choice. But it's still there. Still nagging in my head and heart."

Melanie reached out and put her arm around Ree's shoulders. "What else?"

"And I'm worried about Tristan." The air fell out of Ree's mouth and she felt oddly deflated. "This whole time, I've tried to not focus on him. Not focus on the fact that it is Tristan. But tonight, there is no turning back. Tonight I have to kill my brother."

"Ree." Melanie turned Ree to face her, a hand on each of her shoulders. "We're all worried for each other. This is a huge deal. A massive thing we have to accomplish. But we can't focus on those things. We just have to focus on what we're doing and why."

The sound of a motor drifted over the water and reached their ears. Both of them looked out at the water and saw the glint of the setting sun on the boat hull. Ree felt a little tension in her stomach release. At least these families would be safe for now.

"Tristan always wanted more, Ree." Ree jerked back to look at Melanie. "He hated that he went to school on scholarship. He chose this, Ree. You know it, and I know it. He was never a bad guy; not a bully or cruel. But he wanted more. Maybe he didn't understand why they wanted him. Maybe he didn't know what it would do to him, but he chose it. And we all have to accept the consequences of our decisions."

"Do you think he knew? Knew he would have to kill me?" Ree lowered her voice. "Did he know that the consequences would affect us too?"

"He's the only one who knows for sure, Ree." Melanie squeezed her shoulders before letting go. "It really doesn't matter now."

Ree shook her head and looked back at the water. It

really didn't matter anymore. He had made his decision and Ree was making hers. She couldn't let the Earth fall into the dark gods' hands. Even if that meant she had to kill her brother. Even if it meant killing a piece of herself in the process.

Sighing, she headed for the dock. She wanted to welcome the new people to the island, help them feel safe. The closer the boat came, the more she could feel the fear and worry of the humans. She caught the rope Met threw to her and tied it to one of the cleats. Ree brushed her hands off when she stood and offered to help the first family off the boat.

"I'm Ree. Sorry for the suddenness of everything, but you will be much safer here on the island." She smiled at the father, but he just looked at her hand.

"Who's in charge here?" He hopped onto the dock and held his hand out to his wife and young children.

Ree looked at Met and Niall for a minute. She hadn't really thought about it, but if she was being honest, she was the one in charge now. And she had a feeling she needed to assert that fact right away.

"That would be me. You're the Thornton family, right?" Ree smiled at the kids. "Why don't we go on to the house where you'll be more comfortable? We're expecting more people and it would be easier to explain it once."

"We're not moving off of this dock until you tell me why we're here." He looked at Ree, his face stubborn. "That little guy stuck me with something and the only reason I haven't done something about it is because I didn't wake up until we were on the boat."

"Um, excuse me." A small grey-haired woman with bright blue eyes looked at Ree. "Does this have anything to do with the vampires?" The little old man holding her hand rolled his eyes and the angry father cursed under his breath.

"You've got to be kidding me."

"Actually, yes, it does." Ree smiled at the old woman. "The Dark Ones are looking for people that have a little something extra in their blood. Both of your families were at risk."

"You're out in the sun. You aren't a vampire." The man crossed his arms over his chest. "Are you planning on using us as hostages? We're not joining any cults or worshipping monkeys. Just give me the keys to the boat and we'll be out of here."

"Met? Would you mind a demonstration?" Ree nodded at the Guardian who smiled.

Before Met could say or do anything, Niall looked at the father and opened his mouth in a wide smile. His Guardian fangs slid free and gleamed in the remaining sunlight.

"Nom, nom, nom."

Ree wanted to slap herself on the forehead, but decided it would be better to slap Niall instead. Grabbing his shoulder, she pulled him back behind her with a glare. The Guardian was still smiling, but Ree didn't have time to deal with him. The little old woman was crossing herself and her husband looked close to a heart attack.

The father had taken a step back, blocking his children from view, but his expression said he clearly didn't think Niall was all that dangerous. More like he was extremely annoyed by his sense of humor. Ree heard someone approaching from the house and sighed in relief. Kay came into view and smiled at everyone. There was a dishtowel hanging over her shoulder, and something in her expression seemed to ease the tension on the dock.

"I'm not going anywhere with that little freak. Not sure why you think showing me you're vampires would make me want to go with you." He stared at Niall, but his words were for Ree.

"Oh, those aren't the bad vampires." The older woman stepped up. "They have such a nice aura. Even the cheeky one."

From the look on Niall's face, Ree felt like he had just gotten better than a slap.

"Hi! Welcome to Sanctus Island!" Kay pushed her way past Niall and held her hand out to the father and mother.

"So are you in charge? These kids aren't making any sense." The father shook Kay's hand with a look of relief.

"In charge? Oh, no. That would be Ree." Kay smiled at Ree over her shoulder and moved her hand to the man's elbow. "However, I am the one that will be helping you guys all get comfortable and making sure you're fed." She smiled at the mother and children over her shoulder, all the while guiding the man past Ree and toward the house.

Ree looked at Kay, feeling surprised. The woman that had popped her and Melanie's butts with a wooden spoon for stealing cookie dough had just told everyone Ree was in charge. Turning back to look at the older couple, Ree was relieved to see Melanie helping the woman navigate the dock. She smiled at the two and nodded her head at the man trailing behind them. He stopped and looked at Ree.

"Do you have those teeth, too?" He adjusted his glasses and glared at Ree.

"No sir, I don't." Ree clasped her hands in front of her body, trying to look innocent.

"Then why would you be in charge?" His gaze never wavered, making Ree feel very young.

"Because there is a war happening, and I am the only one that can end it." Ree's words seemed to cut through the wind coming off of the water, even though she had said it softly.

"Heh." The man looked away from Ree and followed his wife's progress. "She's been going on about vampires and magic for a while now. I just thought her mind was goin', you know?"

"I can understand why you would think that." Ree shifted from one foot to the other.

"But she's right?" The man looked back at Ree.

"Yes. She's right." Ree pressed her lips together and met his stare.

"Well, then. And this island is safe?" He looked back toward the house.

"Yes, sir. As safe as I can make it."

"Thank you for bringing us here, then. I'm glad to have as much time as possible with Libby." He smiled at Ree. "And I'm very glad to know she is still in touch with reality."

Ree smiled at him, but the sound of more boats nearing the dock drew her attention. The old man patted her shoulder and headed for the house. Ree looked back in time to see him grab his wife's hand. Very clearly the woman looked at him and said, "I told you."

Melanie came back to the dock chuckling, but the sound died away the closer the boats got to the dock.

There was something stuck in the side of one of the boats and small holes lining another.

"Go get Paden." Ree moved toward the end of the dock and the sharp, copper smell of blood grew stronger. Melanie was gone in a second and Ree could hear her calling for Paden.

One of the Guardians had several holes in his shirt, the black material slick with blood. Magda was standing on the prow of the other boat, the rope in her hand and ready to throw to Ree. Snatching the heavy rope out of the air, Ree quickly tied the boat down and moved to the next one. There was a girl around twelve or thirteen crying on the floor of the boat. There was blood in her hair and she had her hands pressed to a wound on her leg. Ree's eyes raked over the passengers, some of them in shock, others trying to help those that had been injured.

Paden slid next to Ree, his eyes taking in the scene. He ducked back to the other boat to take stock.

"Guardian! Over here." Magda dipped down to pick up a woman from the floor of her boat. She had an arrow jutting out from her right shoulder and another from her leg.

Paden's hands were glowing by the time he reached them. Carefully, he brushed the hair back from the woman's face and checked her eyes.

"Oh, thank the gods. You're a healer." Magda laid the woman down on the dock and left her in Paden's care. "I had hoped one of you were."

Ree jumped into the boat with the girl and knelt down next to her. "What's your name?"

The girl looked at her with glossy eyes and Ree's heart squeezed in pity. Very carefully she looked into her eyes again and asked, "What's your name?"

"Sabrina." Tears slid down the girls cheeks. "Where's my mom?"

"I don't know, Sabrina. Right now we just need to help get you fixed up." Ree slid her arm around the girl's waist and helped her stand. The Guardian that had been driving the boat came to the other side and they carefully lifted her over the edge of the boat and onto the dock.

"I've never seen so many darklings, Alastriana." The Guardian looked at her with serious eyes. "I did everything I could."

"Where is your partner?" Ree knew the answer already, but had to ask.

"He fell so that we could get away."

Ree reached out and squeezed his shoulder. It wasn't much of a condolence, but all she had time for. Going back to the boat, she helped several other people off that seemed to only have minor injuries. They were all in shock. Being shot at by a gang of supernaturally fast criminals is not something anyone can expect or be prepared for. One of the women seemed to be coping well, her toddler stuck on one hip, while she helped another woman out of the boat.

Paden made his way through the victims, blood covering his hands. For a random moment, Ree wondered if he should clean his hands between victims, but then figured he probably cured any blood-carried diseases. When he got to the young woman holding on to the Guardians' shoulder, he looked at Ree and she could see the drain from all of the healing. He looked away, obviously sensing her worry. He didn't want her to focus on him, and, for the moment, he was right.

Her friends had all come to the dock to help transport the wounded to the house and Ree looked up in worry when she heard more boats nearing. The sun was quickly getting lower in the sky and Ree knew they would have to leave soon. Three more boats pulled up to the long dock, but, thankfully, the people and Guardians looked to be in much better shape. There were a few humans limping or sporting scrapes, but nothing like the two boats that had been shot at while escaping. The Guardians from those boats did their best to herd the newcomers around the wounded.

Someone hollered from the direction of the house and Ree looked up to see the mother that had been helping people run back toward the dock. A man helping a boy out of a boat turned around, his face a mask of relief. The woman flew through the crowd and launched herself into the man's arms. As they held each other sobbing, the Guardians worked around them.

"Alastriana, we brought everyone back that we could. I also brought back some of the others' extended family members. Two of the families on the list were not at home or their work places." A tall Guardian leaned down to look at Ree. "It is my hope that they had left town or were unable to return because of the looting."

Ree nodded her head. Hoping they could get everyone back was wishful thinking, but at least they had managed to get this many to safety. Ree stepped out of the way so Magda could help the woman who had been hit by two arrows toward the house. Surveying the rest of the victims, Ree was relieved to see most of them up and moving around. Yet, there on the dock was one body covered in a blue tarp. A human who had not made it safely to the island.

Ree walked over to the draped figure and knelt down. "I'm so sorry we weren't in time."

Without lifting the cover to see who it was

underneath, Ree scooped the slight figure up and carried it off of the dock and down to where the pyres had been set up not that long ago.

Chapter 27

A few of the new Guardians had gathered near the beach. Niall looked at Ree and for the first time, she saw something other than disdain and pain in his eyes. Walking swiftly to Ree, he held his arms out and took the body.

"Let me, Alastriana. I will make sure she is well tended." Ree looked down at the covered form. She had guessed it was a woman, based on the size and weight, but she didn't even want to know the gender. Maybe that wasn't fair, but with everything else she had going on, it was one more sad detail in a storm of misery. Nodding at Niall, she turned around and walked back to the house.

She looked up at the sky and was surprised to see the purple tones of dusk dominating the world. Picking up her pace, she darted into the house and was relieved to see that Kay had managed to get everyone in order and no one was waiting to attack her with questions. Nodding her head at the families as she passed, Ree went straight to her room. She could feel Paden in her bathroom, so she went to her closet and flipped through the clothes. Grabbing a black long-sleeve shirt and dark jeans she turned back to her bed but hesitated. She kicked her shoes off and contemplated Paden.

Something felt weird and she wasn't sure why. He was doing something to try and keep her from sensing what he was feeling. Throwing her clothes onto the bed, she walked over the bathroom door and knocked.

"Paden?" Ree leaned her head close to the door. The sound of glass falling onto the floor sent her into action. She moved back and planted her foot solidly on the door in a mighty kick. Her bare feet skidded on the glass, but she barely noticed. Paden was slumped on the floor, his back pressed to the wall, his eyes closed.

"Go, please." His voice was hoarse. He didn't open his eyes to look at her.

Ree slid across the floor, dropping to her knees and cupping his face. "What's wrong, Paden? What happened?" She ran her hands down his chest and over his arms, looking for whatever was hurting him. Now that she was touching him, she could feel his extreme lethargy and pain. It was as if his entirebody was completely depleted.

"Fine. Just need rest." He cracked his eyes open and attempted a smile. She scowled at him, not willing to be pushed away so easily.

"Paden, what happened? Was it healing all of those people?" Ree brushed the hair back from his forehead.

"Poison, I think." He tried to move, but Ree pushed him back down. "Took a lot to heal. Was everywhere. Couldn't let her just die."

"Who?" Ree ran her hands over his shoulders, anxiety making her feel jumpy.

"Arrows." Paden shook his head a little. "Don't know her name."

Ree thought back to the dock. "The lady with the two arrows? They were poisoned?"

"Meant for Guardians." Paden's eyes closed again and his shoulders sagged. "Difficult to heal from."

"But you healed more people after her!" Ree shook his shoulders gently. When he didn't respond right away, she looked around the bathroom and grabbed a towel from the basket next to the counter. Shifting Paden, she pushed him down onto the floor and placed the rolled up towel under his head. Rubbing the heel of her hand across her forehead, she shook her head in worry.

"Just too much. Couldn't let them hurt." Paden didn't open his eyes, his words barely a whisper.

"Can you heal from this?" Looking at Paden, Ree's worry turned to fear.

"Yes. Need a little time." Paden cracked an eye. "Fine in a few minutes. Then go."

"Dammit, Paden. We're not going anywhere like this." Ree shook her head.

"Ree, you cannot wait much longer." Aphrodite's voice coasted along the walls. Ree jumped to her feet, while Paden struggled to sit up.

"We can't go if he is hurt." Ree looked at the goddess warily.

"Ares managed to escape." Aphrodite's words sent a shiver of fear through Ree. "You need to end this now."

"Can't go without me." Paden managed to lever himself up and slumped against the wall.

"What help would you be right now?" Aphrodite tsked. She walked toward Paden and knelt down so she could look him in the eyes.

"I will always go where she goes." Paden stared at the goddess, his words vibrating with certainty.

Aphrodite looked back at Ree and smiled before looking back at Paden. "Of course you will."

"Aphrodite, how did Ares manage to escape?" Ree looked at the goddess where she knelt.

"He has exchanged blood with the dark gods." Fire circled in Aphrodite's eyes. "He was able to break the chains used in Hades."

"He had fangs." Ree looked at the goddess. "And he knows—"

"Say nothing, Alastriana." Aphrodite's voice turned sharp. "Some things are better left unsaid. I've guessed at your plight, which is why I am here. I bear a gift for your hero."

The goddess turned back to Paden and pushed his hair away from his forehead. The look she gave him made Ree's anger simmer and the power hummed in her chest. Taking his face in both hands, the goddess leaned forward and very gently placed a kiss on his forehead. Sighing softly, she ducked her head and pressed her lips to Paden's. Ree's immediate reaction was to stab the goddess with something pointy, but she tried to stay calm. However, she couldn't help the flow of power that gathered around her feet. Her agitation only increased when she realized that she couldn't move.

The goddess pulled back and looked down at Paden, a seductive smile curling her lips as she trailed her hand down his chest. "I've always had a soft spot for heroes." Standing up, the goddess brushed her hands together as if removing dirt and turned to look at Ree. "Stop trying to hiss at me, Alastriana. I did you a favor. Seems like I should get a little something out of the deal."

Aphrodite smiled at Ree, her amusement almost palpable. "Besides. Now you're even."

As soon as the goddess left the room, Ree was free from her restraints.

"You bitch." Ree almost fell forward, her muscles set on moving as her mouth formed the words she had been mentally chanting. Dropping down to her knees, Ree lifted Paden's chin and looked into his eyes.

"Are you okay? Paden?" Ree's entire body went still as Paden's eyes met hers.

"Come here." Paden lifted one hand and pressed it to the back of her neck. Heat seemed to shoot down Ree's spine and her body immediately curved into his.

"Paden?" Her breathing became heavy, her words a whisper. His thumb rubbed small circles just over the pulse point below her ear and she found it hard to think coherently.

"Ree. Do you trust me?" His voice was husky and his fangs slid down, to make indents on his bottom lip.

"Always." Ree leaned closer to him, something pulling her forward. As if everything else in the world had fallen away and they were the only things left.

"I want to taste you." His words sent a shiver over Ree. She knew it would hurt, that he would never ask, but she couldn't deny the pull emanating from Paden. Underneath everything else, she also knew it would help him.

"Yes." Pressing even closer, Ree turned her head and brushed the hair from her neck.

He leaned forward and trailed his lips slowly over her throat, before opening his mouth wide. When his fangs pierced her skin, her back bowed and pleasure ripped through her body. Nothing mattered but the feel of his mouth on her. With each sip, she could feel his strength return. Paden's hands moved to slide along her back, pressing her even closer. When he finally pulled back, it was to look at Ree in shock. Her body still humming from the pleasure, she was confused at the look on his face.

"Oh, God, Ree. I'm so sorry." He looked down at her throat and his jaw tensed. Gently, he ran his thumb over the punctures and wiped away the blood.

She had to bite her lip to keep from purring when touched her neck, her body caught in after-shocks. Taking a deep breath, she leaned back and shook her head a little in an attempt to try and clear it. She could feel his fingers work their healing magic while he touched her.

"It's okay. You needed it." Ree closed her eyes for a moment, before opening them to look at Paden.

"I could've hurt you. You need your energy just as much as I do!" Paden leaned his head back against the wall. "Now we have to push the attack back. You can't go if you aren't one-hundred-percent."

"You didn't hurt me." Ree narrowed her eyes. "I'm guessing we have Aphrodite to thank for that."

Paden's cheeks turned pink. "Ree, I didn't—"

"I'm not mad at you, Pay." Ree leaned forward and pressed her forehead to his. "It is what it is. And, if this is the trade off, then we didn't come out too badly."

"How do you feel?" Paden lifted her chin so he could look her in the eyes. "Be honest. You aren't helping anyone by rushing out of here and not being at your best."

Ree took a minute to answer, honestly trying to assess how she felt. She reached up and touched her neck, but there was no lingering pain. She moved off of Paden's lap and stood up. There was no dizziness or exhaustion.

"I feel a little tired, but not much." Ree held her hand out to Paden and pulled him to his feet. "Nothing a little food won't cure. How about you?"

"Much better." He looked at Ree, his mouth pulling to the side in a grin. Obviously he was feeling better now that he knew Ree hadn't been hurt. "That was… interesting."

"You could say that." Ree smiled at him. "Definitely different."

"I wonder why it didn't seem to affect you as much, the blood loss I mean." Paden squatted and started cleaning up the broken glass and blood from the floor. He looked at her feet and frowned. "Did you cut your feet?"

"They've already healed." Ree looked down at the blood that was soaking her socks and shrugged. "Maybe you just didn't need as much of my blood because I have an extra dose of the power."

"Maybe." He stared at her feet. "Why didn't you put shoes on?"

Ree just stared at him. Did he really think she was going to worry about a little glass when he was lying on the floor hurting? He looked up at her, obviously sensing he had said something wrong.

"What?"

"Would you have put shoes on if I had been on the floor?" Ree raised an eyebrow.

"Of course not." Paden stood up and dumped the

glass in the trash can. "But, I'm the man and—oofh!"

Ree grabbed him around the neck, pulling him into a headlock. "You might not want to finish that sentence."

"It was a joke! I swear!" Paden's laugh made Ree smile, her heart fluttering in relief to hear him back to normal. She let him go, but grabbed his hand and pulled him into a hug.

"Don't do that again, Paden. You scared the hell out of me." She closed her eyes and breathed in his scent.

"I'm sorry." He pressed his lips to her hair.

After a moment, Ree pulled him into the room so they could change. She kicked off her clothes and pulled on the ones she had picked out earlier. Paden stood watching her for a minute, his eyes serious.

"I think your clothes were moved into my closet, if you want to change. We've got to leave soon." Ree pulled on her boots and smiled while Paden rustled through the clothes.

"Well, it's really starting to get creepy on the island." Paden's voice was muffled as he traded his dirty shirt for a new one.

"What do you mean?" Ree grabbed her dagger and sheath from her bedside stand and rolled up her jeans. She tightened the straps around her calf and zipped up her boot.

"They show up everywhere, move our things around without asking, and have weird ideas about what is acceptable." Paden shook his head. "It's like living with giant-sized toddlers."

"I try to pretend that they're ghost butlers. Taking care of things, but with a hint of mischief." Ree stood up and grabbed a jacket out of the closet.

As they headed out of Ree's room, Paden chuckled. "Ghost butlers, huh?"

"Yeah. Makes it seem a little less creepy."

"Ghost butlers aren't creepy?" Paden bumped into Ree with his elbow.

"I said less creepy. You can't make it completely creep-free." Ree pulled at the sleeves of her coat as they walked, trying to make them a little loose.

"You know I love you, right, little one?" Paden smiled down at her. His old term of endearment warmed Ree's heart.

"Yeah, yeah. If you mess up my hair, I'm going to stick you in a shield and leave you here." Ree looked up at Paden and smiled.

Chapter 28

Roland sniffed at the air when they entered the training room, his eyes running over Ree and Paden. Ree couldn't help but notice that his eyes lingered on her neck. It wasn't something she really wanted to discuss with everyone and certainly not right now.

The others were ready and waiting. Ree felt her good mood melt away to something harder, rougher. Her body seemed to become tighter, her steps more deliberate as she walked toward her weapons. Goosebumps erupted along her arms, as if the air around her understood what she was getting ready to do.

Ree walked over to where she had stored her sword and took it down from the rack. Carefully, she unsheathed the blade and checked for anything she might have missed when cleaning it. Once she was certain it was in good shape, she returned it to the scabbard and attached it to her hip. Next she pulled down the two short swords that hung from pegs. Paden helped her slip on the harness that would hold them tightly against her back. Once she had been loaded down with weapons, she turned to look at the others.

There was a sense of calm, a feeling of rightness in Ree's heart. It was now or never. Would Tristan wake tonight and feel the change? Would he know she was coming for him? In a few short hours, the fate of the world would be decided. Ree nodded her head and closed her eyes for a moment. She focused on her love and respect for her friends, her faith in all of them, and knew that they would be able to feel it.

When she opened her eyes, everyone was standing, ready to leave. "Let's do this."

"What, no team cheer?" Weylin smiled at Ree.

"One for all! And all for one!" Melanie held her sword up in salute.

"Death to the demons!" Roland lifted his own sword. When everyone turned to look at him he shrugged. "That's what they said back in my day."

"Death to the demons!" Ree drew her sword in salute, but couldn't help the grin that slid over her face. When everyone else joined in, their battle cries shook the room and Ree could feel their energy growing with each reverberation. A sharp smile pulled at her mouth. No matter what happened, they were going to give the Dark Ones hell.

As they exited the house, some of the refugees watched from different windows. Kay ran after them, grabbing Melanie in a tight hug before kissing them all on the head. She never said anything, didn't tell them to stay safe or to be careful. Ree squeezed the woman's hand. She knew if they failed tonight, things would be bad for everyone.

The extra Guardians were lining the dock. As Ree and her group approached them, they all smiled. Met and Niall were standing next to the boat they had taken to the mainland. Met's cheerful face was set in a serious expression, her dark eyes fierce.

"Alastriana, we would like to come with you." Met's words were formal, asking that Ree grant them permission to fight.

Ree stopped and looked at the faces that were shadowed from the setting sun. When she asked Athena for help, she hadn't considered using the Guardians for anything but protecting the people that had been targeted. Now, as she stared at the people along the dock, her stomach tightened. She looked back at Met and jerked her head once.

"Half of you stay here and protect the island and the people on it with everything you have, everything that you are. This is the last haven available." Ree didn't have to tell them it would come under attack if she lost the battle. "The rest can come and help clear out the city. There will be people stuck in the middle of all this that will need your aid. Tristan is mine, though."

Met bowed her head to Ree. "As you say, Alastriana."

Niall grinned at Ree and spun his knife on his palm. Pointing at the Guardians along the left side of the dock, he motioned for them to get in the boats. Ree moved into her spot next to the console and waited for everyone else to board. Paden stood behind her, one hand on her waist as Roland pulled them away from the dock.

Ree felt, more than actually heard, the crack of thunder. As the boat pulled away from the island, Athena, Brigid, and Hecate watched. Their eyes tense and serious. Brigid held a bow at her side while both Hecate and Athena clasped their hands in front of them. Ree looked away from them and toward Savannah. The goddesses couldn't help them now. It was up to Ree to do what needed to be done.

The ride to the coast was long and cold. The winds whipped the surf against their hull and sprayed them all with fine mist. Paden moved closer to Ree, his warmth helping to keep her centered and not get lost in her thoughts. No one said a word as the sky turned from red and orange to purple. When the coast came into view, the trees were black with shadows, street lights glittering like fireflies in the distance.

Ree could sense the darklings that lined the nearby docks and had gathered in places she and her friends had used to dock in the past, but Roland never stopped. The closer they got to the city, the more darklings Ree felt gathered together. Without stopping, Roland pushed on until Ree could feel them nearing the historic district. The boats containing Niall, Met, and the other Guardians sped up and took the lead. Ree looked at Paden and Roland, wondering if this had been discussed at some point, but neither made an indication either way.

When Roland slowed the boat, Ree frowned at the dock. There was one darkling, sitting on the edge. His les legs swinging back and forth above the water as if he didn't have a care in the world. It didn't take Ree long to understand why he seemed so nonchalant. A piercing whistle drew more darklings from the shadows. In less time than it took Ree to understand what was truly happening, she had erected shields over boats.

Arrows bounced off of her green energy and fell into the water. The darklings weren't very organized in their attack, despite having a lookout. Met's calm voice drifted over the water to Ree's ears, drawing her attention. She had a bow at the ready, arrow knocked and ready to fly.

"On my mark, Ree!" The Guardian stood at the front of her boat, her feet in a steady stance. As the darklings' arrows fell harmlessly away, an amused snort reached Ree's ears. "Now!"

Ree dropped her shield immediately and watched as Met's arrows flew like lightning bolts to strike their targets. There wasn't time to try and turn any of them, to see if being a darkling was something they had chosen or been forced into. At this point, the only thing she and the other Guardians could do was focus on surviving and helping those that couldn't on their own.

In a matter of moments all of the darklings had been dispatched. Roland slid the boat next to the dock, and Weylin quickly tied it down and ran down the dock toward the trees. Ree and Paden were next, the others following close behind. The sound of sirens and the smell of smoke filled the early evening air.

"We need to get to the school as quickly as possible and with as little attention as possible." Ree looked at Paden and Roland, but it was Magda who spoke up.

"A distraction would be good. I looked at the map you had in the office." Her eyebrows drew together as she mentally went over the details. "What if we hit the houses around one of the nightclubs? Let them believe we've targeted the wrong place."

"Could work." Roland nodded his head.

"Okay. Hit the ones closest to the boats, but let us get a head start." Ree started to head down the road.

"What about people that are being attacked? Do you want us to split up and try to corral some of the worst offenders?" Niall looked at Ree through hair that hid his eyes.

"Sounds good." Ree looked at everyone. "You guys are on your own. Draw their attention away from the college and protect those you can." Ree started walking backward down the street. "Take care of each other."

The streets were eerily quiet. Only the sound of the

occasional siren or fire alarm seemed to pierce the cloud of silence. The group had fallen into their running pattern without thought. It felt natural and easy, moving like one organism as they slid though the shadows and through people's backyards. Ree concentrated on the darklings that seemed to be patrolling the streets, steering their group away from any that could be avoided. When it wasn't possible to move around one of the looting darklings, someone would make quick work of the problem.

Ree could feel the frustration of her friends mounting with each kill. None of them liked killing the darklings, but accepted that there wasn't another solution. Ree refused to use the power until she had no other options. When they neared the school center, Ree noticed the flyers for the special effects convention lying on the ground or taped to the old-timey light poles. When a cop car turned the corner onto the square they were surveying, the group ducked into an empty coffee shop. The door was hanging open and several of the windows had been broken, obviously a casualty of the looting that had taken place through the city.

Everyone kept quiet as the police cruiser slowly made a loop around the square before heading to the next block. Ree knelt behind an overturned table, her fingers rubbing the hilt of her sword. Paden crouched next to her, his green eyes sliding around the empty room.

"It will be dark soon." Roland's quiet voice rumbled through the room.

"What's the plan, Kemo Sabe?" Weylin moved so he could see Ree.

"We need to get in…" Ree trailed off and looked out the window. The silver glow from her eyes reflected off of some of the shattered glass on the floor. "We have company."

A group of darklings were walking down the road, the leader sniffing the air as he followed their trail. She wasn't sure if he knew who he was following or if he was just looking for trouble, but there was no mistaking that he was after Ree and her friends.

Ree pulled her power in and concentrated on getting rid of her glowing eyes. There was no reason to announce the Alastriana was in town. The darkling smiled when he stopped outside of the coffee shop, and his pasty skin and black eyes made Ree cringe. He wasn't far from turning; Ree could smell the death coming from him even from where she sat upwind, the light of his soul, weak and flickering.

"Come out, come out." The darklings behind the sickly-thin man chuckled. One of them picked up a rock from the curb and threw it at the broken window. The remaining glass shattered, crashing to the ground in a sound that seemed much louder in the silence of the city.

Roland stood up from where he had been crouching. He bared his fangs and hissed. "Leave, unless you want to replace my dinner."

"My apologies… Dark One. I smelled something off and came to investigate." He edged closer to the building. While his hand was blocked from Roland's view, Ree saw him twitch his fingers at the other darklings in a signal to run.

Before anyone else could move, Ree stood from her spot and threw the knives she had in reach. There was a sickening thunk as the blades found their mark. The flash of more blades flying from the other corner of the room pinned the darklings Ree couldn't see.

The ringleader didn't waste time retreating. Bryce

was out of his hiding spot immediately, grabbing the darkling by the back of his shirt and spinning him against the brick exterior of the building. Hissing, the darkling scrambled against the wall, trying to free himself from Bryce's grip.

"Ree?" Bryce looked at her and nodded to the darkling.

Ree looked at the darkling and contemplated for just a moment. Unfortunately the sound of running feet made up her mind. "Do it."

Bryce made it quick and painless, but Ree would always remember the look on her friend's face as he snapped the darkling's neck; disgust and pity warred violently, leaving him to look almost depraved. Ree shivered once, but put away her thoughts. Drawing her sword, she moved from behind the table went to retrieve some of her throwing knives. Darklings were coming from every street, somehow alerted to their presence.

"Operation Sneaky doesn't seem to be going so well." Weylin scooted one of the darklings out of the way with his foot.

"Time to move on to Operation Make an Entrance, then." Ree looked at her friends. "The sun is down and I can feel the Dark Ones waking. Our window is gone. Now we just get in there and raise hell."

"I like it." Weylin pursed his lips and nodded his head once.

"You know how I like to make an entrance." Juliette tossed her knife in the air before catching it and sliding it back into her sleeve.

"Where do we go, Ree?" Paden looked down at her, his eyebrows pulled together. "Can you sense where Tristan is in the building?"

Ree looked at the building and squinted while trying to figure out just where Tristan would have bunkered down. "There's a big concentration of Dark Ones in the center of the building. A large classroom, maybe. "

"Then let's go." Paden moved for the door, Ree quick on his heels. As the darklings neared, their greed and excitement was thick in the air.

"Where are the cops when we need them?" Weylin huffed under his breath.

"Fastest route possible, Ree." Roland moved behind her, shielding her back as the darklings rushed forward.

"Seriously? Do they not get they don't have a chance?" Juliette brushed the hair out of her eyes and glared at the people coming their way.

Ree looked over her shoulder at the twenty or so people coming from a back alley and back to the people walking down the empty road. Kneeling down, she put one hand on the ground and pushed the power into the earth. It flared out from their group like a tidal wave, the pavement pitched and rolled, the wave growing larger as the power flew toward the approaching groups. Most of the darklings that were in the earlier stages of the transformation were knocked off their feet or sent scrambling out of the way. The darklings that were a little faster or stronger jumped over the first wave and came on.

"Let's go." Ree stood up, grabbed one of her knives and threw it at an approaching darkling as she sprinted for the front door of the building.

Chapter 29

Ree skidded to a halt, looked at the chains on the double doors of the building, and took a deep breath. There was no light emanating from the building; nothing but darkness, the foreign feel of cold, soulless Dark Ones, and the crackling power that announced the presence of at least one god. All of this ended tonight. One way or the other, things would be decided.

Paden looked over at her and nodded his head. It was time and everyone was ready. She looked at her friends and felt her mouth pull back in a grin of pride. These were the people that had stood by her from the very beginning. They all wore fierce expressions, intent on taking down their enemies and Ree was grateful they were on her side. No more waiting for the right moment, no more hiding what she was capable of, and no more running from what must be done.

There was no use in trying to sneak into the building. The Dark Ones would have been able to sense her at this point. Turning to look at the entry, Ree lifted her hands and unleashed her power, sending the doors flying off their hinges and down the hall, gouging chunks of plaster as they tumbled. Each of her friends let out a war cry, and Ree felt her own voice lift in unison. In no time, they had crossed the threshold of the building and were shooting down the long hallway. Dark Ones came from shadowed corners, offices, and classrooms. Ree let the power rush ahead of her, shoving the crumpled doors even farther down the hallway, and obliterating the Dark Ones directly in her path.

Her friends fought and killed the enemies that came from the darkness with deadly quickness. The sound of the Dark Ones hissing and growling filled the corridor and combined with the sound of weapons meeting flesh. By the time they reached the doors to the large auditorium in the center of the building many of Ree's friends had blood splashed across their clothes or faces. There was no denying the ferocity of the group. Thankfully, none looked to have taken any damage. Ree could feel the black hole of ice that meant Tristan was awake and waiting for her. Looking at the doors, Ree held her sword in her right hand, letting it angle away from her body and pointing it toward the floor. She sent the power whirling away from her, and the loose hair around her face whipped forward angrily as the power slammed the doors open to reveal a large room, lit only by the moon filtering through the skylights.

Tristan was standing on the stage between Loki and Ares, his face set in a dark look. Ree's heart squeezed at the familiar face and she tried to remind herself that he wasn't her brother any longer. He clapped three times before taking a step toward Ree. "So, you've come to try to kill me."

"I'm here to end this war." Ree let the power flare out around her so that the green light slid along the floor in all directions.

"You think this is about a war?" Della stepped into view. She was lurking near the shadows of the stage, her elegant face wreathed in amusement. "This is about a brother and sister set against each other. About one embracing a new way of life, while the other clings to the past."

"This is about you setting my brother against me. About you killing everyone on this planet or making them cattle. This is much bigger than Tristan and me." Ree's anger had the power swirling around her feet. "I know enough of the situation to understand he made his choice. He isn't my brother any longer. He's merely your pawn."

"I'm no one's pawn, Ree." Tristan stepped gracefully off of the stage to land in the aisle directly in front of her. Something felt different about his energy. Instead of being the cold, empty spot most Dark One's generated, power crackled along his edges, like frozen lightning.

Ree's eyes darted to the gods still standing on the stage. Ares was glaring at her with hatred, but Loki wore his customary look of amusement, his blond hair glowing an eerie silver-white in the moonlight. Off to the side of the stage was someone Ree hadn't thought about much over the last few days. Shannon leaned against the chest of Michael. Her hair was lank, her cheeks hollow, and her dark eyes rimmed in red. Michael's mouth was open just enough to let his curved fangs peek out, pressing over his bottom lip. He snarled at Ree and she had to squash the desire to kill him right then.

"Who gave you the toothpick?" Tristan looked at the sword Ree gripped. "Paden, you're doing a terrible job of keeping her safe. She's so clumsy she'll probably cut off her own foot." Tristan laughed, his face transforming into something closer to what Ree remembered from when he was alive. There was a flash of something warm from the corner Shannon and Michael were standing in and Ree couldn't help but let her eyes dart in that direction. The black of Shannon's eyes had diminished and Ree was surprised by the love the girl felt when looking at her brother.

"The only feet you need to be worried about are you own." Ree focused on Tristan.

"Oh, that's rich." Tristan looked over his shoulder where Della stood laughing. He looked back at Ree with a small smile. "You know, since I'm your brother, I'm going to let you practice a little before we do our thing."

Ree narrowed her eyes and raised her sword. "Scared, Trist?"

Tristan snarled at Ree, his fangs ripping free of his gums. The cold energy around him snapped and churned. "I have nothing to fear from you, Ree."

Ree let the energy that had been sliding along the floor rush toward Tristan. He jumped out of the way quickly, leaping back onto the stage in a move that shouldn't have been possible. He growled again and Della jumped onto the stage. The tall woman slid next to him and ran her hand up and down his arm possessively.

"Then why do you keep running away?" Ree stared at Tristan. She felt her friends tensing behind her as they fanned out a little wider. Dark Ones were slipping into the room, their eyes glittering in the shadows as they made their presence known.

"Now, why would he do that? He promised the others they could have a crack at you before he finished things." Della smiled at Tristan, her double fangs pressing into her own lips to leave small spots of blood. "He's merely keeping his promise. I knew Tristan would make a good leader." She leaned forward and nuzzled his neck. There was a spike of raw anger that came from Shannon, but Tristan's face was neutral. "I learned from past mistakes." Della looked over at Roland, her eyes swirling with black.

Roland didn't respond, but Ree could feel the barely-checked rage as he stared at the woman who had stolen his life.

"Looks like she still has some things to learn." Ree could see Weylin shake his head from the corner of her eye. "Pissing off Roland never ends well for the other person."

Della looked at Weylin and hissed, her fingers tightening on Tristan's arm. Her back arched like a cat's, and her face transformed into something inhuman. Her overly large eyes seemed to almost glow, and the skin stretched over the severe angles of her face tightened, showing the sharp bones underneath. Her fingernails drew blood from Tristan's arm. His lip curled when he looked down at her hand. Reaching over, he pried her curled fingers away from his skin.

"Looks like someone hit a sore spot." Melanie's voice cut through the room.

"She looks a bit like a cat with mange." If it had been anyone other than Bryce to make that statement, Ree wouldn't have been as amused. The corners of her mouth pulled slightly up.

"Attack." Tristan's voice brought the seriousness back, and Ree was thrust into fighting. Dark Ones swarmed from the shadows, some dropping from the beams that lined the high ceiling. When one landed in front her, she quickly spun, using her sword to cleave the Dark One's head from his body. He fell to floor in a fine dust, no blood or gore to be seen.

Dark Ones seemed to never stop coming, and Ree realized Ares and Loki had opened portals. Ree moved so she was back to back with Paden, carefully avoiding the attacks of the monsters nearest her.

"Portals." Ree said as she ducked underneath a blow to ram a dagger between the Dark One's ribs.

"I see them." Paden's voice was calm and to the point. "How do we stop them?"

"Don't know." Ree moved again, this time relying on her sword to dispatch her opponent. "Maybe if we block them as they exit?"

"I got it." Weylin jumped from the back of one chair to the next row, moving quickly toward the nearest portal. When he neared the shimmering doorway, he pulled something out of his pocket and tossed it into the opening. The sound of the explosion was almost deafening, the fire that washed out of the portal was blinding. Ares roared and made to jump from the stage, but Della held up her hand.

"You cannot engage, war god. It will bring your brethren." Della's voice reached Ree's ears and she realized it was only Loki controlling the portals. The gods of Earth must be looking for Ares's power signature. If he used his god abilities it would bring the pack of them down on the school immediately.

"Della is mine." Roland's cold voice touched Ree's ears. She didn't have time to respond before he disappeared from view.

"The rest!" Ree shouted at Weylin.

"On it."

Ree broke away from her group, set on making her way to Tristan.

Her brother's eyes never left her face as she killed

Dark Ones on her way to him. Paden was following closely behind her, protecting her back. The others all fought to keep the remaining Dark Ones away. The sounds of Weylin's explosions and the screams of the dying filled the room with chaos. Roland appeared on the stage near Della. His face was dark and stormy, fangs extended, and he carried two swords black with old blood.

"The prodigal son returns." Della moved away from Tristan and flashed her fangs at Roland. Ree couldn't follow everything that happened next, but she was certain Roland had been on the offensive while Della did her best to get an advantage. It was as if the world had slowed when Della and Roland met blade to blade. Della seemed to hold the upper hand for the most part, her strength and agility giving her an edge over Roland. She bent and moved in a manner no human body, even turned with the alien disease, would ever be able to.

Time seemed to slow as Della and Roland danced around each other. Their movements were in sync, telling that they had spent time training together while on the same side. No matter how much Roland pushed and gave to the fight, Della returned with the same amount of vigor. The only difference was the rage that simmered under Roland's skin. His hate for Della was a physical force, letting him hold his ground. When she flipped over his head to swipe at his back, he barely reacted, despite the blood that ran from the wound.

Tristan moved toward Ree drawing her full attention, his dark eyes glittering with something that made her shiver inside as he stared at her from the stage. Gripping the power, she let it fill her until it swirled in the very tips of her fingers and toes. Her feet left the ground and she floated up so she only had to step onto the wooden floor of the raised platform. Tristan pulled the sword from the scabbard on his back and looked at Ree. Holding her own sword by her side, Ree gathered the power in her hand and threw it at Tristan. He moved deftly out of its path and tsked at her.

"Your only bet is to stick me with your toothpick." Tristan moved forward, faster than any of the Guardians or the Dark Ones that Ree had fought. His thrusts had her stumbling backward toward the edge of the stage. Paden was on the stage immediately, moving between Ree and Tristan. He seemed to fare much better than Ree had, his footing much more sure and his blows just as fast as Tristan's. Paden's dual immortal lineage gave him an edge over the other Guardians.

Michael seemed to come out of nowhere, completely forgotten in the battle. His knife flew past Ree as she caught her footing and stuck in Paden's thigh. It was just enough to slow Paden down, and Tristan seized his opportunity. His sword was a blur of silver as it swung toward Paden's neck.

The power soared out of Ree without a thought, flying through the room in a rippling wave of green energy. Caught in the killing move, Tristan wasn't prepared for Ree's attack. The only people left standing were Ree and Roland, who was never touched by her power. Roland never stopped his movements, and drove his sword through Della's stomach, pinning her to the wooden floor. Ree dropped to her knee and yanked one of the short swords from her back and flung it at Tristan's chest.

The flash of Shannon's dark hair was the only warning Ree had before her short sword embedded in the girl's chest, knocking her back into Tristan. For a long second, it was as if the entire world had gone silent. Every hair on Ree's body stood up and her heartbeat echoed in her ears.

"Why?" Tristan clutched Shannon to him, shaking

his head, a dark bloody tear falling from one eye.

"Love you." Shannon's words were so soft, Ree could barely make them out, even with her enhanced hearing. Her heart stopped the moment the last word left her lips and Tristan's roar of rage matched the outburst of cold energy that washed out of his body. It was similar to what Ree held, but cold and dead. The most shocking feeling was the complete and utter grief that came from her brother's hunched form, and the realization that if he could grieve it meant he could feel love.

Paden slid back along the stage and grabbed Ree's hand. His fingers squeezed hers as they scrambled to not fall off the edge. Paden's wide green eyes met hers, and she knew exactly what he was thinking. She didn't know where that burst of energy had come from either.

Tristan was brushing the hair away from Shannon's face, his bloody tears falling on her pale skin. Michael moved into view, his expression one of disgust as he looked at Tristan. Tristan seemed to feel his old friend's eyes on him, because he looked up at Michael and growled. Laying Shannon down, he stood and was on Michael faster than Ree could follow. With a savage yank, he pulled Michael's head from his shoulders and threw it across the room, where it trailed ashes in its wake.

"Tristan!" Della's voice cut through the room. Roland was kneeling next to her, a sharp piece of wood lodged in his side. Ree's heart hammered in her chest as she felt for her friends. They were all alive, but hurting. She couldn't help them because Tristan's rage had shifted back to Ree. His dark eyes bored into hers, and she knew that there was no stopping the fight now.

"Loki!" Della's voice cut through Ree's bones. Melanie jumped onto the stage and made her way to Roland. He pulled the wood from his side with a gasp and sat back on his heels, shaking his head a little.

"Oh, this has been much better than I thought it would be!" Loki's laugh made Ree want to crawl away, and the hairs on her body vibrated with disgust.

"You're supposed to be on our side now, god!" Green splattered out of Della's mouth as she snarled.

"I'm a god of chaos. That doesn't change no matter who I've aligned myself with." Loki's voice was chiding. Melanie looked at Roland before yanking the sword out of Della's chest. Quick as lightning, she loped the original Dark One's head from her shoulders and quickly turned to drive the sword back through the very center of her heart. Della's body didn't disintegrate like the others. Instead of a fine ash, or even the gooey ash of a freshly fed Dark One, her body seemed to age. All of her long years ran over her body, turning her alien beauty into something from a crypt. Her screeching howl was an eerie accompaniment to her painful demise.

Tristan picked up his sword as he advanced and Ree stood, bringing her own to the front. Paden rose next to her, pulling the knife out of his leg and tossing it to the side. She could feel him vibrating with tension. Ree listened to the instincts she had inherited from Sophie and ran at her brother. This was no time to be on the defense. His blows jarred Ree's arms and her muscles strained to not let him get the upper hand.

"This will be decided by the two of them." The flash of Loki's power surrounded Ree and Tristan, his voice laughing as he kept everyone else from interfering. Paden's angry voice beat at the shield, but Loki only laughed.

Tristan never acknowledged the shield; his sole intent was killing Ree. She fought with everything she had, never stopping, even when she thought her arms would fail. With each blow she received, she was reminded that Sophie had barely survived an attack from Tristan. Blow after blow weakened her arms until she was certain they would fall off of her body. Her legs shook with the effort to keep up. The pain and hate coming from her brother was almost enough to choke her, despite the effort she put into blocking. It was almost as if there was some connection linking them; some kind of blood or magical tie.

Ree stepped back, her foot slipping in some of Shannon's blood. It was the smallest moment, the tiniest loss of concentration, and Tristan's sword slashed across her hip as she scrambled to get her footing. Paden's howl of rage and fear made Ree's soul shake as she looked up into Tristan's eyes. His backhanded strike lifted her from her feet and sent her careening into the shield. Her sword flew from her hand and landed feet away. The flash of Loki's energy seemed like fireworks to Ree as she tried to shake her brother's strike off.

Tristan advanced, his eyes set on Ree. As she tried to skirt along the edge of the shield, she slipped on the blood from her hip and thigh and had to catch herself with her hands. Her fingers touched something hard and she grasped it between her blood-soaked fingers like it was the key to a very important lock. Standing up, Ree looked at Tristan and a feeling of calm settled in the pit of her stomach.

Chapter 30

"I love you, Tristan." She threw Michael's knife as hard as she could, but before it had even hit her brother, she pulled as much power as she could and let it follow the blade. The knife stuck between his ribs, but it wasn't a killing blow. However, the impact had been enough to surprise him so he didn't sense Ree gathering the power. His head flew backward and she pushed with all of her might. There in the center of his chest was a shining sliver of soul, wrapped tightly in dark bands of hate. Whether all of the magical blood had breathed life back into his soul, or if it had never been wholly snuffed out, Ree didn't care.

The realization that her brother was not completely lost almost destroyed Ree's concentration. She grabbed at that tiny little piece of soul and fed all of the power she could into it, it was like trying to feed a dying child. That tiny little piece of soul twisted and turned, fighting for itself, trying to be free. She dropped to her knees with the effort, so tired she could barely see straight, but Paden's voice reached her ears.

"Me, Ree. Take from me." Her friends' voices joined Paden's and she did as they said. She reached out toward them and Loki's shield shattered around Ree. It didn't stand a chance when she made up her mind. All of their energies called to her, but her eyes stayed on her brother's glowing form. Paden's fingers closed on her shoulders and she felt his energy pour into her body. Through him, Ree grabbed at her other friends' energies, but it still wasn't enough.

Tristan writhed where he was held; his eyes glued to Ree's face. Ree did the only thing she could think to do and pulled from the strongest sources in the room. Ares and Loki were like never-ending pools of energy and Ree's body convulsed with the power she channeled from the gods into her brother.

Ares's roar barely registered with Ree, but she felt his hate and anger as he tried to attack her friends. She felt the moment he called his remaining energy, no longer caring if the other gods found him. Ares threw a bolt of power at Ree and her friends, his attack meant to distract. Closing her eyes, Ree simply pulled that energy into herself as well. Fire ran over her body and she felt when Paden was pushed away. Her body lifted from the floor, her feet dangled above the ground. Loki's amused laughter had changed into something inhuman as he howled in shock and rage. In his need to cause chaos, he had missed just how at risk he truly was. She pulled and pulled from the gods, taking everything from them, even the energy that animated their cells. She drew until there was no more, directing every little bit of energy she could at the growing piece of Tristan's soul.

The blue glow spread out over his body, wrapping him in an embrace of light. Something shifted in his face, the cruel mask disappearing, replaced by the face of an exhausted teenager. He opened his eyes, all traces of black gone. Real tears ran down his face and blood poured from where the knife was lodged in his chest. He fell to his knees the moment Ree released her power and let him.

"TRISTAN!" Ree's feet were moving by the time they hit the floor. She fell to her brother's side and cradled his head in her lap.

"Ree." He coughed, blood coming from his mouth which she quickly brushed away.

"Paden!" Ree didn't look away from Tristan. For the first time in years, she was looking at her brother and she didn't want to lose one second. "Please, Trist. Hang on. Hang on."

Paden's hands moved toward his friend's chest, but Tristan batted him away with one hand. "No."

"Tristan. You're hurt. Paden can help you." Ree's tears ran down her face and she grabbed Tristan's hand but he tried to pull away. "Stop it! I can't lose you again. Not again, Tristan. I've missed you. Mom has missed you so much."

"No." Tristan stopped fighting Ree and squeezed her fingers instead. "I'm sorry. Tell mom and dad."

"Please, Tristan." Ree's body shook with sobs, her words barely coming out.

"No crying, sis." Tristan coughed, but smiled a little. "My choice."

"Ree." Paden touched her shoulder, but she shook him off.

"No! Heal him! He doesn't understand!" Ree shook Tristan as his eyes drifted closed. "Wake up, Tristan."

"It's over, Ree." Tristan's words were a whisper. "Thank you."

"I love you, Tristan!" Ree shook, her head bowed over her brother.

"Love you." He never opened his eyes and his heart stuttered on the last word. The grief hit Ree so hard she lost control of the power and everyone was pushed away from where she sat, holding her brother. No one said a word while she sobbed, her body shaking as she unleashed every bit of pain she had locked up.

Finally, someone pulled Tristan's body out of Ree's hands. She fought them, pushing at his shoulders and smacking at his hands. Roland touched her face to get her attention. She looked up at him through blurry eyelashes, not sure what he wanted.

"Let go of the power, Ree." Roland brushed the hair back from her face. "There are a lot of people here that want to hold you."

Ree looked around her, surprised to see the rippling energy that had kept everyone else at bay. Taking a deep breath that ended on one of those awful hiccups, she let go of the power. Paden was beside her instantly. Sliding an arm under her legs and the other around her shoulders, he pulled her against his chest. Melanie slammed into them both, her arms wrapping around Ree as best she could.

"You did it, Ree." Melanie's strained voice reached Ree's ears, but she didn't really understand. Tristan had died. "You did it, Ree. I'm so sorry about Tristan, but you did it."

Ree struggled in Paden's arms so he would set her down. He put her on her feet but kept an arm wrapped around her waist. Ree hugged Melanie and absorbed what her friend was telling her. The war was over. Her eyes darted over her friends and knew tears were welling in her eyes. They had all made it. There was blood, and wounds that would heal with time, but they were all alive. They were the last ones standing.

The thunder claps announcing the arrival of gods made Ree jerk against Paden's chest. Every nerve ending in her body felt raw, her heart and brain weak from overload. She looked over to where Athena stood with several gods Ree didn't recognize, and then over to where Brigid stood next to Hecate.

"I told you they had been dealt with." Athena kicked at the pile of ashes at her feet with disgust. "The evidence."

"This was your doing?" Zeus's voice made Ree's heart rate accelerate. He was a tall man, wearing a business suit that hugged his muscular body.

"By my command." Athena didn't look remotely bothered. "I told you I would not suffer a traitor, Father." She sniffed as she looked over to the other pile of ashes. "Much less two."

"This is finally over then?" A man with bright yellow hair asked from where he stood next to Zeus.

"Yes, Apollo. The children have saved our planet." Hecate's voice rang through the auditorium.

Zeus looked over at them as if just realizing they were there. "Good job, then."

Just as quickly as they came, they disappeared. Brigid and Hecate lingered just a moment longer. Hecate winked at them and Brigid offered a small smile, but they, too, left quickly and without any more words. Roland ripped off part of the curtain hanging from the rafters and placed it over Tristan's body. He scooped up Ree's brother's body and nodded at her.

"I really want out of here." Ree looked at Paden.

"I second that." Weylin limped toward the stairs for the stage.

"What about the Dark Ones? Where did they all go?" Ree looked about the room, not sure if there was enough dust and ash to make up all of the monsters that had been trying to kill them.

"They ran the moment you broke through the shield." Bryce squeezed Ree's shoulder as they made their way down the hall. "We couldn't leave you there to follow."

"Don't worry, we picked off some for you." Niall was standing just outside of the broken doors to the school.

There, in the pink hues of the coming morning sky, the remaining Guardians who had come to Savannah with her friends waited on the stairs. They all looked tired, a little battle worn, but in far better shape than anyone who had been in the school.

"Thank you." Ree shot Niall a half smile.

"I think we should be thinking you, Alastriana." Met nodded her head at the school. "You sure did put on a hell of a light show."

"What do you mean?" Ree looked at the Guardian in confusion.

"The night sky lit up like the aurora borealis when you did whatever you did in there."

"Oh." Ree blinked. The sound of sirens in the distance, made Ree sigh.

"I guess we're still on the wanted list." Weylin shook his head.

"Probably." Bryce smiled.

"We kept them busy for as long as we could." Magda said. She was sitting on the low wall next to the steps.

Some of the Guardians had commandeered vehicles and there was plenty of room for the ride back to the boats. Ree leaned against Paden, still too conflicted to feel relief at having finished the biggest task she had ever been given. Deep in her soul was an ache that nothing but time would heal.

When the boats made it to the island, Ree took Tristan's body and carried him to the pyres that had been set up in their absence. Not all of the Guardians had been as lucky as Ree's friends and there were two bodies to be laid to rest next to Tristan's. The humans that were on the island had gathered a respectful distance away, but were there to show their support.

As the flames ate the bodies of the Guardians and devoured what remained of her brother, Ree did her best to let go of all the pain she felt. After a while, the others drifted away, but Ree refused to move until the flames had completely died away. Someone brought her a blanket and Paden wrapped it around her shoulders before pulling her into his lap.

Neither of them said anything until the last flame had gone out. The sun had risen hours ago, but Ree stayed in the exact same position as she watched her brother leave the world for real. Paden hadn't complained once about the damp ground or the cold air. He sat there quietly, his love for Ree the only real warmth she could feel that morning. Finally, he shifted so he could see her face. Very gently he kissed her lips and touched his forehead to hers.

"I want to go somewhere warm." Ree's words were quiet, but she smiled softly at Paden.

"Where do you have in mind?" Paden kissed the tip of her nose, his relief for her washing over her.

"I don't care. Somewhere with a lot of sun and a

beautiful beach." Ree picked up small rock and rolled it between her fingers.

"You just want to see me in those little trunks." Paden narrowed his eyes at Ree and she laughed. It warmed her from the pit of her stomach and flowed out to get lost in the sound of the crashing water.

Paden stood up and pulled her to her feet. "C'mon. There are a lot of people who want to talk to you."

"Oh?" Ree let him pull her toward the house where she could hear people laughing. She wasn't sure that she was ready to talk to anyone but Paden.

"I think there's cake." Paden smiled when she picked up her pace.

"Well, I can't let good cake go to waste, can I?" Ree squeezed his fingers.

"Not you, little one."

"I wonder where I can order some of those little shorts. Do you prefer a certain color or do you just want green to match your eyes?" She laughed when Paden made a grab for her and threw on the speed. His growl turned into a chuckle as they entered the house and were immersed in hugs from their friends and the people who knew just what they had gone through.

Ree looked back at Paden as Kay pulled her to the kitchen for cake and held out her hand. Lacing his fingers with hers, Paden stayed with Ree, just like she knew he always would.

Chapter 31

Ree pushed her plate away and leaned back in her chair. Her friends were the only ones left in the kitchen. Everyone else had gone to bed, or disappeared to spend time with their families and friends. Paden and Weylin were arguing over the last piece of cake, which Bryce took without notice. Juliette and Melanie were watching them with amused eyes.

The humans had all been settled into the little houses in the center of the island, and the extra Guardians had been offered passage back to their own homes. Most of them had stayed though, to help clean up the mess that Savannah had been left in. There were still Dark Ones running around and darklings that needed to be healed. It would take a lot of work and time to rid the Earth of the alien disease.

Taking a deep breath, Ree closed her eyes and enjoyed the bickering that meant things were a little more normal. The chair next to her scraped against the floor and Roland sat down. She opened her eyes and smiled when he handed her a spoon and pointed at the carton of ice cream he had gotten out of the fridge.

“This was Sophie’s favorite.” Ree scooped a big spoonful out.

“Yep. There are four more containers in the freezer.” Roland laughed. "I’m going to miss her. She was my family.”

Ree reached over and squeezed his hand quickly. “We’re your family too.”

He smiled at her and touched his spoon to her nose. “You poor people.”

“Where the hell did the cake go?” Weylin stood up and looked around the room. “What the hell?”

“Sorry man, the cake looked so good and it was getting cold while you argued.” Bryce put the last forkful in his mouth and closed his eyes. “So good.”

Weylin dropped his fork on his plate and fell into his chair, utterly defeated. Ree shoved the ice cream in his direction and smiled. Sighing he took a big bite and shrugged.“It will do.”

“So, what’s the plan now?” Melanie asked.

“What do you mean?” Ree leaned forward and looked at her friend.

“I mean, do we go back to school? We missed weeks.”

“I don’t know.” Ree frowned. “I really didn’t think about much past the final battle.”

“Well, it’s over now.” Paden bumped her shoulder with his. “And there’s no telling when we’ll have to answer one of their favors.”

“Maybe we can just take online classes? I’m not sure I could go back to school and look at everyone. Besides, the news station said the school had been closed for repairs." Ree frowned around the room. "Plus, last I talked to Mom and Dad they said that they're not sure when they're coming back. They've been in upstate New York and Mom loves it."

"So what? They want to move?" Juliette leaned forward and frowned.

"No, but our house is destroyed. They want to wait until it's fixed before they come home. I don't really blame them. It doesn't feel like home anymore." Ree shrugged "And, I don't know, but I think that knowing Tristan is really gone makes it even harder on them. They had just seen him again." She hadn't told them that he had been turned back to human in the end. She couldn't bring herself to tell them that she had killed her own brother. Tears gathered in her eyes and she shoved another spoonful of ice cream in her mouth. Tristan had made his choices and she had done her best to live with the consequences.

"What about a vacation?" Paden looked at Ree, obviously wanting to draw her thoughts back to something happier. It worked. His eyes glowed with something that made her want to drag him back to their room.

"I've heard that Bora Bora is pretty nice." Juliette smiled.

Epilogue

"You have got to be kidding me." Paden's voice drifted out of the bathroom in the small hut they were sharing next to the beach. "Ree! I'm not wearing these!"

Ree bit her lips to keep from laughing out loud. She tucked his swim trunks under the bed and tried to swallow her laughter. "What are you talking about?"

Paden stepped out of their bathroom, his towel hanging low on his hips. Obviously fighting a smile, he held up the tiny, green swim trunks Ree had switched out with his normal pair.

"What? They match your eyes." Ree's mouth twitched.

"I'm not wearing these, Ree. I would never hear the end of it." Paden stretched them between his hands. "Roland would die from laughter. And Melanie and Jules! They would feel unsatisfied for the rest of their lives! Imagine knowing this much hotness was right next to them, but they could never have it?"

The laughter burst from Ree and she covered her mouth with both hands. Paden flung the shorts across the room, slingshot style. She ducked and let them hit the wall over her head. Paden was across the room in a second, pressing Ree down onto the bed. He kissed her until she thought her heart was going to explode.

When he finally leaned back, he nipped at her nose and smiled down at her. "I love this."

"What?" Ree smiled up at Paden, enjoying the happiness that radiated from him and warmed her soul.

"Being with you, right now. Seeing you happy and relaxed." Using the fingers on his left hand, he pushed Ree's bangs out of her eyes.

"I'm happy too." Ree wiggled under him, finding a more comfortable position.

"Good. Now tell me where my trunks are. They're going to be waiting for us." Paden narrowed his eyes sternly.

"I have no idea what you're talking about." Ree grinned broadly.

"They're under the bed, aren't they?" Paden moved to look under the bed, but Ree grabbed his shoulders and yanked him back.

"Let them wait a little while. We have forever to go snorkeling." Ree pulled his head down to hers and kissed him soundly.

"Hard to argue with that kind of logic." Paden mumbled.

An hour late, Paden and Ree finally showed up on the beach where the others were waiting next to a small boat. Weylin was lying on his back in the surf. The water was making his growing hair lap around his head like octopus arms. He pushed his sunglasses down on his nose and glared at Paden.

"Not cool, dude."

"We're not that late." Paden kicked some water at him and dropped their snorkeling gear into the boat.

"If you had been late because you had run into evil, blood sucking monsters it would be understandable." Weylin sat up and glared at Ree and Paden. "But, noooooo. You were doing the pogo stick dance and there is no brain-bleach to be found anywhere on the island."

Ree blushed, but couldn't help the sputtering laugh that came out of her mouth. Paden shook his head and sat down on the edge of the small boat. Bryce walked over and high-fived Weylin before pulling him to his feet.

"It's too late to go snorkeling now. We'll have to go tomorrow." Bryce went back to Juliette and picked her up over his shoulder. She squealed and smacked at him, but everyone knew she wasn't serious. Jules could have made him put her down if she wanted.

"Where are Melanie and Roland?" Ree helped Paden pull the boat closer to their little stand of houses.

"They went to go get snacks, because you guys were taking so long." Weylin grabbed his towel from one of the white lounge chairs. He plopped down into his seat and glared at the water. "There was a really hot chick on the other boat. I was hoping she would lose her snorkel and I could offer her mine." He wiggled his eyebrows and Ree groaned. Paden laughed and grabbed the soccer ball that was next to the chairs.

"C'mon. Maybe I can teach you how to look cool before she comes back." Paden kicked the ball at Weylin's chair.

"You wouldn't know cool if it bit you on the ass."

Weylin stood up and dribbled the ball down the beach away from Paden.

A dark-haired blur sped past Weylin and took the ball. The sun glinted off of Roland's bronzed skin, his mouth wide in a happy, carefree grin. "Did I hear you say you wanted me to bite you on the butt? That's sick man."

The boys started hollering, laughing, and posturing. Ree just shook her head and enjoyed the sight. When Melanie sat down in Weylin's empty chair, she turned to smile at her friend. Melanie pulled out a soda from the picnic basket she had been carrying and handed it to Ree.

"Now, this is the life. A beautiful beach, our favorite soda, and a show with hot guys. Doesn't get much better than this." Melanie winked at Ree. They clinked cans in a toast, and Ree felt her smile grow.

***

"They have left." Athena looked at Brigid over her glass of scotch.

"For now." Tossing her red hair over her shoulder, Brigid sat down next to the Greek goddess. "They believe we cheated."

"Bah. They're just angry that we won." Hecate sipped from her silver chalice, her bright eyes twinkling. "But you're right. They'll be back."

Narrowing her eyes, Athena glared at the fire crackling in the hearth. "We'll be ready for them."

"More importantly, so will our heroes." Hecate waved a hand at the flames and formed the small of images of Ree and her friends. For a few minutes they watched as the group splashed in the warm waters at the beach.

"It's nice to see them relaxed." Brigid's expression softened.

"They deserved it." Hecate smiled at the small figures. "Ree has rid us of two traitors and in the process gained even more power."

"That she did." Brigid smiled as Ree and Paden ran hand in hand.

"Don't forget our other plans." Athena flicked her own fingers at the fire. The friendly scene by the beach was replaced by the image of a young woman. She resembled the Alastriana, except for the short dark hair. "I believe she will be quite useful."

"Quite useful, indeed." Hecate lifted her glass in salute.

Acknowledgments

I've thought about this moment for a long time. I'm through with the Dark Betrayal Trilogy and it is one of the most bittersweet moments of my life. To say that I love these characters would be an understatement. They have been part of my family for years. So, it's with a certain amount of sadness that I bid them adieu… for now.

I owe so many people thanks, I find it hard to know where to start. My husband deserves the lion's share of the cake, for believing in me, pushing me, and never letting me down. My daughter, who has been incredibly patient for a three-year-old, deserves a year at Disney World. (The other day she told me that she wants to write books. My heart almost exploded with pride.) My sister, also, deserves thanks. Without her, I may never have finished Mortal Obligation. She has been my Writing Warden. My friends, Heather and Tina, deserve huge shout-outs for believing in me and being my personal cheerleaders. My parents will always receive thanks for encouraging my crazy imagination. I'm thankful for my friends, Shawn and Laurie, who designed my website and put up with crazy requests. I am eternally indebted to Liz Reinhardt for going through my book and picking apart my grammar and weird phrasing. (And didn't once threaten to put me in her pocket while doing it!) It took a lot of time from her own projects and I hope that her fans can forgive me. Elizabeth Hunter, who is an inspiration and my writing hero, for going through and reading my work, even when I thought it sucked. Thanks to my wonderful friend and editor, Anne, who never pushed me to hurry up and finish. Anne, you'll never know how much your support meant when I was trying to make this book the best that it could be. Kathie from Kats Eyes Editing was a god-send in my moment of need. She has been spectacular to work with and I'm grateful to have met her even through difficult circumstances.

For my writing family: thank you, thank you, thank you. The FP has been an incredible inspiration and source of support. Not only are you all amazing authors, I'm honored to call you friends.

Thank you to my readers. The ones that have gone out of their way to tell people about my books. The ones that left reviews or just thought about my characters when they should have been doing something else. You guys are the reason that I write. Thank you for your support and thank you for your patience.

About the Author

Nichole Chase is a daydreamer. No, really, just ask any of the math teachers that had the misfortune of seeing her name appear on their class schedule.

For years she has had storylines and characters begging for attention, but she resolutely pushed them aside to focus on more normal (read, boring) jobs. Well, no longer! She is currently heeding the voices in her head and frantically writing their stories. In the last two years she has penned the *Dark Betrayal Trilogy*, *Flukes*, and the upcoming novel, *Suddenly Royal.*

Nichole resides in South Georgia with her husband, energetic toddler, loyal dog, and two cats. When not devouring novels by the dozens, you may find her writing, painting, crafting, or chasing her daughter around the house while making monster noises.

If you would like to learn more about Nichole and her projects, check out her website. You can also subscribe to Nichole's newsletter to be notified of new releases.

www.NicholeChase.com
www.nicholechase.blogspot.com

Books by Nichole Chase

Mortal Obligation (Dark Betrayal Trilogy, Book One)
Mortal Defiance (Dark Betrayal Trilogy, Book Two)
Immortal Grave (Dark Betrayal Trilogy, Book Three)
Flukes (Flukes Series, Book One)
Suddenly Royal (Suddenly Series, Book One) – Coming 2013

Printed in Great Britain
by Amazon